Praise for Lauren Dane's
Cascadia Wolves: Wolf Unbound

"This is one hot page-turner!"

~ *Romantic Times Magazine*

"...These books are action packed and full of love and romance, along with loads of alphaness and women who know how to handle all that testosterone."

~ *Sandy, The Good, The Bad, the Unread*

"...Ms. Dane's storytelling just gets better and better. Wolf Unbound has everything it takes to make this an exciting read – thrilling suspense and mystery, humorous and witty dialogue, paranormal elements, and most of all deliciously, hot sexual encounters."

~ *Nikita, Erotic Escapades*

"...This book had everything I like suspense, love and romance, paranormal flavor, and hot sex made all the hotter with the BDSM elements. ...The suspense made it a page-turner, and the love story will tug at your heartstrings. When I turned that last page I had to sit there for a minute, I was so disappointed it was over."

~ *AMG, The Romance Studio*

"...Ben and Tee make a great couple, loving and supportive – inside and outside the bedroom. Fourth in the Cascadia Wolves series, the focus is on Tee and Ben, but the stakes in the National Pack have just been amped up and there is a lot of action."

~ *Amy, Ecataromance*

"I can't get enough of Lauren Dane's Cascadia Wolves and Wolf Unbound is no exception. I read this book like a junkie looking for his next fix. ... I blushed at their encounters and cheered their victories. Wolf Unbound was written in such a way that I could hear their words and feel their emotions."

~ *Talia, Joyfully Reviewed*

"...This story is full of all of the passion, emotional angst and wolfie wonders you could possibly want in a fantastic storyline. ... One of my favorite things about this series is how each story builds on the last one and you feel like part of the family. If you haven't yet experienced a Lauren Dane book then you're missing out!"

~ *Chrissy, Romance Junkies*

Look for these titles by
Lauren Dane

Now Available:

The Chase Brothers Series
Giving Chase
Taking Chase
Chased
Making Chase

Cascadia Wolves Series
Wolf Unbound
Standoff

To Do List
Reading Between The Lines

Coming Soon:

Always

Cascadia Wolves: Wolf Unbound

Lauren Dane

A Samhain Publishing, Ltd. publication.

Samhain Publishing, Ltd.
577 Mulberry Street, Suite 1520
Macon, GA 31201
www.samhainpublishing.com

Cascadia Wolves: Wolf Unbound
Copyright © 2009 by Lauren Dane
Print ISBN: 978-1-60504-098-1
Digital ISBN: 1-59998-847-X

Editing by Angela James
Cover by Dawn Seewer

First Samhain Publishing, Ltd. electronic publication: January 2008
First Samhain Publishing, Ltd. print publication: January 2009

Dedication

Ray—thank you for listening to me babble for the last twenty-one years. H-A-U-L Haul baby, haul...

Megan and Anya, um, yeah, more thanks for listening to me babble. And thank you for your help critting, supporting, lifting me up and kicking my booty when necessary.

Just a shout out to Emma Holly, who yes, I know, is not reading this, but thanks nonetheless for writing The Velvet Glove. My first step in to reading D/s romance and it spoiled me.

Beta Readers, Friends and Fans—y'all rock.

—XOXO, Lauren

Chapter One

Tegan ran. Heart bursting with the joy of the forest, with the elation of wolf, her paws hit the warm earth, claws scrabbling to keep balance as she rounded a curve and saw the edge of the land that was safe to be wolf in.

Collapsing at the base of a large tree, she stretched to rub her spine along the bark, a growl of pleasure darting from her muzzle. Sighing, she put her head on her paws and closed her eyes.

"Hey. You're late." He smiled up at her, blue eyes twinkling, short blond hair set off against sun-kissed skin.

Startled, she froze a minute. Watched as he sliced mushrooms with competent speed. In three steps she was close enough to touch him. Feel the vibrant warmth at the back of his neck, the straw-colored softness of his hair tickling her fingers.

"Lucas." His name tore from her painfully. "What?"

He put the cutting board heaped with vegetables aside and gave her a quick kiss. "That's all I can do." Turning back to the sink, he began to peel potatoes. "God, I miss you. But you know what makes me saddest?"

"What are you doing here?" Impotent rage flooded her. "You're dead!"

He put the potato down and dried his hands on a nearby towel. "I'm dead. But not here." Warm fingers brushed her temple. "Or here." Another fleeting brush over her heart. "In your memories and your heart I'm still alive. Our love lives on in your memories. But just because I'm dead doesn't mean you have to be. I've been telling you that. Why haven't you listened?"

She shook her head, tears sprang to her eyes and the pain of his loss welled up like a familiar ache. "The other dreams...were you trying to tell me?"

He nodded. "Okay the deal is, I can't be here long. So listen to me, please, honey. You're wasting your life. Damn it, you're wasting your heart. A heart I know has room to love again. I'd be so ashamed if my death was the reason you never moved on to love another man."

"I...there's only you. Why, Lucas? Why did you leave me?"

He closed his eyes and the room dimmed a bit. "I didn't. It wasn't like that. But there's no more time. Tee, it's coming and you have got to be ready. Lots of stuff. Big stuff. You can't deal with it, may not survive it if you don't let me go and move forward."

She felt her consciousness begin to rise, fought it, moved toward him. He took her hands in his, kissing her fingertips. Her desperation faded into resignation and then calm flowed over her.

"I have to go. I'll always be a part of you, Tegan. But you need to move on. It's time."

And she was alone in the forest. But the faint scent of him still rested on the air and for the first time in four years, when she walked back into the house wearing her human skin, she felt whole again.

℅

"You know what, Lex? I think my time-out is over. I want to move back to my own house." Tegan Warden continued to clean her weapon as she spoke to her brother, the Enforcer of Cascadia Pack.

"This isn't a punishment for God's sake! Tegan, we know Pellini is out there and looking for a way to hurt one of us. It's not safe for you to be back at your house on your own." Lex spoke through clenched teeth.

"Lex, by all that is holy, if I put coal in your ass it would turn into a diamond! Loosen up! I'm twenty-eight years old. In case it hadn't occurred to you, I'm a fucking werewolf guard on your damned Enforcer team. I can take care of myself." She put her weapon back into the case and locked it.

Her sister-in-law, Nina, leaned against the counter and drank her coffee, watching them both.

"I think you should do what Lex says on this, Tee." Cade came into the room and shoved Nina aside playfully, getting himself a cup of coffee.

"Of course you do, your ass is as tight as his. Look, I like being on my own. I only lived here because after Lucas...well it was a place to come and it was part of the job. But now I have my own place. It's filled with my own things. It's where my bed is, and my sheets and my plates. No offense but I don't want to live my life by committee anymore."

"How's she ever gonna get any action if she's here anyway? God, you guys, she's been alone for four years. It's time she gets back out there and starts dating. She deserves a real life and you making her stay here isn't going to keep her twelve years old." Tegan couldn't risk looking at Nina just then. Nina's intuitiveness and insight were scary sometimes.

"It'll just keep her from ending up dead!" Lex's jaw clenched and unclenched.

Tegan stood and shook her head. "I'm not going to die if I'm not under your nose every minute of the day. I appreciate your concern, Lex. I love that you all want to keep me safe and protected but I don't want that. I want to be on my own."

"To have hot monkey love!" Nina joked.

Tegan rolled her eyes at her sister-in-law, suppressing a smile. "If I choose, yes."

"Tegan, what's gotten into you?" Lex didn't wait for an answer as he turned back to his wife. "I can't believe you're taking her side on this, Nina." He began to pace.

"There aren't sides here, Lex." Nina reached out and touched his shoulder and he stopped, leaning into her. "Let her go. It's just twenty miles."

Lex threw his hands up in the air. "Fine! No one listens to me. I'm only the Second and all. What would I know about security?"

Tegan squeezed his forearm and stood, picking up her weapon case. "I'll be back for my shift at nine. My stuff is packed and in the car." She walked out of the room.

It was silent for long minutes until Nina turned to Lex and Cade, who glowered at her from the table.

"She wants to move on. She *needs* to. Can't you see that?"

"Did she tell you that? Because the woman who just walked out of here isn't one I've seen in a very long time," Cade said.

"You know she didn't. She doesn't tell anyone anything she doesn't have to. But I have eyes. She's lonely. I didn't know Lucas but I *do* know what it's like to have a mate. I can't imagine losing one. Worse having her anchor bond, Abe, mated and therefore unavailable to her romantically. Sure she didn't lose her life when her mate died, but to not have the fallback of an anchor to replace the original mate bond would be difficult. Like losing a mate twice over.

"But I *have* noticed her actually seeing men for the first time since I met her. She's more..." Nina shrugged her shoulders, "...alive than I've seen her. I know you all say she was vivacious before Lucas was killed but she's been on lockdown since I came into this Pack and I've seen her starting to open the doors a bit. This is good. Let her move on. My God, she's only twenty-eight, she has time to find love again."

"That's what this is about? Her getting out to get laid?"

Nina narrowed an eye at Cade. "Hey, fuck you. That'd be like me saying, *so, this is about you not having a guard at your beck and call?* Unfair and petty. This isn't about her sex life but so what if it was? You know better and you're all grumpy and talking like an ass because you're worried about her. It's your way."

Cade harrumphed in her direction but Lex still glared.

Undeterred, Nina leaned back and sipped her coffee. "She's getting back out to live her life. She's been here living as a guard for all these years. She needs friends, she needs her own schedule and things to do. And she needs a man. Is it so wrong to want that? Don't you want that, Cade? Someone to snuggle with in front of the TV at night after your day is over? Someone you can take to dinner, who makes your heart beat faster?"

Problem was, Cade was more than a little in love with Nina. She probably shouldn't have asked but these two males were myopic on the issue of the women they loved.

"I suppose the other females are in your corner on this?" Lex raised an arrogant brow at his wife, saving his brother from answering.

Nina stood with a slow smile. "Lex, my most luscious

Scooby, you want to protect everyone. It's who you are. And your big dumb brother too. I haven't consulted the Warden women but if I did, I'm sure they'd all agree Tee needs this. Let her have it or I'll kick your ass."

Lex sighed and sat back in his chair, eyeing Nina appreciatively. "You owe me."

"Like that's a punishment?" She laughed as she left the room.

"Keep an eye on her, Lex." Cade's voice was low.

"I already had a better security system put in at the house and her car has bullet proof glass and reinforced doors."

Cade patted his brother's arm. "Good."

ॐ

Tegan walked into the front doors of Wild Ginger and saw her sisters already seated with Nina. Waving, she moved to sit with them.

"Thanks for getting my back with Lex and Cade last week." Tegan smiled at Nina.

"Well if I'd been doubting it was the right choice I'm convinced now. You look great!" Nina grinned.

"You do. Man, Tee, I don't think I've seen you in makeup in—"

Tegan interrupted her twin sister, Megan. "Four years. I know. I'm working through it."

"What happened? Why the sudden turn around?" Their oldest sister, Layla, looked up from her menu.

Out of all her siblings, Tegan was closest to Layla. It was Layla who'd held her as she wept when they'd come with news of Lucas's death in Afghanistan. Layla who helped her choose the casket and the headstone. Layla never pushed, she just let Tegan deal with it in her own way and that meant so much to her. Layla truly listened to Tegan in her grief. While others tried to fix it, Layla had a mate, she'd known there was no fixing it. Layla never compared how Tegan was before the death to the way she was afterward. No one but Layla seemed to understand that a part of her died that day when those uniformed officers had come to her door.

But it was time to live again.

"I had three dreams in the last month and one a year ago. Lucas was in all of them. The first ones were sort of hazy, but I got the feeling he was telling me something. The one I had two weeks ago was clear. We were in the kitchen of our old house and he was peeling potatoes. He turned to me and he told me to move on. He said that I was wasting my life and my heart and that he would be ashamed if his death was the reason I never found love again." She stopped, hands trembling a bit as she took a sip of water.

"Anyway, he said it was coming. A bunch of big stuff and that I had to be ready for all of it. Told me to live my life again and that love was out there and a piece of him would always be there but it was time to let him go. And so I have. Or I'm trying. I'll always love him. He was my mate. But I went out two nights ago. And I liked it. I've had dinner with our old friend Ryan and his boyfriend. It feels like what I'm supposed to do."

The women, her sisters, all leaned forward and touched her. In that way of wolves, they gave comfort and support through caresses and hugs and then broke away.

Unshed tears shone in the eyes of everyone at the table. "You're so strong. I love you, Tegan." Megan's voice was shaky but clear.

"Ditto." Nina used her napkin to dab her eyes.

"Yep," Lay agreed. "But what did he mean when he said it was coming? Love?"

Tegan sighed. "I don't know, Lay. Partly, yes. But something else and I think it might have something to do with Pellini."

The table silenced for long moments until Nina said, "Then we'll have to be ready. And then we'll kill him and he'll stop being a threat to the people I love."

"Amen," the others echoed.

Chapter Two

Tegan Warden walked confidently into the club's front doors. In the months since she'd moved back to her house she'd found solace in a few things and the Club De Sade held one of them. Tonight, her fiery red hair cascaded around her face and shoulders in fat curls, in contrast to the sleek black lace-up vest she wore, breasts nicely pouring over the top. A creamy expanse of her stomach showed just above the low waist of her leather pants. High-heeled boots completed the outfit.

"Yo, Tegan! Honey, you look *fine* tonight!" Max, the nearly seven-foot-tall bartender, whistled low as she approached.

A smile curved her lips. "Oh Max, why can't you play on my team?"

"Because my team is better." Max's partner and the owner of the club, Ryan Post, hopped onto the stool next to where she stood. "It's been a week. You promised to call me! How are you this evening, buttercup?" He kissed her cheek when she leaned down to hug him.

"I'm looking for someone to play with. It's been a very rough week. Pellini seems to be moving again. Big time Pack politics and my brother, ugh! He's all up in my business now. I love him, you know that, but Lex could drive a saint insane."

"Now, don't get me wrong, I love male werewolves. They're terrific in bed, but they are a bit...overbearing sometimes." Ryan winked and grinned. The gleam of one of his incisors marked his otherness. The Club De Sade was run by vampires, which was fine with Tegan. It was private, membership only and those who were allowed in were extensively screened. It was safe for paranormals to play there, that's what she was always concerned with.

"Human or Were? Vampire perhaps?" Ryan asked.

"No wolves! The politics of dealing with a wolf who's lower in Pack rank is too annoying. Other than that, I want someone who can wield a flogger with expertise, Ryan. The last time I came in, the Were who flogged me had the worst hand ever. Like he'd never even seen a flogger before. And honey, I do not want to educate a Dom. I'm not a tutor for God's sake."

Ryan laughed. "Hmm. Well, we've got a relatively new member. I've seen him in action a few times. Human. Quite yummy. He's looking for a regular submissive though."

"Regular?" A shiver went through her and she flashed onto her dream. She knew she got her belief in that sort of stuff from her grandmother but she felt like Lucas was there, pushing her.

"Get that note of terror out of your voice, Tegan. You admitted that you wanted to move on. He wouldn't want you to be alone for so long. You were meant to be cherished." Ryan and Lucas had been good friends. In fact, Tegan and Lucas had gotten involved in D/s through Ryan. Ryan had been a regular fixture in her life until Lucas's death and then she didn't see him very often, although he kept in regular contact. When she'd shown up at his and Max's apartment three months before, he'd welcomed her back into the world with a big hug and a glass of wine.

She could have made a flippant remark to hurt him but she knew he was right. Still, how could she replace what Lucas had been to her? He'd been her everything, her best friend, her partner, her mate. When he'd died, she knew she'd be alone as her anchor had already found his mate. At least she stayed anchored and should she ever find anyone again, she'd be spared the necessity of the tri-bond.

So all she did was shrug.

"Why don't you at least let me see if he's available this evening? If it works, if you click, great. If not, what's the harm?"

Heartache. Devastation. Loneliness. *Connection.*

"Okay. I'll wait here."

He smiled, hopped off the barstool and headed toward the back where the play rooms were.

"I think you'll like Ben, he's a nice guy. Tough but not the kind of Dom that talks in all caps and stalks around like he's got lead balls."

Tegan nearly choked on her club soda as she laughed at Max's comments. "You know me well."

He shrugged with a grin and turned to fill drink orders.

Before long, Ryan came out and beckoned Tegan toward the back. Once in the hallway it was a lot quieter than out in the main bar area.

When he raised his hand, she saw the blindfold he held. "He wants you to be blindfolded the first time. I'll observe even though I've watched him before and you know I'd never let you play with anyone I didn't trust. The safeword is rubberband. I've informed him you're more high capacity than most other women and that you're Were. I'll be there on the other side of the glass."

A shiver of delight at the hint of danger slid through her system unbidden. She hadn't allowed anyone to blindfold her since Lucas. "All right. If he gets out of line I'll just rip his head off." And she could. Even the strongest human couldn't stand against a werewolf.

Ryan rolled his eyes and walked behind her, sliding the blindfold over her eyes and adjusting the straps to make it totally light tight before securing the Velcro.

The first hint of submission settled into her body. Calming and soothing her.

Ryan took her by the elbow and led her into the play room. She scented the man there. Smelled soap and clean skin, a hint of leather, his shampoo. Just clean, hard man. Nothing better.

She felt Ryan move away and the other man touch her with surety. Not rough, not presumptuous. Sure.

"You've got a beautiful body." His voice was hoarse as his hands stroked over her bare shoulders and down her arms. "I want to see your back bare."

She knew Ryan had specified just play and not sex so she nodded, giving him permission to remove her vest.

"I'm Ben." His hands worked the lacing up the front of her vest and she felt the cool air of the room as he slid it from her body. He hummed in satisfaction. "I'm going to love how pink your nipples get from the flogger."

She shivered and a low sound broke from her lips. God how she craved this, craved being taken in hand. Craved having a man like this one, like Lucas looking at her, finding her beautiful.

"Tell me your name." He circled her, she felt the heat of his body as he did.

"Tegan." Her voice sounded breathy, like a low purr.

"Unusual and beautiful, like you are. I love redheads, Tegan."

She heard the slither of the tails of a flogger and she arched her back. He chuckled. "You like that? Good. I like it too. I like watching your nipples tighten as you anticipate where I may touch you first."

Lightning quick the very tip of the tails licked her nipples and she moaned at the bright, hot sensation that stole over her. Her knees nearly buckled and her pussy bloomed.

Three more times in quick succession the tails bit into her breasts with expert precision. Not too light, not too hard. It was more the sound than the actual feel, the air as it rushed ahead of the leather of the flogger, the scent of the leather, the creak of the handle in his hand.

He moved around and the flogger found her back as heat spread, narcotic and sensual, over her skin.

After a time she was aware of nothing more than his presence and the slither and snap of the flogger, the heat of her body as the flogger warmed it and the heat of his body as he moved.

She began to sway as the sensation hypnotized her.

"Good God, you're fucking amazing." She heard him lay the flogger down and his hand was at the small of her back like a brand. "I'd like to do more. See what shade of pink your ass turns." He waited for her response and she struggled upwards through the layers of serotonin to answer without a slur.

"Yes."

His hands moved to the front laces of her pants and he bent her forward, gently. A sturdy padded table sat in the middle of the room. She'd been in there before so she wasn't surprised to feel the edge of it dig into her stomach as her breasts touched the cool of the leather. She felt him pull off her boots and then her pants followed. He left her thong on but she felt more naked than she'd been in a very long time.

"Your skin is so pretty." His whisper was like sandpaper dragged lightly over her skin as he trailed the flogger over her ass and thighs. "I think you might need a little restraint."

She wanted to say *sure* but all she could do was whimper and make it sound affirmative. How this man affected her so deeply she didn't know, but he did. She might have been scared if she weren't already on the edge of subspace, if it hadn't been so long since any man had made her feel so alive.

As he leaned over her body, she felt his cock at her hip while he used a wrist cuff to attach one hand and then the other to the table legs. Hard and thick. Her mouth watered and her pussy clutched.

Before she could be ashamed at the wantonness of her response the blows began to rain on her ass and thighs. At one point he used the toe of his boot to spread her legs wider and she moaned and then hissed at the sharp pleasure that radiated when he flogged her pussy like a fucking expert.

She wanted to writhe and beg but the top half of her body was fairly immobile and she didn't want to move her legs lest he stop. The heat spread up into her cunt. She caught her bottom lip between her teeth until she tasted blood.

Until orgasm hit her so hard and by surprise her head shot back and she cried out. Dimly she heard his intake of breath and the tails of the flogger continued to tease the wet seam of the thong between her thighs.

"God damn, so fucking beautiful," she heard his astonished whisper.

She wanted him to ask for sex. She would have agreed in a heartbeat. Wanted to feel his cock slide into her, wanted to please him.

But he didn't. Instead, he murmured to her softly as he undid her wrist restraints and helped her to stand.

Gently, he led her to the bed in the corner of the room and lay down beside her, letting her lay on her stomach as he rubbed scented oil into her skin, soothing the burn.

Tears pricked her lashes and she stayed face down, trying to hold it together. How long had it been since anyone had made her feel this way? Beautiful and desired? The times before when she'd sought out the hands of other men to satisfy her need to be dominated it hadn't felt deep or intense. Sometimes she'd felt really good, most of the time it felt like eating fast food, she was satisfied but an hour later, empty again.

She felt the movement as he undid the blindfold. Swallowing her tears, she turned to look up at him. His eyes were a startling blue, almost a steely gray. His features were intensely masculine, nearly feral. Sharp nose, beautiful lips, chiseled chin and sharp cheekbones. A scar marked the skin just above his left eyebrow. Salt and pepper hair that was just a bit too long came to his collar with a natural wave.

Licking her lips she searched for something to say.

He smiled. "You okay, sweetheart? You were amazing."

Her insides warmed and she nodded. "I feel amazing."

"Can I take you to dinner? Tomorrow or Saturday? I have a meeting to go to in two hours and I don't want to have to rush with you. I..." he shrugged, "...I'd like to get to know you a bit better."

The moment stretched long and at last she nodded. "All right." Relief filled her. She'd taken a huge step and the world hadn't ended.

"Can I buy you a drink now?"

"It's awfully loud out there and I have to be at work in a few hours myself. But you can buy me a cup of coffee if you like."

She felt her nudity acutely contrasted with his being fully clothed. As if he sensed it, he got up and handed her her clothes.

"I will miss knowing that those welts would be on you when you woke up. But on the other hand, knowing you're Were makes me feel a bit better that I won't hurt you."

She got dressed while watching him put his gear into his toy bag. She gasped when she caught sight of the rope. He turned to look at her, concern on his face changing to understanding. Ryan tapped on the door.

"Everything all right, cupcake?" He kissed her cheek.

"Yes, thank you. Ben and I are going to grab a coffee."

"Well, my goodness, those baristas are going to thank their lucky stars when you walk in wearing that." He winked and Ben laughed.

"Are you ready?" Hefting the bag in one hand, Ben held his other out for her to take.

Nodding, she reached out and held on.

He dropped the bag into the trunk of his car and they walked three blocks to Café Diva. They took a seat near the front windows and he went and got their drinks. He put a plate of six layer chocolate death between them. Two forks.

"You like chocolate?"

"Ever met a woman or a werewolf who didn't?" She laughed.

"I didn't really know any werewolves until two years ago."

"And?" She watched him as he sipped, wiping away the foam in his mustache with a quick swipe of his tongue. A delicious shiver worked up her spine.

He shrugged. "It wasn't the most auspicious of occasions but now I work with you all on a regular basis."

"What do you do?"

"I'm a cop."

Her fork fell to the plate with a clatter. "Oh shit."

"What? Hey, if I can set aside my prejudices about werewolves, you can get past my being a cop can't you?" He leaned toward her. "Especially because I saw the way you looked at the rope."

She had to close her eyes a moment at the thought of the rope.

"It's not that." Waving that away, she picked up her fork and took a fortifying bite of chocolate cake. "You're Ben Stoner, aren't you?"

"Yeah, how did you know my last name?"

"I'm Tegan Warden."

"Shit, you're Lex and Cade's sister? Cousin?"

"Sister. And why is that bad?"

He chuckled. "Hey, you're the one who was all shocked. And well, Lex is a big ass dude, I'm having very, very untoward thoughts about his sister. I better stock up on silver bullets."

It was Tegan's turn to laugh and the richness of the sound flowed over them both. "I can't believe I've never met you. In two years, you've been doing all this work over Pellini and the Packs, how did I miss you? Because trust me, I would have known if I'd seen you before."

Ben sat and watched the statuesque redhead across from him talk. Goddamn she was the sexiest woman—werewolf—he'd ever met. Beautiful, sensual, breasts that made every straight man on the planet give thanks for women. Her ass had turned the most beguiling shade of pink when he'd flogged her and she came prettier than he'd thought possible.

And it was clear she was a submissive in the bedroom but a strong woman outside. He liked the contrast. A lot. Those feline green eyes and the fiery red hair completed the package.

Tegan Warden was as close to perfect as he'd ever imagined a woman could be. Except she was a werewolf and her brothers were the Alpha and the Enforcer of the local werewolf Pack. Boy could he pick women or what? He might as well hang out in alleys with dollar bills pinned to his clothing and get his ass kicked that way.

Still, he'd bet Tegan Warden was worth it. He greedily soaked in the sight of her bringing the forkful of cake to her lips and eating it. His cock ached when she licked the tines before putting the fork back down. Holy shit, the woman was walking sex.

"I, uh, what was the question? Oh, why we hadn't met before. I don't know. I've gone out to the house a few times but we usually meet down at my office so we can conference in the representatives of the other Packs and the feds."

"I'm not usually patrolling in the house when I'm on duty. I prefer to be outside. That may be where I was if you came to the house. Or I was off or something."

"You still want to go out with me?"

"Yes. You still want to go out with me? Knowing who my brothers are? Because I'll tell you up front, they're both nosy old women about this kind of thing and it's been a while since I've dated and so they're both liable to be a bit, um, forceful about it."

"Because I'm human?"

She waved that off. "Nina was human. No, because like I said, I haven't dated in a while and they're both just very protective. And you know yourself that right now things are very hinky with Pellini out there."

He nodded. "There's a story there, isn't there? About the not dating?"

"Yeah."

"Okay. Dinner. Tomorrow night. Perhaps a movie? And if things go well... Well, there are other things we could try." He loved the way her eyes widened and then her pupils enlarged and her breathing quickened. "And you can tell me then. I want to know you."

He walked her back to her car and she gave him her address and phone number.

As she moved to get inside, he stepped close, his body caging hers against the door. One hand slid up her waist and over the side of her neck, essentially collaring half of her with his palm and fingers.

She fought the limpness that her body wanted to give him. Not in public. She didn't want to give in to him all the way just yet. But she sure as hell wasn't going to turn away when his lips met hers.

Her arms slid around his neck as the soft, gentle kiss became more intense. The edge of his mustache tickled her top lip, his scent, the scent of an alpha human male, strong and spicy, filled her nose, rode her senses.

His tongue stroked over the seam of her lips and she opened her mouth to him, letting him inside. His taste, chocolate and coffee and man nearly knocked her off her feet.

Oh how she wanted more but he broke the kiss and took a step back, slowly letting go of her neck. "I could do that all night. But you deserve better than a parking lot. I'll see you tomorrow night then. Seven."

She resisted touching her fingertips to her lips until she'd gotten onto the 520 bridge heading back into Seattle.

Chapter Three

Ben walked off the elevator and saw Lex and Cade there with two guards. He saw the resemblance then between the other Wardens and the one he couldn't get his mind off.

He'd quickly driven home and showered, changing out of his jeans and T-shirt and into khaki pants and a button-down shirt. Her taste was in his mouth like it belonged there.

Shaking his head to try and dislodge her, he reached out and shook hands with Lex and Cade and waved them into his office.

Lex sat and leaned in. "Why do you smell like my sister?"

Megan raised a brow and hid a smile.

"I, uh, well your sister and I have started to date I suppose you could say." It was disconcerting that they could smell her on him even after a shower. He was glad they hadn't had sex, he wasn't ready to have to explain that to them.

"You could say? What the hell does that mean?" Cade's voice was a low growl.

"Oh for cripe's sake! She's an adult. He's an adult. Stop it or I'll tell Nina."

Ben wanted to thank Megan but he just leaned back in his chair. He had to approach this as an equal. He wished he'd had more time to think on it but it was something he had to deal with right then.

"I just met Tegan this evening. I've asked her to have dinner with me because all we had time for was coffee. I'm sure she'll tell you more if she feels it's necessary."

"What are your intentions?"

"Cade!" Megan stomped to him. "I'm telling you this as your sister, not as a member of your Pack. Let Tee tell you all this if she wants. If you meddle...look, please. Let her have a life."

Ben wondered what that comment meant. He supposed it had something to do with Tegan's saying she hadn't dated for a long time.

"I want to respect Tegan. I'm not asking to marry her. I just met her. But I like her a lot. I enjoyed her company and I want to spend more time with her and get to know her. I'm an honorable man, my intentions are not something I'm going to share with you other than I'll treat her with respect and honesty. And now we're moving on to our conference call with Nick, Gabe, Tracy and Agent Benoit."

Once the other three Alphas and the FBI agent were on the line they began to compare notes.

"Today I received a call. Jack says Pellini has been pressuring Tina, the Fourth in National, for more control. Templeton is holding Pellini off for now but I think it may be time for some of the Packs to break with Jack. It'll be authentic and keep Pellini thinking National and Templeton are still in his pocket. Tina is too weak to challenge Jack so all this internal politicking will keep Pellini busy for a while." Ben sighed. Templeton Mancini was the National Alpha and right at the moment, Warren Pellini believed him and the National Enforcer, Jack Meyers to be in his pocket when really they were working with the FBI and some of the other Packs to try and bring him down. This was complicated by the fact that their Fourth was in fact a Pellini pawn and they'd recently lost their Third to Pacific when he became Tracy Warden's mate. Damned werewolves were more complicated and political than humans.

"I'll go first," Gabe Murphy, the co-Alpha of Pacific Pack and Cade and Lex's brother-in-law, spoke over the phone line. "It'll mean more coming from me because I was Third for a long time and used to count Jack as a good friend." They were still good friends in fact. But the plan was for Jack to look dirty, which put Gabe in the position of publically holding his old friend up as a liar and a fraud. Kept Pellini feeling in control while they looked for ways to take him out.

"Pellini has pretty much taken over Sargasso and Quinta. It's very strategic, they're both on the border and he can move drugs and guns through a lot easier now." Ben sat back and took notes.

"He's working on Michigan and Maple Leaf for the same reason. We need to move on him and soon. He's like a cancer, the deeper he gets into the Pack structure the more dangerous he becomes. We can't let it happen," Cade added.

"We can't move just yet. Not until we know if he's got the virus, Cade. If he's got the virus and we move prematurely we're endangering wolves and humans alike. We have to take this slow." Ben understood Cade's wanting-to-get-in-and-end-it-now attitude, he felt the same way but the stolen lycanthropy virus was too big a threat. They had to be methodical and smart, too many lives were at stake to rush or be sloppy.

Cade sighed, sitting back.

The conference call lasted another twenty minutes before breaking up. At the conclusion, Megan stood and went to the door, looking outside and conferring with Dave, the other guard who'd come to escort Lex and Cade.

"Keep me apprised." Cade nodded sharply at Ben who nodded back.

"You'd better be good to my sister. She's been hurt and I'd have no problem ripping your head off and beating your body with your spine."

Ben had been a cop for fifteen years; he knew when a man was telling the truth and Lex was not lying. He put his hands up.

"I'm not an asshole and your sister is a werewolf, she can kill me herself if I get out of line. Now go on. I'm willing to talk with you in detail about Pellini but not about my love life."

Megan reached in and yanked Lex toward the door and Ben heard Cade chuckle.

When they'd finally gone, Ben sat in his chair and looked at the stack of papers on his desk. He knew he should back off. Cade and Lex were going to be a big hassle if he continued to see Tegan but he couldn't help it. There wasn't anything he wanted more than to see her again.

℘

Tegan knew they'd heard about her and Ben the minute she walked into the house. They must have smelled her on him when they had their conference call.

Trying to ignore it, she checked in with Dave, who filled her in on all the details she'd need for the midnight to six a.m. shift. It wasn't much. She'd spend most of that time as a wolf anyway, patrolling the grounds.

That's why she took the midnight shift one day a week. It was solitary, she didn't have to talk to anyone and she could be outside in wolf form. It was a nice gig.

But when Lex came around the corner wearing the big-brother-in-charge face, she knew she wouldn't be able to get out the door any time soon.

"Good luck," Dave murmured. "I'll get Peter out on your patrol, you can do inside tonight."

Damn. Stuck inside. With her brothers who knew she'd been rubbing up on Ben Stoner. Her heart sped as she thought of that kiss and the way he'd taken her in hand at the club. Thank goodness they didn't know about *that*.

"Evening, Lex. It's a bit late for you isn't it?" She was almost amused by his frowny appearance.

"Why didn't you tell me about Ben?"

"I just met him. I'm an adult, Lex, I don't run home to tell you about every man I meet."

"He's human, Tee. It's very complicated to date humans. I don't want you to get hurt."

"Lex, I like him." She shrugged. "He's funny and nice and very sexy. He asked me to dinner. He made me feel beautiful."

"I'm just saying that perhaps dating wolves would be better. Safer."

"Which must be why you did it, huh? Lex, I haven't had a romantic thought about anyone in over four years. I have not been touched by a lover in all that time. Not kissed because I was so lovely he couldn't stop himself. Do you know how lonely that is? Tonight I met someone who made me feel alive after being numb for a very long time. I don't care if Ben is a human or a wolf. He's a nice man and we're going out to eat. It's not the prom, it's just a date."

He moved to her, hugging her, and for the first time since the weeks after Lucas's death, she not only let him but she returned it.

"I just worry about you. I love you, Tee. I saw you nearly lose it after Lucas. I don't want you to ever have to be hurt again. You've had enough in your lifetime. I'm going to try and not interfere too much. I said try. I just want to protect all of you."

"Aw, Lex, you know what? Nina is the best thing that ever happened to you. And I know you want to protect us all. And I love you too."

"Why does she get all the credit?" Lex teased as he stepped back, kissing Tegan's forehead. "I was a fabulous guy before she came along."

Tegan laughed. "Yeah. A fabulous control freak. But, since you've been together you've relaxed a bit."

Cade walked in and put his arms around the two of them briefly. "We're all getting better. I can't say I'm pleased about this new development but Ben is a good guy for a human. And it's so good to see the old Tegan again."

"Older and wiser, with a few bumps and bruises but I'm trying. Lucas wouldn't want me to just roll over and give up."

"No he wouldn't. So you like Stoner huh?" Cade sat at the table and looked at his sister.

"As I was telling Lex, I just met him tonight. He's a nice man. Handsome. We hit it off and had coffee. He asked me to dinner. It's just a date. Stop engraving the wedding invitations already. And what difference does it make if he's human? Why are you both making such a big deal out of it?"

"He's not going to understand our culture or our rules. You remember how it was with Nina."

"Well, uh, yeah! Someone tried to kill me at the first dinner I attended as your mate. Excuse me but that's an issue with *you* people, not with humans." Nina came into the room, looking pissed off.

"You can't deny it's been difficult because you were human when we mated. That's all I'm saying," Lex countered.

"No it isn't what you're saying at all. What made things difficult, Lex? Werewolves burned my house down, killed my brother and turned me without my consent in a fight to the death because someone insulted my dead brother and I was supposed to apologize. That's not an issue of me being human. That's an issue with just how undemocratic werewolves are and how they cling to the old ways that used to protect them but aren't necessary now."

Tegan listened to her sister-in-law and agreed. Had agreed, especially since that night Nina had been torn apart and no one could move to help her.

"I'm not having this conversation again, Nina. It's been two years. Let it go." Cade made a cutting motion with his hand.

Nina looked shocked and stood. "You're right. And I said afterwards that I'd never be able to trust you again on the level I did before that, Cade. Thank you for reminding me."

"Nina! That's unfair." Cade stood and Tegan sighed.

"I'm done here. Nina's right about whose issue all of that really was. Cade, you're wrong. You did what you did that night and I understand why, but we need to change our ways. I'm going to get to work. Goodnight." Tegan leaned in and hugged Nina, who was caught off-guard but accepted the support gratefully.

Silent and surprised, they watched her leave the room before she heard them taking up the argument anew.

Tegan walked through the house and did a security check. Everything was fine and after an hour, she went out and chatted with Peter for a while, listening to night sounds.

But something wasn't right. Tegan changed into wolf form and moved around the perimeter that surrounded the house until she got to a spot on a vista about a quarter of a mile away.

Someone had been there. Another wolf. Two. She didn't recognize the scent so it wasn't a Cascadia wolf. Tegan went over the whole area, scenting a trail down from the vista to a dirt road that they often used when the Pack came up for casual weekend runs.

A car had been there about three hours before. When she'd first arrived. Damn. Peter should have noticed this and she didn't relish having to deal with Lex over such a huge failure. Peter would surely get his ass in big trouble.

Worse, she smelled gun oil at the vista where it was obvious someone had been camped to watch the house. It wasn't a close enough spot to snipe through the windows. Lex had been very meticulous with the plans when he'd designed it, taking great care to situate the house on a high point, out of all but surface to air missile range. On top of that, their security existed in concentric rings, layer upon layer of failsafes for protection of the house and the property around it. Still, the spot where she'd scented the intruders was close enough to monitor the comings and goings into the property.

She followed the trail of the car out to the road and lost the scent once she hit the entry to the drive to the main house. Too many other vehicles had been in and out to keep track.

Trotting back the way she'd come, Tegan rechecked to be sure no one else was around before getting back to the house and changing back.

Knowing Lex would want to hear of this immediately, even if it was four in the morning, she gave Peter a glare and motioned him inside. She then buzzed Megan and Dave and the other guards, telling them to meet in Lex's office in ten minutes before finally contacting Lex.

He came into his office five minutes later, stone faced.

Tegan knew that face, she wore it then herself.

"Tell me," he said simply as he sat down.

"Intruders. On the vista up the road. I scented two. They'd been camped there for a few hours, probably starting at eleven or so and stayed until about two. I followed their scent to the back road and down to the main road, losing it when I got to the main drive. They weren't our wolves and at least one of them had a gun."

Lex's eyes narrowed. "Who had outside duty tonight?"

Peter walked forward, eyes down. "I did, Enforcer. I failed. I'm sorry."

"Two strangers with a gun within a mile of this house. That's a failure all right." Lex looked to Tegan. "Why is it you discovered this and not him?"

"I went outside to compare notes for the shift. It was in the air. It just wasn't right. I shifted and checked the outer perimeter." Tegan shrugged. There was no way to sugarcoat it. Peter had fucked up. Every outside shift should include a run around the outermost perimeters. "There is no excuse for such a lapse and I take responsibility for it. The team is mine when I'm working."

"I appreciate that, Tegan, but this is not yours to own. Peter has been in the Enforcer guard for fifteen years. He got lazy and that could have gotten someone killed. We know Pellini is out to hurt us. We can't afford this kind of lapse."

Tegan had to fight her wolf not to completely submit to the Enforcer wolf. The anger radiated off him in waves. This was not her sweet and concerned brother. This was Lex Warden, legendary Enforcer, boogeyman to all naughty wolves everywhere.

Peter fell to his knees and put his forehead to the ground in utter obeisance. Lex's arm shot out and Peter was on his side, bloody but still breathing.

"Rise, Peter. You took your punishment. You'll be on probation and moved to administrative work. I can't trust you in the field."

And that was worse than a cuff to the face. Having your Enforcer tell you he didn't trust you to keep the Alpha safe was a deep blow and Tegan watched as Peter flinched but kept his eyes down.

"Yes, Enforcer. I'm so sorry."

"I want the teams to expand to five. Let's go with three shifts of eight hours. Tegan, I want you on the day shift. Eight to four. Lead it. Megan, you're on midday. Four to midnight. Dave, you'll take midnight to eight. Choose your team carefully. Put two extra guards on Cade and one more on Nina at the nursery."

Nina was going to love having another bodyguard hanging around her all day as she dealt with customers. Tegan was glad Lex and Megan would have to deal with her.

Lex stood. "Shift change starts today. Tee, grab some sleep so you can get started at eight, please."

Nodding shortly, she moved around him to the door. She gave brief instructions after consulting with Dave and Megan about who would take over for her and get outside, she headed toward the guest room that had been hers for some time.

"Tegan."

She turned around to see Lex moving toward her.

"You did an excellent job tonight, Tee. Thank you." He touched his hand to his forehead and heart and it moved her. He'd thanked her as Enforcer to his subordinate wolf instead of brother to sister. It meant a lot.

"Thank you."

She changed into some clothes she'd left behind, knowing there'd be times like these when she'd have to sleep over, and slid between the sheets. Even though she was amped from the situation, she knew she needed the rest and meditated until she was able to shut down and fall asleep.

Ben's steel-blue eyes were the last thing she thought of before she fell into sleep.

Chapter Four

By the time Tegan got home that evening she was tired. But not too tired for dinner. She had an hour and a half so she decided on a quick, forty-five minute nap and then she'd get ready.

People often didn't realize just how good a short nap felt but when Tegan awoke at six-fifteen she felt refreshed. Even more so after a shower and a cup of coffee as she got ready.

Dinner and maybe a bit of play, he'd said. Tegan shivered as she remembered just what a fine hand he had at play.

It was January but wolves were very warm blooded. Foregoing a coat, she chose a scoop necked cashmere sweater. It was a coppery-brown that Tracy had given her for her birthday the year before. A long black wool skirt and knee high boots with a nice heel completed the outfit. She decided to leave her hair down and went with just a little makeup. She generally preferred a bit of lipstick and some mascara.

She'd just fastened some pretty earrings when she heard her doorbell ring and with trembling hands, she smoothed down her skirt. "It's going to be all right, Lucas. Right?" she asked herself in the mirror before moving to get it.

Checking to be sure it was someone she knew, she opened the door and his presence hit her, tightening her entire body. He stood on her doorstep in a black turtleneck, jeans and boots.

So damned sexy she wanted to skip the dinner part and go to the sex part.

Instead she smiled and motioned him to come inside.

He brushed a kiss over her lips as he passed. "You look beautiful tonight, Tegan."

She turned to him after locking the door. "Why thank you. You look quite handsome yourself."

He looked around the room at the pictures and art hanging up. "Wow, this is amazing." He indicated a painting hanging over her fireplace.

"It is, isn't it." She smiled. "It's my brother-in-law Sid's work. He's a very talented artist. He gave that to me as a wedding present."

Shit. Well, she hadn't planned to tell him about Lucas right then and certainly not like that but he was a cop and she knew he hadn't missed what she'd said. Especially when he looked her in the eyes.

"You were married before?"

"Yes. He died, four years ago."

His face softened. "I'm sorry. How?"

"He was an Army Ranger like Lex used to be. He was killed in action in Afghanistan."

Ben whistled low. "Wow. He must have been young."

"Twenty-three. He'd just gotten through Ranger school about eight months before. He loved it."

"How long were you two together?"

"Four years. I was twenty when we mated. He was nineteen."

"So young. I'm sorry for your loss. I really am."

Looking into his face, she knew he meant it. What a

genuine man he was. So totally different looks and personality wise from Lucas, who'd been a wiry blond who was always moving and joking.

"Well, I didn't mean to bring the date down right off. Sorry about that."

In three steps he was on her, his arms around her waist, forehead against hers. "You didn't bring the date down. You were sharing about your life. Now, are you hungry?"

"Starving. It's been a crazy twenty-four hours, let me tell you."

"I heard part of it earlier. We can talk about it later. Does Thai sound okay with you? Lotus?"

"Love it."

Keeping his arms around her, he moved his mouth to hers. Kissing her slow and sweet. His body was hard and warm against her own and there was no ignoring the brand of his cock through the denim of his jeans against her stomach.

When he pulled away, she was lightheaded and need for him pulsed through her. Each taste she got of him made her want him more. The raw nature of that need edged her senses.

"You do something to me," he murmured, stepping back.

She nodded and they walked out the door without commenting any further. What else could she say? It was true but she couldn't just let it go. She wanted more of it, more of him.

Dinner at the small Thai place in Wallingford was nice. Just a few miles from her house, the restaurant was one of her favorites.

"So how was your day?" Tegan asked, liking the way his sweater stretched over his upper body.

"The usual in the human crime world. An assault, car theft.

All the excitement came after I got a call from Lex." He spoke quietly but not in a whisper that would get attention.

"Yes. It's been a very busy day. Nina is pissed at Lex for putting extra security on her. We had a very long meeting this afternoon about the new teams."

"I know what it means to pull a double shift. Would you like to call things a night early so you can get some sleep?"

She slowly shook her head. She knew what she wanted and it wasn't sleep. Not then. Not for hours she hoped.

"Well, perhaps I can help relax you." There was a question in his eyes and it wasn't about a massage.

Tegan watched him for long moments. She'd never really submitted to anyone other than Lucas before, except for the hour long play sessions she'd engaged in a few times at the club. She knew, watching this man and the determined way he handled everything from ordering food to flogging, that he was not a man of casual appetites. If she took this step, she'd be taking a step with him above and beyond a few hours of slap and tickle.

And one couldn't submit if one didn't trust the dominant. Tegan was a woman who went by gut instinct. It served her well and kept her alive during the time she'd spent as one of Lex's Enforcer guard. And her gut told her two things. One that she could trust Ben Stoner with her very life and two, taking this step would mean something monumental. He was not merely a date if she let him top her. He'd see her as more and she would see it that way too.

Something about the man called to her, made her respond in a way she hadn't in a very long time. And she didn't want to ignore that.

"I'd like that," she said at last, taking a leap and hoping like hell she wouldn't be sorry.

"Good." He smiled warmly.

After dinner they decided to skip a movie and go back to her place. Once inside, they sat on her couch and he turned to her.

"Tegan, I don't top anyone casually. I don't play outside a club unless I'm sure the woman is going to be a regular person in my life. And me in hers. I think it's important to say all of this up front so you know what I need and I expect. And so I know what you need too."

"Okay."

"So laying it all out—I'd very much like us to see each other regularly. And exclusively. Some doms can separate the sex from the play but I can't. Leaving you last night without being inside you was very difficult. Is that what you want?"

"A relationship with you? Exclusive?"

He nodded.

"I haven't been with anyone other than Lucas. Not as a submissive anyway. I dated before I met him but I was twenty when I mated and then after he died there was no one. Not until you. I've dated a few times in the last three months but nothing serious. I've played three times at the club but none of it was anything approaching how it felt last night. So yes, I'd like to see you exclusively."

"Good. We can work out your limits as we go. You have a safeword and I expect you to use it if you're in trouble or overwhelmed. We can also work up to new levels of things we do. I'd love to see you in my collar but it's something I take very seriously so I wouldn't collar you until we'd been together a while and I knew you were truly willing to submit to me."

"Okay, that sounds appropriate."

They spoke for some time, outlining boundaries and

expectations. Tegan liked that he seemed to place so much importance on open communication. D/s wasn't something to be taken lightly in the context of a relationship. She was relieved to see he thought so too.

"Now, I don't have any desire to top you twenty-four hours a day. I only want your submission in the bedroom."

"Good. Because I don't take orders except there."

He smiled in a way that promised very wicked things.

"I want you to get up, remove your clothes and then lead me to your bedroom."

Standing on somewhat shaky legs, Tegan leaned over, pulled her boots off and slid out of her skirt. The sweater followed and Ben looked her over as she stood in her bra and barely there panties.

"My God, you're so beautiful." His voice was smoky and hoarse, it stroked over her senses and soothed her even as it seduced.

One hand popped the catch between her breasts and her bra fell to the ground. She stepped out of her panties as she walked from the room, feeling absolutely gorgeous. He made her feel so beautiful and sexy just by looking at her.

Once in the bedroom she stood next to her bed, waiting.

He came in and dropped the duffel just next to the bedside table and walked around her body. "Let's get warmed up, shall we?" He turned her body so that she was facing the bed and stepped away.

Moments later she heard him unzip the bag. Leaning around her, he laid several items on the bed in her view. Wrist restraints. Rope. A fuzzy-lined blindfold. A flogger and a paddle.

Standing behind her, he pressed his body against her back. "Do any of those tickle your fancy, Tegan?" His breath was warm against her ear. "I know you like the rope. I saw your face last night, heard your gasp. Did it make you wet? Imagining it against your skin?"

He leaned down and she watched his hand, wondering what he'd pick up. The wrist restraints.

"Hands behind your back, Tegan."

With the warm honey of subspace beginning to brew within her, Tegan moved her hands, clasping them at her back.

The restraints were lined and slipped on easily. He tightened them just shy of pain. "Is that too tight?"

She shook her head.

"Good. Now bend forward. I've got your wrists."

He grabbed the restraints and helped her bend forward, her upper body against her mattress. The paddle and flogger were in her line of vision and he picked the paddle up. She took a deep breath.

The edge of the paddle drew a line down her back where she heard him twirl it in his hand just before the first crack sounded and the surface hit her square on the ass. Over and over the blows rained down, each in a different place until a warm glow covered her skin and the heat built up toward her clit with each smack.

The paddle came back to the bed beside the flogger and he leaned over and blew over the stinging skin of her ass and thighs.

She felt him go to his knees behind her, pushing her thighs wider.

"So wet. Your pussy is pink and pretty and glistening." His thumbs pulled her labia apart and she cried out when his tongue took a long lick, dipping into her gate and then back to swirl around her clit.

Her fists clenched at her back where they were restrained and she pressed back into his mouth as he feasted on her pussy with expertise. It had been so very long since she'd felt a tongue on her pussy she'd forgotten how good it felt.

One of his hands shifted, and his thumb slid into her pussy as his middle finger stretched up to stroke over the tight pucker of her rear passage. A moan ripped from her lips.

"Please," she gasped.

He stopped, pulling his face back and she whimpered.

"Please what, Tegan?"

"Please make me come."

"Why?"

Confused a moment, she was silent. "I need it. God, please, I need it."

And he went back to her, the combination of tongue and lips and hands, even the scrape of his teeth against the sensitive nerves of her clit all went into synchronized overdrive until she began to come so hard she saw stars against her eyelids. Pleasure washed through her in wave after wave, knocking her down into a place where all she could do was feel good.

His hands petted and caressed her as he stood, undoing her wrists. The paddle and flogger went back into the bag and he looked at her and she nearly came again at the look in his eyes. Intent, raw and naked there. Intent to take her places she'd only dreamed of the last four years.

All she could do was nod slowly and say, "yes."

"On your feet then, Tegan. Undress me."

She stood on slightly shaky legs and he put a hand to her arm to support her. Once she was standing and looking at him, knowing he'd be naked soon, she began to feel much more solid and the hands that reached to take his sweater off were sure and steady.

His upper body was hard and wrapped in tight muscle. Not bulked up muscle but he clearly worked out and used his body in his job. Her palms smoothed over the hard planes of his chest and abdomen, through the salt and pepper hair there. She laid a kiss on his chest, over his heart and dropped to her knees, her hands going to his waistband.

The jingle of his belt buckle made her pussy clutch with need and the *pop, pop, pop* of the buttons on his fly skittered down her spine.

When she pulled the jeans down, his cock sprang free, so hard it lay flat against his belly. No underwear. Good gracious the man was sexy. Grabbing the denim, she pulled the jeans off and he stepped out of them, having already taken his boots off when they'd come back from dinner. His socks were the last thing to go and then he stood before her, gloriously naked and incredibly masculine.

His scent made her lean in and rub her cheeks over his thighs. She'd thought she'd never burn for a man as much as she had Lucas and it felt almost like cheating that she craved Ben's touch so much.

"Stay on your knees."

He pulled the coil of rope off the bed and let it hit the ground but for the bit in his hands. The dull thunk made her moan softly.

"Get comfortable." He tossed her a pillow and she put it beneath her and clasped her hands at her back. "Mmm. Now there's a sight. I like that very much."

He began to wind the rope around her body, slowly and methodically. The feel of the hemp rope against her bare skin was heaven and shivers broke over her. He fit it snug, creating an upper body rope corset that framed her breasts and pinned her upper arms and down around her wrists.

The familiar heaviness came over her as her body released serotonin and ropespace hit her like a warm cloak. She felt what he was doing but within the confines of the rope she felt as if she were floating.

She wasn't sure how much time had passed when he finally straightened and stood back. Her hands throbbed in time with the beat of her heart and his cock was right there, within reach of her mouth.

"Fuck. I've never seen a more beautiful sight than you tied up and on your knees before me. Are you with me, Tegan?"

Looking up from his cock and into his face she nodded, licking her lips.

"Good. Suck my cock." Taking a step forward, he held himself at an angle where she could take him into her mouth.

His taste burst though her, lighting up all her nerve endings, making her feel so alive it was shocking. She had to have more of him. Eagerly she rocked herself back and forth, taking as much of him into her mouth as she could, over and over.

"Yes. Oh yes, Tegan. Your mouth is so good. Keep me nice and wet. Oh yeah, that's the way."

She fell into a dreamy rhythm as she sucked and licked his cock, wanting to bring him as much pleasure as he'd given her.

Ben looked down at Tegan and while she might have been the one physically on her knees, she'd taken him emotionally to his. The sight of her here—bound for his pleasure, her lips wrapped around his cock, that gorgeous hair tumbled about her shoulders—spoke to him.

He was forty years old. She wasn't the first beautiful

woman he'd topped or been with naked but he'd never, ever felt this level of intensity for anyone before. Not even Sarah had made him burn this way.

A deep, nearly feral need burned within him for this woman and he had no idea where it came from but he could not get enough of her. The taste of her honey still coated his lips and hands and he wanted more.

When her eyes opened and she rolled them up to catch his gaze he sucked in a breath and pulled away from her, delighting in her disappointed pout.

"I need to be inside you, Tegan. Are you still with me?" He wanted to be sure they were on the same page. Later on he'd rely on her use of the safeword more but he wanted to know her better first, know her limits and her likes and dislikes. It would take a while for them to both get comfortable with each other completely.

"Oh God, yes. Please."

He smiled. "Let me help you up. I want you to ride me with the ropes on." He helped her to stand and then got on the bed, taking her weight as she got on after him and moved to straddle his body.

"Wait, let me get a condom."

She shook her head vehemently. "No. You don't need one. I'm not at my fertile time and we don't carry STDs. Please."

Like he was going to argue with that?

She straddled him and he held the head of his cock so she could sink down on him, and each let out a long, shuddering moan as he filled her completely.

He watched the muscles in her thighs bunch and flex as she pulled her body up his cock and then ease back down. Her breasts swayed slightly with the movement, nicely framed by the rope. His hands burned to touch her and he gave in, sliding his palms up her thighs and belly, over the rope to her nipples, pinching and rolling them until she writhed on him.

"Such sensitive nipples. I'm tucking that away for next time. I wonder if I can make you come just from licking and playing with them?"

Her only response was a desperate whimper.

But he was already close from paddling that ass to a pretty shade of pink, seeing her honey rain down her thighs. And he'd eaten her sweet pussy until she'd come screaming into the blankets. By the time she'd undressed him, his cock literally throbbed for her. The forty minutes he'd taken to bind her had sent her right into ropespace and he'd gotten off just watching, feeling the rope in his hands, against her skin, listening to her breath slow. And then she'd sucked his cock like she was starving for him.

Ben was quite sure he'd never been so fucking turned on in his entire life. Wetting two of his fingers, he found her clit, still swollen and begging for attention. Slowly but surely, he teased it with the tip of his finger, adding a bit more pressure each time until she rocked forward, grinding herself against him. When he gently plumped her clit between his thumb and forefinger, her head fell back and she bit her bottom lip as he felt her pussy begin to clutch and flutter around him with orgasm.

He took over then, thrusting up into her, holding her hips as he did to get as deep as he could until climax burst through him with blinding intensity as he emptied himself deep into her, naked cock to naked pussy.

But it kept on, wave after wave until he felt as if he'd surely drown in her and when he opened his eyes, the world shifted and he saw a look of utter wonder on her face just before he lost consciousness.

"Shit!" Tegan didn't want to break free of the rope but she was worried about Ben so she reached down and pulled her wolf toward the surface enough to muscle through the ropes. Hands tingling and arms asleep, she pulled herself off his cock reluctantly and shook herself to get feeling back while saying his name.

Jumping out of bed, Tegan rushed into her bathroom, coming back with a wet washcloth that she pressed over his face until he began to return to consciousness.

Smiling at him, she kissed his forehead. "Are you all right?"

"Did you just fuck me into unconsciousness?" Startled, he sat up and saw the rope.

"Sorry. I broke free, I was worried about you. We can go to Monk's together and buy some new rope. Are you feeling better?"

"What the hell happened?" He put a hand to his forehead and then looked at her, realizing how different he felt. "Tegan?"

She took a deep breath. "Well, uh, do you want a drink first?"

"Did you just change me into a werewolf?"

She rolled her eyes. "I'd never do that without your permission! Okay, so the short of it is, you and I have just mated."

"What?"

"I know. It works like this. Werewolves mate for life. It's a very long story but Lucas was my mate and I had an anchor bond, I still do so we don't have to deal with that. But Lucas died and my anchor saved me from dying too. When Lucas died, I was able to mate again. But of course I was devastated and I haven't dated or even had sex in the last four years."

"My head hurts, Tegan. Anchors, mates? What the hell are you telling me?"

"Hey, don't be an ass. I didn't plan this but it sure explains why I was so damned attracted to you from the start." She gave him a narrow-eyed look and he relaxed, putting a hand on her thigh. "So anyway, it works like this—there are genetically compatible people out there. Not like only one person on earth but it's rare enough. Anyway, when the semen of one of the genetically matched people enters the vagina of the other person it creates a, hell, I don't know, it's sort of magic. It changes the DNA of each party to something else entirely, something matched and coupled. It creates a bond between the two people. In my culture, it's marriage. When you came inside me, you sealed the bond and Claimed me as it were."

"Tegan, I won't deny that I am really attracted to you and have been from the first moment I laid eyes on you. But I'm human."

"Nina was too." Tegan shrugged. "I won't make you do anything you don't want to do. I won't force myself on you. You have to accept it in your own way."

He stood and began to pace, alarmed at how much he wanted to get back in bed and roll around with her. "Why did you do this to me without telling me?"

"I didn't know. I wouldn't have done it if I'd known. I'd have waited to get to know you better. I know you don't know me very well, but I would not have done this without your consent if I'd known. I'm not like that."

And instinctively he knew that was true. But he didn't know anything else from there. He grabbed his clothes and began to get dressed. She watched him from the bed with sad eyes.

"I can't handle this. I've got to go home and think."

She nodded. "I understand."

"What does this mean?"

Sighing, she stood and pulled on a robe. "What do you mean, what does this mean? Do you want me to use the rope to keep you here? You're freaked, you don't trust what I'm saying and you're overwhelmed." She shrugged. "But, Ben? When I mated with Lucas, I wanted to be with him all the time. Wanted to touch him and be touched. When we were apart for any long period of time, like when he was in Ranger school and when he was shipped out to Afghanistan, it was incredibly difficult. I expect you'll feel it too. The need to be with me."

She put her arms around herself. "I am sorry, Ben. I've chained you to me without your consent and I apologize for that. I didn't know."

"Is it reversible?"

She shook her head. "No."

He felt the need to comfort her and reached out to caress her face. "I believe you didn't know. I'm not angry. But I'm confused. I was ready for a regular sub and a girlfriend, I don't know if I'm ready for a wife. I have to get out of here. I will call you. I promise."

She stood in the doorway to her bedroom, watching him pull on his boots, grab his bag, and head for the door.

"Goodnight, Tegan."

Even before he'd gone she felt him leave. Felt him pull himself away from her and the emptiness that had been her constant companion for the last four years suddenly consumed her again. Having that warmth of connection to a mate again after the aching hole inside herself, only to have it stolen again, left her bereft.

Lowering the hand she'd raised as he'd gone, she slid to the

Lauren Dane

ground and began to weep.

Chapter Five

Tegan dragged her ass to the house, knowing there'd be a shitstorm once she got there and they scented that she'd been Claimed. But there was no way around it so she went, hoping Nina was there to get her back.

She called Layla on the drive over and, as always, Lay was calm and cool and said she'd head on over to the house as well.

It was seven thirty when Tegan rolled into the kitchen and thanked her lucky stars to see Nina at the sink and Megan sitting at the table. No Cade or Lex in sight.

Both women spun as Tegan entered the room, nostrils flared. Before they could exclaim, she put a finger to her lips to silence them both. Nina's brow rose as she turned to pour a mug of coffee for Tegan and hand it her way.

"Sit. Lex and Cade are in the office so we don't have a lot of time. What happened?"

She told them the whole story, glad she'd cried all her tears the night before.

Nina looked shocked and then shrugged. "Shit. Well, Ben is a great guy. He'll come around. He was shocked. Hell, I remember. I was shocked too."

"I hope so." Tegan took a sip of her coffee, thankful for her very common sense sister-in-law.

"Don't you need to take care of the tri-bond?" The tri-bond was a second male who had sex with the female and formed an anchor, like the third leg to a stool. The anchor kept the female alive should her mate die. In some cases, a mated female who refused the tri-bond went insane from the intensity of her feelings for her mate and without the stabilizing influence of the anchor. It was an accepted and honored position for males to hold in the lives of the mated couple.

Tegan shook her head. "No. My anchor is still alive. In cases where the mate dies and the anchor is mated to someone else, the wolf who moves to another mate doesn't need to do the tri-bond again. So no insanity for me."

Megan laughed and squeezed her sister's arm. "I'm glad to see your sense of humor back. I've missed it." She looked up. "Ah the rest of the cavalry has arrived I see. Hey, Lay."

Layla came in, dropping her bag before delivering a kiss to each woman in the room. "Have the control twins heard yet?" Her voice was low.

Tegan shook her head. "No, but they will soon enough. And we have to find a way to keep them off Ben's back. It's hard enough for him to have to deal with this, the last thing he needs are Cade and Lex on his ass."

They all agreed to that. "Okay, but I need to talk to Ben. Because I've been where he is and because I love you, Tee, and he needs to deal. If I'm guessing right, he's got to be jonesin' pretty bad for you right now. He may listen to me easier than anyone else," Nina said.

And that's when Cade and Lex came in. At first it was howls of joy until they heard the whole story. That's when all hell broke loose.

Cade stalked to the door, ignoring Tegan's cries to wait. Until Tegan pulled a weapon and put it to Cade's head. "If you leave this room and go to harass my mate, I will kill you, I swear it."

Cade stopped and turned to face his sister slowly. Nina, Layla and Megan held Lex back. "You best be putting that gun down, Tee. I'm not joking. He needs to deal with his responsibilities."

"I'm not! Don't piss me off any more! He's my mate and I'll protect him. This is not your affair."

"The hell it isn't. You're my sister and one of my wolves. He can't just fuck and run."

"He did not fuck and run! My God, we'd just started to date and then this metaphysical thing happens out of the blue and ties him to me in this rather permanent way. He's shocked and trying to deal with it. Let it be. I mean it, Cade, don't do this. I lost one mate, I will not lose another. I won't." A ragged sob tore through her and Cade took the gun, tossed it to Lex and pulled his sister into his arms. He rocked her back and forth, smoothing a hand over her hair as she wept tears she didn't know she had inside her anymore.

Suddenly all of them surrounded her and comforted her, giving her love and support.

Some minutes later Cade pushed her into a chair and shooed the other guards who'd come running at the commotion, sending them off to patrol.

"We can't let this go on, Tegan." Cade's voice was gentle.

"I'm going down there to talk to him about it." Nina stood. "I've been where he is. Maybe he'll listen to me. Certainly he'll hear me easier than you two."

"Nina," Lex started but just stopped, knowing she'd made her mind up and that she was right. "Okay, I'm going too. As a guard. I won't go into Stoner's office or anything. I swear."

"Fine. Let's go."

Ben's stomach hurt. His back ached and he'd thought of nothing but Tegan since he'd left her place the night before. He'd heard her start to cry once he walked out, and wanted to go back to comfort her but not more than he needed to be away.

He'd driven for hours before going back to his house. Sitting in the dark of his living room, he'd thought about the situation until the sky had begun to pinken with dawn. While he really didn't like the idea of this mate thing, he couldn't deny that he'd been strongly attracted to her from the start.

Ten years ago there'd been Sarah. The great love of his life. Or so he'd thought. They'd lived together and planned to be married. He'd given her his love and a home and his trust. Until she'd broken it and betrayed him, cheating with his partner at the time.

He'd been utterly destroyed. Thrown himself into his work with such dedication that he'd been promoted to detective the next year. But he'd shut off his heart and his emotions, moving from one several months' long relationship to another. He deliberately chose women who didn't challenge him, who didn't stir him. It was nice to sleep with them and then move on with no engagement of emotions on his part. But there had been one woman about a year ago, who'd been his girlfriend for nearly seven months. In her, he'd found his will to top a woman again.

In the last six months or so, he'd come to the conclusion that he wanted a woman in his life again, a girlfriend and a submissive. When Tegan Warden walked into that room at Club De Sade, he'd known she was meant for him.

Certainly not in the sense that it apparently meant now. He didn't love Tegan. He liked her, desired her, wanted to know her more, but to him, marriage meant love.

He'd gone to work in a daze and sat looking at the papers on his desk in between phone calls and meetings until Nina Warden tapped on his door.

Warily he asked her to come in and motioned for her to sit down.

"So wow, huh? That magic semen is something else," she said brightly and he blinked rapidly. "Ben, you know why I'm here. You may not have known that any werewolf can scent the bond on Tegan and now you, but we can. She walked into the house looking like death warmed over and we smelled you on her and the bond and oh boy was it an exiting morning at my house! Tegan held a loaded gun to Cade's head when he threatened to come and talk to you."

He stared at her. The woman just chattered and chattered.

"Oh all right, down to brass tacks. The deal is that I was human and had no real idea of the mate bond thing either when it happened to me. Here I was enjoying some, uh, horizontal interaction with Lex and then bam! I passed out and then he tells me his magic sperm has now changed my DNA. Oh man was I pissed off at him." She snorted. "Anyway, it took a lot of adjustment. There aren't a lot of things about my first few months with Lex that went smoothly. But I'll tell you right now, Ben, he's the best thing in my life. I know this all seems very woo-woo and spooky and you probably resent your lack of choice in the matter, I did too. But she's meant for you. Give it a chance. You don't have to love her yet, but you want her. I know you do. So why not go with that for now while you get to know her?"

And she made sense. Suddenly it all made sense. He could do that. They could continue to date and get to know each other. There was no harm in that. And if they were meant to be like everyone kept saying, it would happen the way it was

59

supposed to.

"Do you think that would work for her? That she'd go for it?"

Nina nodded. "She understands you're upset. She didn't know, she wouldn't have just bound you without telling you. She's a good woman, Ben. One of the best people I know. I trust her with my life. With Lex's life."

He sighed. That was high praise. He knew how much Nina Warden adored her husband. "She's off at five?"

Nina grinned. "Yep."

"Your family, er, Pack will be okay with it too?"

She shrugged. "Look, I'm not gonna lie to you, wolves are pushy about Packmates. They're downright annoying when it comes to their family. Tegan's brothers are the top dogs, um, wolves. So they wanted to come here, beat your ass and drag you back to the house and give you to their sister to make her feel better. That's what they do. That's what brothers do. But as she quite unabashedly held a Glock to Cade's head at the very threat, he's backing off for the time being to try and let you two work it out. I'll do what I can to help. But if you hurt her, you'll wish Cade or Lex had found you first because I'm not playing around here. Tegan is special, you will not harm her. You have her heart, you *will* be careful with it or I'll hack your balls off with a plastic spork and feed them to feral ducks while I make you watch."

He shifted in his chair uncomfortably. "All right. I'll call her when her shift is over and arrange to see her."

"Call her now. She'll feel better and you will too. I promise." Nina stood and went to the door. "Oh and Ben? Welcome to the family." She winked and left.

The woman was fucking scary. He snorted as he picked up the phone and dialed the number Tegan had given him.

She must have seen his name on caller ID because she answered, "Hi." He felt her sadness and relief through the phone lines. Weird. Still, he wished like hell he could touch her to ease her worry.

"Hey. I'm sorry about last night. I didn't know what to do or say. How are you today?"

She chuckled. "It's been a day. I held a gun to my brother's head earlier."

"I heard."

"Ah, Nina's been by."

"She said a lot of stuff. Most of it went over my head. She talks a lot. But some of it made sense. Can I see you tonight? Make you dinner at my place so we can talk?"

"Yeah. I 'd like that."

He gave her directions and she arranged to come over at seven. And he did feel better when he hung up.

Tegan took a deep breath as she got out of her car and stood in Ben's driveway. She liked the look of the unassuming rambler. The front yard was nicely landscaped with Japanese maple trees and pretty shrubbery. Nothing fancy, but it was kept up and Tegan felt like the place was taken care of by someone who cared about it.

For her, the matter was simple. He was her mate. But at the same time, she didn't think she could deal with waiting around until he figured out just what he wanted either. She was a patient woman, the years after Lucas's death had taught her a lot about waiting and truly being ready for the big things. Ben was her big thing.

How she'd balance her need to respect herself and let him find a way to accept what was between them wasn't something she'd worked out. She wanted to give him time. Wanted to help him through what had to be a very confusing situation. That would be her starting point because he was hers and she knew the joys of having a mate connection and she very much wanted it again.

Tegan had spoken with her grandmother earlier that day. All Grandma would say for sure was that things are thrown in our path for a reason. Ben was there and it was Tegan's destiny to deal with him.

And while she respected her grandma very much, Tegan felt like she'd had her damned share of things thrown in her path for a reason and wondered why something easy couldn't be her destiny instead.

Brushing the front of her clothes, she gave herself a mini pep talk and headed for his front door.

He opened it before she even knocked, standing there looking masculine and sexy. "Hi. Come in."

She walked past him, trying to ignore how much the scent of his body made her weak in the knees. The place was warm inside and a fire was going in the fireplace on the far wall.

The feel of his body behind her washed over her as she tried to hold herself together, wanting to touch him but not knowing if she could bear to be rejected.

"You look beautiful. Even in jeans and a plain shirt you knock me out," he murmured as his arms encircled her waist and she allowed herself to lean back into him.

"Thank you."

Gently, he turned her in his arms until she faced him. "It feels so good to have you in my arms." Leaning down, he kissed her quickly and then returned to her lips for a more thorough kiss, his tongue sliding into her mouth like a lover.

She moaned softly and molded her body to his, putting her arms around his neck as she opened to him.

His taste rushed through her as her senses recognized him, her mate. Her loneliness was gone then, replaced by home and warmth. He filled the Ben-shaped space in her heart.

When he broke the kiss he looked into her eyes for long moments before smiling. "I hope you're hungry. I cook when I'm nervous." Keeping hold of her hand, he pulled her toward the dining room and sat her in a chair. "I'll be right back, the salmon should be done."

He ducked outside through sliding glass doors and opened a grill on his back deck. The man had grilled steaks in January. Okay, then.

Smiling, she watched him come back inside and put a plate of heavenly smelling salmon on the table between them. Plates and bowls filled with all manner of vegetables and other side dishes littered the entire table top.

"Wine?" He held up a bottle of white wine and she nodded. Pouring it, he indicated the table. "Dig in."

If she'd been human, Tegan doubted she'd have much of an appetite. Her nerves jangled and she felt wary and concerned even as being with him was comfortable. But her wolf needed the calories and protein so she dug in.

"This is really good. You're an excellent cook."

"Thank you. My mom and dad owned a restaurant in Renton for twenty-five years. My sister runs it now. We're all good cooks."

"Really? I'd love to go there. That is, well, if you're going to expose them to me."

Sighing, Ben put his fork down and looked at her. Surprise bit into him as he realized he felt her agitation acutely, like it was his own. "Can I feel what you do?"

Wary, Tegan nodded. "There's a link of sorts between us. When we're in the same room we should be able to feel emotions from the other one. Strong emotions more so."

"Okay. Then I can feel how upset and uneasy you feel. And I'm sorry. I don't want you to be hurt or upset. This is all way over my head but even if you were a woman I was merely dating I'd want them to meet you. I'm very close to my family. I haven't told them about this mating thing, but it's more that I don't quite know how to describe it than my being ashamed of you. I'm not. Confused as hell, but not ashamed of you. You're beautiful, Tegan, strong, smart."

Her eyes met his and she let out her tension, nodding.

They ate and talked around the elephant in the room until Ben stood and held his hand out. "Let's just talk about all of this. Okay?"

Standing, she took his hand and followed him into the living room where they sat on the couch together.

"I'm still shocked after last night. I can't lie. It took me by surprise and I don't quite know how to feel about it all. But I know that I'm strongly attracted to you and I want us to see each other. I meant it when I said I wanted to get to know you. I can't say I love you. I don't know you. But I want you. So much my hands start shaking in the middle of my day when I think about you. And I like you. That's a good start, isn't it?"

"What are you saying?" Tegan eyed him cautiously, afraid to hope just yet.

"I'm saying I'd like to continue seeing you. If this is some kind of magical fated mate thing, it should work out that after we've known each other for a while, things will just move to the next step. Everything we talked about last night before we had sex still holds true for me now."

"And what if I don't want that?" Tegan pushed up from the couch and began to pace. "What if I don't want you to toy around with me while you decide if I'm worth being with?"

Panic surged through him for a moment at the thought of her walking away.

"Tegan, I don't plan to toy around with you. Well, I'd like to use toys *on* you, but I truly want to get to know you. I think you're worth being with. But for me, marriage is for when you love someone. And I don't love you. I'm sorry if that's hard to hear but I just met you. It takes time. I want to spend that time. Can't you meet me halfway here?"

Sighing, Tegan went to look out the window and he followed, needing to touch her. He stood behind her, his hands on her shoulders. The scent of her body, the sweet smell of her shampoo tickled his senses and made him slightly crazy with need.

"I can't say I understand what this is like for you. I'm not a werewolf. I only know how I feel and what I can sense through the link. I believe in this mate thing more every second I'm with you. I don't want to hurt you. Can you help me get through this?"

"Yes. I'll try." Her voice was quiet and he wanted everything to be okay, wanted her to turn to him with joy in her eyes.

"Are we okay?"

She shrugged. "How the hell should I know? I hope so. I think so. I can't not be a werewolf, Ben. My family is going to want to meet you. Those who haven't already. We have a ceremony. I can put that off for the immediate future, but my family is important to me and I want you to know that going in."

"I understand and respect that. I'm close to my family too and I want you to meet them. Let's take this one step at a time. We didn't start off in a traditional sense but we can make this

65

work."

She turned into his embrace and he buried his face in her hair, the tension and panic waning as her scent lulled him.

"Will you stay over tonight? It's closer to Cade's from my house than from yours," he spoke softly, his fingers sliding through her hair.

"I want to try and help you through this but I have feelings too. I *need* to be with you. If we're going to be serious and have a relationship, I can. But I need to know for sure what you want."

"I told you what I want. You and I, exclusive, serious. Can we see what happens tonight and go from there? I'm not leading you on. I do want you. Very much." Every few words he paused to kiss a different place on her neck, pushing her hair to the side.

Melting into him she sighed, half contented, half unsure. Each time he touched her, she wanted him more. She knew it would be the same for him. Felt guilty in a sense that part of his attraction to her would be based on their new DNA and the mating than just plain old-fashioned lust. Still, as Grandma was so fond of saying, fate was fate. You sucked it up and got to it or you wallowed but wallowing never got you anywhere.

"I can stay. I always carry a duffel with me. It's in my car."

"Good." He hesitated and looked into her eyes. "Tegan, I need you. I need to touch you, hold you. Be inside you."

A shiver of need ran through her at his words, at the feel of thinly disguised desire emanating from him, rolling off his body in wave after wave. She managed a shaky nod.

Holding a hand out, he kept his eyes on her until she took it. The house was a split level and she followed him up a short flight of stairs and down a hallway to his bedroom. It was warm and masculine, like he was. Black and white prints hung on the wall. Upon closer examination, the photographs were sexual, sensual—the long line of a back, the shine off a black stiletto heel, a wrist wrapped in a cuff. Heat flushed her skin as she slowly walked from frame to frame.

"You've got a whole side to you I never imagined. You're a sensualist, Ben. These are amazing."

"You like them?" Pleasure lit his face.

She nodded. "I really do."

"I took them."

She turned to look at him. "More surprises. Well." One brow rose as she turned to look back at the wrist in the cuff. Jealousy rose within her. How the man could think she'd be sleeping in the room where some picture of another woman he'd dominated hung on the wall was beyond her.

Jealousy knifed through Ben and he realized it belonged to her. "What's wrong?"

She shook her head but he took her chin in his hands. "Tegan, you either submit to me or you don't. I asked you a question. I expect you to be totally honest with me and I'll do my best to do so with you. Now I felt it, I felt your distress and your jealousy. Tell me what's wrong."

"I hate this." She stepped back out of his reach.

"Don't hold yourself away from me, Tegan."

"Fuck you, Ben! God. You know I didn't plan this. I didn't plan to have a nice sexual interlude turn into a claiming. I spent a lot of time on my own, doing my own thing. You fuck me and walk away and want me back on your terms and now you want me to spill my guts on your terms too. It isn't always about you, Ben. Not everything is about your goddamned expectations."

Standing there, Ben watched her through hooded eyes.

"Submission isn't going to be a game, Tegan. We're in my bedroom, this is my domain. Part of our agreement. Your well being is my job just as your pleasure is my job. You aren't letting me do that job when you won't be honest with me. Now, tell me what's wrong."

Her annoyance began to turn into something else as she met his eyes, and even her agitation at him began to fall away as he fully owned his power as a dominant man. His vehemence moved her even as the sharp and yet even tone of his voice made her pussy wet. Suddenly, she wanted to know just what he'd do to punish her disobedience.

Ben's agitation at her refusal to submit suddenly dissolved as he watched her face and knew she was deliberately pushing his limits to see how he'd react. Of course his woman would be a willful submissive. He wanted to laugh but kept his face impassive as he circled her body.

"Are you going to tell me, Tegan? Or—" he leaned in close to whisper in her ear, "—are you being naughty on purpose to see what happens?"

Her bottom lip caught between her teeth and he smiled, standing back. "All right then. Strip off and kneel at the foot of the bed. I'll be back." Without looking over his shoulder to make sure she obeyed, he walked into the hallway, heading into the room next door.

Taking his time, he got hold of his rampant emotions and his near-overwhelming need for her as he looked through his toy drawers to find just what she needed. He'd gone to his favorite toy store earlier, on his way home from work and picked up some things just for her. He grabbed those and the blindfold and looked out the window for another few minutes as he planned out just what he'd do to her.

Tegan removed her clothes with trembling hands. She

wasn't afraid of Ben Stoner. No, she yearned for him, wanted him to take her in hand and let her know he'd take care of her no matter what. Needed to know he'd make things all right and cherish her above all others.

How he handled himself with her that night would set a tone and Tegan hoped like hell it would be the right one. Because that woman's hand in that cuff made her furious in a way only a mated wolf could feel. If she was just dating Ben, those pictures wouldn't have even made her think twice. But her wolf didn't want any reminders of other women before her.

Kneeling, she waited. He took his time and with a small smile, she went inward and found a calm place, her hands clasped at the small of her back.

That's how he found her when he came back into the room, kneeling there looking so beautiful it made his chest hurt, flame red hair loose about her shoulders, eyes closed, peaceful.

But she knew he was there and slowly opened her eyes, focusing on him. "Good. You ready to talk to me yet?"

She rolled her eyes and he had to bite his cheek to keep from smiling. The woman needed to be taken in hand in a major way and he could not wait to do it.

"Fine. Stand up." He moved to a chair near the door and sat. "Come here and bend over my lap."

Gracefully she gained her feet and swayed to him. She was pretty tall but he was as well, so she folded herself over his lap, her ass in the air, belly against his cock.

Tracing his fingertips over the creamy curves of her luscious ass, he delighted in watching gooseflesh rise in the wake of his touch. No one else would ever touch her this way. He stopped a moment as the thought came into his head and pushed it away.

He stroked a hand over her spine until she relaxed

completely, her hands curled softly on the floor near her head.

Quickly, he delivered four sharp smacks to her ass, where thigh met the apex of her pussy and the curve of her cheeks. She gasped and then moaned softly.

"Mmmm. Such a pretty shade of pink. So, tell me, Tegan, why are you feeling jealous? What have I done to make you doubt me?"

When she didn't answer he delivered four more. Her pussy was so wet the backs of her thighs glistened and her honey scented the air. He realized though that, because she was a werewolf, she had a very high capacity and he did not want to risk harming her. So to get around the issue, he realized what he could control.

"Spread your legs wider."

She complied quickly and he drew a fingertip through the slicked folds of her pussy until she arched her back with a sigh.

"No, not yet." He moved his fingers away and smiled at the frustrated sound she made. "Tell me, Tegan."

"No!"

He picked up the vibrator he'd bought earlier that day and turned it on low, just for a moment. He knew she heard it because her body stiffened briefly.

"Stand up and move to the bed, keep your back to me."

When she hesitated a moment he knew he'd finally taken a step in the right direction. He walked behind her, laying the vibe on the bed in her view and pulling the blindfold from his back pocket.

He tightened the blindfold around her head, making sure it was light tight and comfortable. Leaning down, he blew over her nipple and smiled when a soft whimper escaped her lips.

Her skin felt more alive than it ever had. The warmth of his breath over her nipple sent shocks of pleasure straight to her cunt. The inner walls of her pussy throbbed, her clit was swollen and achy and she knew she'd just engaged in a battle with a man who was going to not only make her tell him what was wrong but beg him to let her come.

"Bend forward. Palms flat on the mattress. Stay standing. Spread your thighs."

She obeyed each command, the sensory deprivation adding to the extra sensitivity of her skin. The cool, soft cotton of the comforter under her hands comforted her, the nap of the carpet against the bare soles of her feet brought them alive with sensation.

She heard the snap of a bottle opening. Cinnamon painted the air. Warming lube. Her breath caught as he reached around, his body wrapped around hers, and drew a slick fingertip around each nipple. The tingling began immediately and she sighed.

Until the pinch of first one clamp and then the other bit into her nipples and she drew a breath and pushed it out. Letting the pain flow into pleasure, letting the pleasure rise up and use the pain.

The whir of the vibe sounded again and he must have touched it to the metal chain that held the clamps as the vibrations hummed up through the metal and into her body.

Totally unexpected, the crack of a paddle sounded as the percussive waves moved through her ass and pussy.

Genius. The man was a wicked genius.

The sound of his zipper played down her spine and a whimper of need escaped her lips. That whimper turned into a cry as his cock slammed into the slippery cleft of her cunt, stroking hard and deep three times and pulling out, leaving her breathless.

Then the vibrator, directly on her clit and then his cock. Over and over until she was a quivering mass of muscles.

"Tell me, Tegan. Tell me and I'll let you come. I'll fuck you and we'll make this better." His words, whispered in her ear, echoed through her, playing on her need to confide in him. Her need to come. Her need for his cock inside her body.

"I hate other women you've fucked being on the wall of a room you're fucking me in! It feels like a notch on your bedpost and I want to be more than that!"

The edge of subspace left her words slightly slurred but clear enough.

He placed the vibrator directly on her clit and pressed into her body, fucking into her with short, hard digs. First one and then the other nipple clamp was removed, and blood and feeling rushed into her, *throb, throb, throbbing* with erotic pulsebeats. His free hand moved to grip her hair, holding her in place as orgasm slammed into her with force, subsuming her mind and body as it wrung her out.

She felt the rasp of his zipper on the back of her thighs, against the sensitive skin he'd paddled. It made her feel alive. His body tensed, his grip in her hair tightened and he came with a grunt, holding himself deep within her.

Some long moments later he pulled out and removed her blindfold, placing it with the other things he'd used, at the foot of the bed. He helped her to stand and kissed her softly.

Pulling the comforter back, he motioned for her to get in and slid beside her.

"The pictures are of models. None of them are women I topped. In fact, I took them before I got into the scene. Part of a photography course at a local community college. I suppose it was a sign, something that flipped my switch even then before I fully understood what I was. I can take them down if you want me to. I don't want you to feel uncomfortable here, not ever." He kissed her forehead. "You *are* more to me. Enough that I want you to tell me if you feel bad. I don't want you to hide things from me."

A smile hinted at her lips. "Even if it gets me punished like that?" Oh he'd broken her all right. Well and truly. He was a man she could submit to proudly and completely. Not that she'd suddenly become easy and sweet. That wasn't who she was. But he'd earned her submission that night.

A surprised laugh barked from him. "You're going to be a handful, aren't you?"

Tegan shrugged, feeling heavy and sated. She snuggled into his body and he held her against him easily.

"Alarm is set for five. I'll make us breakfast after a long, hot shower," he murmured into her ear, enjoying the way she hummed her satisfaction and pressed into him closer.

He lay there, her body against his, curved into him like she was made to be there and a sense of totality broke over him. Things in his life were *right* in a way he'd never felt before. Even with the uncertainty about the whole mating thing and Tegan being a relative stranger, he still felt as if things were going to be all right.

Pride warmed him at how she'd finally submitted fully. How she'd trusted him with her emotions as well as her body. Now he had to be careful to always be worthy of that trust.

Chapter Six

Tegan actually found herself humming as she changed her clothes after showering. Ben would be arriving to take her to a movie in a few minutes.

A movie! And he promised they'd make out and he'd buy her the big bucket of popcorn too. It was breathtakingly normal. And wonderful. Two weeks of wonderfully normal dating stuff.

During the day, he called her just to say hello. He sent her flowers. They rented DVDs and watched them, parked on the couch at his house. She hadn't dated since before Lucas. It had been a very long time and she found she liked getting to know Ben bit by bit. They did have their struggles. A man like Ben, despite saying he only wanted control in the bedroom, constantly tried to exert control out of it. Not in a creepy, woman-hating way, but because he liked to be in charge. He pushed, she pushed back. It was sexy sometimes.

She knew without a doubt he was her mate. It wasn't in question but she also realized he was human. He hadn't grown up with mate bonds as a reality. Even though she wanted him to simply accept it as she had, she worked at giving him the space to do that himself and hoped over time he would see it as clearly as she did.

She'd just put her lipstick down when he rang her doorbell and she went to let him in.

"It's my favorite redhead." He handed her a bottle of wine. "I thought we could have some after the movie." His eyes darkened as he pulled her close and his warmth stole over her. "Before you suck my cock and I fuck you."

Her breath stuttered and her eyelids dropped halfway closed. The man was so sexy. He walked the line between sweet boyfriend and super-scorching-hot sex god quite well.

"Okay. We could skip the movie and get to the cock sucking."

He caught her chin, nipping it lightly and laving the sting with the flat of his tongue. "Both. We'll do both."

The way he walked with her, holding her hand, opening her door and taking care of her with small things made her feel cherished and special. It was taking a while to wrap her head around, but aside from the physical and spiritual mate bond they shared, they genuinely enjoyed each other.

In the darkness of the theater, he took her hand and massaged it. Every inch of her hand was treated to a sensual caress, a kneading and God help her, he made such an innocent thing feel like he touched her pussy instead.

She felt like a teenager as he'd kissed her. No tongue even, just a brush of lips here and there.

By the time the movie was over she was primed to be fucked and dragged him to his truck as he laughed.

"I like this side of you, Tegan," he said against the skin of her neck once they'd gotten inside his house and stumbled to the bedroom.

"What side of me?" How did he expect her to think when he did that thing to her earlobe?

His wicked laugh stirred the tendrils of hair at her temple. "Carefree. You're a very serious woman. Driven. I like that. But I like the woman who lets me smooch up on her in the movies and won't share her popcorn even though she had eight gallons of it."

Oh, her shirt had been removed and she hadn't even noticed. She'd keep the part about how she listened to Madonna's *Rain* and thought of him every time. There was only so much a woman needed to let her man know about her inner girl.

"Knees. Now."

And just like that, the sweet man disappeared, replaced by the hot, hard dominant who set her panties on fire.

Dropping to her knees, she made quick work of his jeans, shoving them down and grabbing the bounty within. Oh hello, penis.

Breathing deep, she took his scent into her lungs, the elemental musk of his body, of his sex, tightened her nipples. Nipples he had between his fingertips, twisting and pulling just shy of pain.

With a grunt, he flexed his hips forward, bumping his cock against her lips and she opened up to take him inside. Her tongue slid across the slick, salty eye, dragging over the crown and down the heavy stalk of him and down to his sac.

Those clever hands moved from her nipples to her hair, grasping, guiding but not hurting. His dominance was subtle, not cruel or painful, he took control and used it well. He played her body as well as her brain.

Nothing sexier than a man who understood the key to a woman's cunt was between her ears.

There was something so comforting about being there on her knees, pleasing him. She turned off the warrior in her head, let go of the control she had to exert every other moment in her life and gave it all up to him.

As he came, his taste filling her, he said her name so tenderly it brought tears to her eyes and a tiny bit of fear rose along with the love. Fear of losing him now that she'd found love again.

Tegan awoke refreshed and relaxed. For one brief moment she didn't know where she was but Ben's scent reassured her, and she opened her eyes to see the outline of his bedroom. Sleeping over took some getting used to, but she was slowly growing accustomed to it.

Carefully, she eased out of bed and threw on clothes to quickly run to his truck to grab her duffel bag. The air was frosty and crisp as the quiet of the pre-dawn hour wrapped around her senses.

It was then she felt it. Being watched. Feigning nonchalance, she went back into the house and closed the door, locking it. On swift feet, she went to Ben's side and leaned over to whisper into his ear.

"Mmmm, morning." His arms encircled her and pulled her back to bed. "You're dressed. And cold." Perceptive blue-gray eyes opened and she pressed a finger to his lips, shaking her head.

His body went on alert, tensed, coiled up and ready for action. Her wolf responded and she had to push that aside for the time being. In a very quiet voice she whispered, "There's someone out there. Does your garage have a door into your back yard?"

He nodded.

"I'm going to go out there and change. Take a look. I can sense a lot more as a wolf. Stay here. You may be able to see something if you've got binoculars or night vision goggles but be careful that they don't see you when you look out the windows."

"The hell you are!" he hissed. "You'll stay here. I'm a cop, I'll deal with it and you'll keep safe."

Her head whipped up and one eyebrow rose. "This isn't sex. You can't tell me what to do. I'm not a fragile flower, Ben. I'm a werewolf bodyguard. I'm perfectly capable, in fact more qualified to do this than you are. I just did you the courtesy of telling you so you didn't walk out to see a werewolf in your garage and get spooked."

She pulled away and peeled clothing off as she walked out of the room.

With a muttered curse, he opened the drawer next to the bed and pulled out his handgun, removing the trigger lock. Quickly, he pulled jeans on and followed her.

Nothing could have prepared him to see her transform. He'd seen werewolves in wolf form before but he'd never watched a human change into a wolf. He stood there in his garage and watched, speechless as she knelt and a sharp, electric feeling whipped through him, making his eyes water and his teeth hurt. When it eased, a wolf, a red wolf that on all fours came to his chest took a look back over its shoulder and eased out the already opened door to his backyard. She was beautiful. Otherworldly, fierce. It made his chest constrict to see her there, so not human but his.

"Be careful," he whispered softly.

He'd wanted to argue with her but if they spooked the watchers, it would have been his fault for blowing it. He'd kick her ass when she came back. He just had to trust she'd be all right.

For a big wolf, she was surprisingly stealthy. Tegan put her nose up, scenting the air. Dogs, cats, garbage, perfume and cologne, motor oil, coffee—all normal things to smell in a neighborhood at that time of day.

But gun oil, that wasn't normal. She knew what Ben's gun smelled like, and what hers did. This was different, distinct. The man who carried it was nervous and smelled of stale sweat as he sat up the street in his late model sedan.

Running, she went down the block behind the house, circling around to approach the car from the rear before going back to the house.

Ben waited for her in the living room, looking first relieved to see her and then pissed off. She held her hand up to stall his tantrum. "Two blocks down, dark, late model sedan. License number one, four, seven, Charlie, Echo, William. One man, he's carrying. Nervous. He's not healthy. Didn't seem to have any special equipment. I didn't sense or see any electronics. I say we head out there and ask him what's what."

He stood. "You say? What the fuck? Tegan, you could have gotten yourself killed! I'll go out there after I call his plates in. Sit that pretty ass down right now."

He picked up the phone and called the plate in while she laced up her boots and strapped on her under-arm rig, holstering her weapon and waiting.

"Car is stolen. They're sending over an officer now. I'm going to go make an arrest. You stay, is that a fucking gun? Tegan, do you have a permit for that? Sit down!"

"You did what?" She moved to the door. "I've can't believe you're bringing cops into this. Ben, does the phrase, *you're not the boss of me* ring any bells for you? This is my job. I am a trained bodyguard and if I have to be, a killer. No, I don't have a permit. The ammo is not legal, or well, it isn't even on the human radar. You gonna arrest me? Humans don't want Weres to have guns. Your laws are pretty clear about that. But I don't want to have this argument now. We have to get this guy and

Lauren Dane

bring him in. I want to know who he is and what he's doing."

"Of course I did. I'm a cop! And I said, sit your ass down! This is my territory and my damned job. I'm not only a cop but the liaison between the Packs and the human authorities. If this is one of Pellini's people, he needs to be handled correctly."

"He's human and you don't tell me what to do. This is my territory too. And my damned job as well. I'm going out there before your temper fit ends up making us lose him."

Without another word she headed back out toward the garage and he followed her, grabbing her arm but she shook him off and turned on him, a growl trickling from her lips. "You do not manhandle me, Ben Stoner."

"I'm not manhandling you, Tegan. I'm trying to protect you." He followed her out the back door and they both hopped the fence into the next yard easily and quietly.

"Fuck off," she hissed and stalked out into the alley and headed up, moving to circle around behind the car.

She was fast, faster than he was and he watched, in annoyed awe as she practically ripped the car door off and hauled the dude out, tossing him against the side of the car.

"Who the fuck are you, human?" Her voice was a growl and the hair on his arms and the back of his neck rose as he reached them both.

"What? What's going on? I was just resting here!" The man's voice trembled a bit but he shut up quick when she pulled her weapon and pressed the muzzle into his temple.

"I will blow your fucking head off. You're nothing but meat to me. Understand? Whoever sent you isn't here now but I am. And I'll maim you and take you to someone who makes me look like the fucking fairy godmother. You're not a Were, your kneecap will not heal up quick when I blow it off."

"That's enough. Sir, why don't you tell me why you're casing my house and whether you've got a permit for the weapon you're carrying." He tried to move Tegan out of the way but she wouldn't budge.

Fortunately, the officer he'd sent for pulled down the street and with a sigh of frustration, Tegan moved back, taking care to conceal her weapon and let him be in charge.

"I'm going to follow to question this bozo. You can borrow my other car all right? I'll see you later?" Ben turned to her after the cop had loaded the guy into the back of his car. A tow truck arrived and would take the car to the police impound.

She didn't speak, instead turning on her heel and stalking off toward his house. Her anger and hurt assaulted his senses through their link.

He expected her to slam inside but she was mainly silent as she gathered her things.

"I have to go down there now to talk to him. If he requests an attorney I'll never get anything out of him. I know you're mad but I have to do this by the book."

"You're not going to find out shit. He's already got an attorney alerted. You've put my family in danger." She grabbed her bag and headed for the front door but he intercepted her.

"We'll work this out tonight. I can't let you beat suspects up and threaten to kill them, Tegan."

"I'm just..." she sighed angrily, "...done talking. I'm not borrowing your car, I'll catch a ride with someone."

"What? What do you mean?"

"I mean you have just let the man go who could have given us answers! You undermined me and went macho but had nothing up your sleeve but his Miranda rights. Which is great and all but do you think Warren Pellini cares about the Fifth

Amendment? The Pellini Family is trying to harm my Pack! They tried to kill my sister-in-law and brothers. They have a potential bio weapon that could threaten my entire race and yours too. I'd have gotten that information out of him in less than twenty minutes and you will *never* get it now."

"So I should act like a thug?"

"NO! I should act like a werewolf! I am a werewolf. You should have let me handle this our way. I don't get involved in human affairs, I trust you to do your work. But you threw your dick around and it may very well get one of my family killed."

"I have to go, Tegan. I'm sorry. I want to continue this but I need to get to the station. I *will* talk to you later."

Her two worlds stood in opposition to the other. How could she choose? If she made a mistake could she bear to lose him? But her mistake in telling him had just put her entire Pack in danger. Maybe it was better if she just kept to herself. "Don't bother."

"I will bother, Tegan. It's not that easy to walk away from me. Even if I believed you wanted to. Which I don't."

"Don't threaten me, Ben."

He couldn't help it, seeing her so passionate and deadly turned him on. Made his heart race and his cock throb. He wanted to push her to the carpet and rip her clothes off, fucking her until they both wept with completion. But her change there at the end, as her voice had gone flat and remote, it tore at him.

"It's not a threat. I'm stating a fact. Now—" he opened the door and went outside, "—you can lock up behind yourself if you want to stay. If not, I *will* see you tonight after you get off shift. I'll be at your place at five."

"I said don't bother. I won't be there. I'll be at Lex and Cade's. You've put them in more danger—*I've* put them in more danger. They'll need round the clock protection."

82

"Whatever. I'll see you there then," he called over his shoulder as he walked away.

"We'll see about that," she muttered as she grabbed her phone and called Lex to arrange a ride.

"He did what?" Lex exploded, slamming a fist down on the table.

"I'm not going to repeat myself. You heard me. I couldn't stop him once the other cop got there and they took the human into custody. I'm sorry." She kept her eyes down.

Nina watched, a frown on her face. Seeing Tegan so hangdog bothered her. "You couldn't have stopped him, Tee. He's a cop. There's no way he would have let you go all werewolf on that human. It's not in his make up."

"It doesn't matter now. His make up has put my family in danger, and I didn't stop him."

"You're a werewolf, not a super hero, Tegan!" Nina stood and went to Tegan. "Honey, you can't be anyone but who you are, right?"

"I should have just gone out there myself. Not told him. I should have known." The remoteness of her stance went into anguish, tearing at Nina. She knew what it meant to blame yourself that way.

Nina took Tegan's hands. "He's your mate. You shared with him. That's what mates do. Tee, you cannot make this about *you* failing. That's not what it is. You are who you are. He is who he is. You have to accept that or you'll constantly have problems with him."

"There is no he and I. Not anymore. I told him that this morning."

Lex had been looking out the window but whipped his body

Lauren Dane

around at that. "What do you mean?"

"What is up with that question?" Tegan threw her hands up in the air. "It's made up of six words, all one syllable. What's not to understand? He and I are over. I can't be with a man who puts my family in danger. I was willing to let him mince around and find himself or whatever the hell he needed to do to deal with the mate thing. But this is different. He totally overruled me. At the expense of everyone I love. I can't abide that."

Lex shook his head. "Tegan, as angry as I am at Ben right now, he didn't do this to harm you or me or anyone in the Pack. He's a cop. A human cop with human sensibilities. He did what he thought was right. You can't punish him for that. It's not right and it's not you. You're not thinking about this correctly. Give him a break."

"I'm not punishing him. I'm not sixteen years old! But I have my limits. He crossed them. I'm done with this conversation. I will recommend that you get your ass down to the court house with someone and soon. He'll bond out and be like smoke. A tail might be useful. Now, I'm going out to patrol." Tegan turned on her heel and left the room without saying anything else.

Lex turned to Nina who looked worried. "Okay, I'm at a loss here, beautiful. What do we do?"

"She blames herself, Lex. She takes on too much but there's nothing much we can do but help her figure it out. If I know Ben, he'll come for her. She feels guilty. Like she failed the Pack. That's going to be the biggest thing for her to overcome."

"Does she honestly think I'd blame her for not assaulting some human in front of the cops?"

"I don't know, Scooby. I don't know. We'll have to support her through this. But also keep an eye out too. If Pellini is

84

tailing her, or Ben, well, this just went to DEFCON four."

"Yeah. I'm going to have to bring in Cade and the others. Which means I need to talk to Ben. She's right about the tail."

"Don't hurt him, Lex."

"I'm not going to as long as he does the right thing. I want him to realize she's broken and out of sorts, to give her extra consideration and help her through. I can't bear to see her unhappy like this again. But for now, it's business because we need a clearer picture and I've got a Pack to protect."

Nina nodded, kissing his lips absently as they looked out the window at the lone red wolf trotting away from the house and into the line of trees just beyond.

Tegan slipped back into her human skin once she'd gotten deep into the trees. She went to her favorite spot, a little bench Nina had put at the base of a tree where a creek ran nearby.

Four years she'd been alone. Her only focus had been her Pack, protecting them, putting them first and foremost. Behind the walls she built, her heart was safe. She risked nothing but her life and really, she had no real connections to anyone at that point, didn't allow it, so her life wasn't much to risk.

And then she'd begun to live again. Had taken a small step into the light and had gone out and started to see friends. She'd moved into her own place. Baby steps and they'd been satisfying.

But fuck, like being struck by lightning, Ben had come into her life and turned on all the lights and the walls got kicked down. There wasn't a way to keep him out, wasn't a way to protect herself from the bond she hadn't even known existed until it was created.

She'd waded back into a life with someone, opened herself

up to belonging with, belonging to a relationship and it made her vulnerable. Made her naked to being harmed and Ben Stoner could possibly bring back the kind of pain she felt when she lost Lucas. And she couldn't bear it, not like that.

It wasn't so much that she felt betrayed by Ben for what he'd done that morning. But in her caring for him, in her relationship and connection with him, she'd harmed her family. She'd put something else first and had failed everyone. Failed herself, failed her Pack and failed Ben because she couldn't be what he needed her to be.

Being alone began to be something she missed a lot more than being lonely.

Chapter Seven

Ben stalked back to his office, a roaring headache just behind his eyes. As Tegan predicted, the man lawyered up immediately and they'd gotten nothing from him other than his name.

The lawyer claimed the car was an innocent mistake, the perp said he'd bought it only the night before for cash from a stranger. Ten years ago Ben might have been incredulous at such a story but he heard stuff worse than that on a weekly basis. Still, they charged him with car theft and possession of an unlicensed weapon.

But he'd just walked back from the court house from the arraignment. The guy was released on bond and Ben doubted very much they'd ever see him again. He wasn't sure what made him angrier, that Tegan had been right or that he'd just made her even less safe.

"Stoner."

Ben jumped at the sound and saw Lex standing in the hallway just outside the door. "Look, I'm sorry. He just bonded out. I couldn't do anything else."

Lex walked in and closed the door. "He's got a tail on him. Tegan suggested it earlier."

Ben sighed heavily and sat down. "Good idea. How...how is she?"

"Pissed off. Hurt." Lex shrugged. "Before we get into that, did you find anything out from this guy?"

"No. I was about five minutes behind the arresting officer and by the time they processed him and I got through and into the interrogation room, he'd pokered up after requesting representation. I have a name." Ben paused, looking at his notes. "I'm giving it to you as the liaison, not because of what I am to your sister." He wrote the name down and handed it to Lex.

"And just what are you to my sister?"

Ben scrubbed his hands over his face. "Hell if I know. All I do know is that I want to see her and make this right. I expect she's pretty angry at me right now. But I can't apologize for it, Lex. If I had let her lean on that guy, I'd have been turning my back on what I am. I can't do that."

"And now he's gone and if she hadn't been what she is, you'd have dick. Remember that, Ben. And don't you dare get self-righteous on me. This piece of shit has something to do with a man who's attempted to kill multiple members of my family and who wouldn't blink before harming Tegan to get what he wants. Warren Pellini is a werewolf. This is werewolf business. You can't do anything to him but I can. Back off and let me do it."

"You don't know that for sure. I can't stand by and let you be a thug, Lex."

"I'm not asking permission. And I'm not a thug. Humans are thugs. I'm the Enforcer of the Cascadia Wolf Pack." Lex stood tall and proud. "I do not seek human leave to do wolf business. Make no mistake, we will take care of this threat. You can help or get out of the way. But it will happen."

"If you keep your wolf shit out of my business, I don't see it and I can't stop it. Now, I'm told Tegan is at your place and will be for a few days. I'd like to come up to see her when I get done here. Is that going to be a problem?"

"If you can survive the visit with your dick intact, you go ahead on." Chuckling, Lex held up the scrap of paper and nodded. "Thanks for this."

"See you later."

"Look, she's been alone a long time. She's hurt and more than anything else I think she's scared. So go easy. Oh and she's a werewolf female. There's really no more complicated being in all creation than a werewolf female. Beautiful, magnificent, the world is better with them than without. But you'll never figure them out even as they aggravate you so much you want to drive a screwdriver into your eardrum. Good luck." With a snort, Lex left the office, laughing softly all the way down the hall.

Tegan looked up from the pot of sauce she was stirring. She felt Ben come into the house and sighed.

Nina came into the room about five minutes later.

"He wants to see you."

"I don't want to see him."

"Really? If you're truly serious, I'll send him away. But..." Nina hesitated.

"But what?"

"Tee, you *do* want this to work out right? I mean, you want to be with him?"

Tegan turned and faced her sister-in-law. "I do. He's my mate. You know what that is, what it means. I love him. Even right now I ache to see him, to feel him with me. But I can't be with him if he's not going to respect me. And I can't be with him if he can't accept what we are to each other. I know he's a human and the whole thing is shocking to him so I get that he needs time to process but I need something from him. I need for him to be more than hungry to fuck me. I want him to admit he's hungry for *me*, period."

Nina nodded, leaning against the counter. "I get that. So this is more than just this morning. I see you've been using your day to patrol *and* think. He needs to realize how much you mean to him. And you don't know what you have until it's gone. He can't take your presence for granted. I know it's a shock for him, hell, I was there a few years ago myself. But with all that's going on right now, he's got to deal. You can live apart from him. He can live apart from you. But it's going to hurt and I think he needs a wake up call."

"I'm just trying to process all of this. You know? It's all been about him. How he felt about the mating. Trying to get him to understand and accept the mating. And I realize what a huge shock it is to him and his life. But after this morning, I realize I'm trying to work it out too. I can't do it with him around. I need to think."

"Okay, Tee. I'll send him away. But you know, he is an alpha male, even if he's not a wolf. He won't stand for being separated from you for very long."

"He can bite me." Tegan turned back around and stirred the sauce again. Snickering, Nina headed out of the kitchen and back to the deck below where Lex and Cade had Ben corralled.

On her way out the doors she passed Layla, who dropped a quick kiss on her cheek as the kids ran out to find Megan who laughed as they jumped into her arms.

Ben looked up as Nina came out. "Where is she?"

"She doesn't want to see you, Ben."

"Well it's not up to her!"

Nina's jaw locked a moment and one eyebrow rose. Lex chuckled and plopped down on a deck chair.

"Perhaps you don't know where you are, human. You're in the seat of the Cascadia Pack and this is my territory. I decide what's up to who here and if Tegan doesn't want to see you, she doesn't have to," Cade said before Nina could speak.

"Yeah. What he said." Nina couldn't resist adding. "Look, go home. Get some rest. You'll need it. Try again tomorrow night. Perhaps you'll have better luck then. But she doesn't want you right now. She feels disrespected and guilty and your behavior today hasn't helped that one bit. You're taking her for granted. You're going to have to work for it now."

"I did my job!" Ben exploded. "I won't turn into some kind of lapdog because she's a fucking werewolf."

"She didn't ask you to! But how can you expect her to turn into *your* lapdog just because you're a cop? You two have to get your shit straight and the first thing on your to-do list should be to accept that she's your damned mate and stop this hemming and hawing over it."

"Nina has a big point there, Ben. Yes, it's crazy this whole mating thing. But she didn't plan it. And it still is a fact. You can't wish it away and I'm banking on you not wanting to. I'll admit I have big reservations about this situation. You're human, that's trouble." Cade crossed his arms over his chest and flexed.

"I don't know what you people want. We've been dating exclusively. But I don't love her. It's been three weeks since we met. I'm just barely getting to know her!"

"You've said that a few times. You not loving her. And yet you're here. You're here and your skin is itching with the need to touch her, comfort her. Your heart aches that you've made her upset. You're worried about her, worried she may dump your ass for good." Nina shrugged. "That sounds a lot more like love to me than *gee Tegan, I really like you, you wanna go steady?* Do you want her to wear your frat pin or do you want to be her fucking mate? Because one is love, the other is a shadow of feeling. Yes, it's new and you didn't know and blah, blah, blah. Pull up your big girl panties, Ben! Man up. You do love Tegan, God knows she loves you. Now, what are you going to do about it?"

"I'm not a damned werewolf, I can't just accept all this shit the way you do."

"She's not human. And sometimes, Ben, sometimes things happen that we can't explain. They just are. You can make a leap of faith or you can fight it and still end up in the same place." Lex shrugged.

"You aren't going to see her tonight. Period. Three werewolves stand between you and the door and there are a half dozen more in the house. Just go home. Do some thinking. Figure out what your priorities are and call tomorrow afternoon." Nina motioned her head. "Now go on. I'd tell you to sleep well but you won't. If it's any comfort, she won't either."

"Fuck this. If she wants to play games she can kiss my ass." Ben stormed out and down the steps to the side yard where his car was parked.

"Well." Cade watched him go.

"He's a fool. He'd better get his shit together. She's working on it, scared as hell but she is. He needs to do the same." Nina flipped her hair back over her shoulder and walked into the house.

"He has no idea." Cade shook his head.

Lex laughed. "Well, better him than me for a damned change."

Nina joined Tegan and Layla in Tegan's room. "He's gone. Stormed off in a big hissy fit," she said, tossing herself on the bed. "So, did you tell Layla that you blame yourself for Ben's arresting this Pellini scumbag?"

"Nina, I keep telling you you need to find a way to say what you really feel." Layla grinned. "We just got to that part. The pasta will be boiling soon so let's just hash this out, shall we?"

"Let's not and say we did. Really, I've had enough Oprah moments for the day. I'm all empowered now, I'm every woman. Woot!" Tegan said, sounding exhausted.

"Hey, that was pretty good, my young apprentice. Now, back to guilt. Under the circumstances you couldn't have done anything else. You were at Ben's house. He's your mate. It was only natural you shared with him when you knew you were being watched." Nina's voice was understanding.

"I should have gone out there alone. When I first felt him. I've put us all in danger now."

"We were already in danger and you aren't responsible for everything in the whole world, Tee. Your man is a cop, this won't be the last time something like this comes up. You have to let him do his thing too. You're going to butt heads. A lot. It's actually great for make up sex. I'm just sayin'. Lay doesn't know because Sid is easygoing and he adores her and lets her have her way. But your brother is a pain in my ass every waking moment. Truly, it's only the spectacular sex and the cookies alpha boy makes when he's stressed that keep me here."

Tegan shook her head and began to laugh. It was a rusty sort of sound at first. Not a casual laugh but the kind of laugh that came from deep inside and made your face hurt and your stomach ache. Tears rolled from her eyes and she threw herself back on the bed and let it come until the tears were no longer of joy but pain.

Layla snuggled up to one side and Nina got the other, both exchanging worried looks.

"You couldn't have saved Lucas, Tegan," Layla murmured. "This isn't the same. We're all going to be okay."

Tegan only cried harder. "I should have put my foot down on Ranger school. I should have kept him out of the Army altogether. But I didn't. I let him go and he's dead and I failed him. And now you're all in danger because I let my pussy get ahead of my job."

Layla looked shocked and then laughed. "Oh sweetie, you're giving your pussy an awful lot of power. You're a hot number but really, I think that's pretty arrogant, even for a Warden. As for Lucas? You forget I grew up with him too. He lived and breathed the Army. He wanted it and you wanted it for him. You let him be what he needed to be. And he got killed and that sucks rocks but it was not your fault! I'm pissed off at you for even thinking that all these years. And Tee, if Ben gets hurt, or if someone in the Pack gets hurt, it's not your fault either."

"That's why you gave us yourself twenty-four/seven! Man-oh-man, Tegan. I honestly thought I had the guilt thing down with Gabriel but you got me beat. Your mate gets killed in Afghanistan and you blame yourself. Cut yourself some slack. This guy who cased Ben's house? Not your fault. Ben being a cop? Not your fault. He's your mate. Again, not your fault. But it is what it is and you have to deal. And you are not allowed to feel guilty about this. I'm Second and I say so. So there. You'll let Ben stew because you know he will, he's a man. And then he'll come around." Nina rolled her eyes.

"I'm starving. We're going to eat dinner and you're going to let your family pamper you." Layla stood and pulled Tegan up.

Tegan felt lighter than she had in a very long time. Just

having someone know how she felt, even if she wasn't quite ready to let go of the guilt, made her feel better. Less burdened.

Chapter Eight

Five days went by and Ben tried to pretend nothing was wrong. But it was a losing battle. He saw Tegan in the fiery red leaves on the maple trees in his yard, he smelled her in his house, on his sheets.

He thought about her all the time. At first it was physical. A deep ache to touch her, to be inside her. But then it turned into something else. He wondered how she was feeling. Wondered if she was hurting and felt guilt at not trying to get in contact. She'd called and left a message on his voicemail a few days before but he hadn't replied and she hadn't called again. At first he'd battled that guilt with anger at her refusal to see him but as the days passed, he began to understand her more. He had to, he could only think about fucking her two-thirds of the time, the rest of the time ended up being about her as a person and her motivations.

He wondered how he'd have felt if he'd been in her place. At first he told himself it wouldn't have been the same but he was beginning to have trouble believing that. He felt strongly about being a cop. He did it to protect people. If he was a cop for his family and she'd stepped in and put them in danger, how would he have reacted? He wouldn't have done anything different necessarily but he could see why she was upset.

What he couldn't see was her refusal to even talk to him that next night. He had to get her out of his head, that was it. Getting into his car, he headed to the club to work out some of his feelings and perhaps if he found himself a sweet human submissive, he'd be able to break his feelings for Tegan once and for all.

Except he sat in the parking lot for thirty minutes, remembering the time he'd been with her there. Gripping the steering wheel, he realized he needed Tegan Warden. Not just in his bed but in his life. Whether it was some werewolf mumbo jumbo or not, it was inescapable.

He pointed his car toward Cade's place and swallowed his pride.

"She's not here." Cade looked down his nose at Ben.

"What? What do you mean?"

"She's off shift. I made her go home. Nick and Tracy are here with some Pacific members, they're out at Tee's place. No, get that look off your face, she's being watched and pretending she doesn't know it. Pacific's Enforcer, the one who took Nick's place is also there. She's fine. Pissed at you, but fine."

"I'm getting her back."

Cade shrugged. "Of course you are. The question is, Ben Stoner, how much the bill will be for ignoring her for five days. At first she was hurt. Moped around. Now? Now she's pissed off. And have you ever seen a pissed off female werewolf? No, you're thinking you saw her mad at you five days ago. My sisters are all quick to anger but just as quick to let it go. You saw a spat, and some hurt because you didn't respect her with liberal amounts of guilt thrown in."

"She should feel guilty for not seeing me! I came here to work it out and she wouldn't even do me the courtesy."

Cade had the audacity to chuckle as he leaned back

against the railing of the deck overlooking the woods. "You're an idiot. Guilt because she felt she'd failed her family. Her Pack. She went to her *mate* to share her concerns and the guy got away. She tried to talk to you about it but you gave her guff and reminded us all how much you didn't love her. Remember that?"

"You're a smug bastard."

"I am. I'm the motherfucking Alpha of one of the most powerful werewolf Packs in the world and you hurt my sister. You have no idea how much that makes me want to rip your head off. And I can. You'd best remember that. You'd best remember that you're drawing breath right now instead of bleeding out in the woods behind me because my sister loves you and you love her, you stupid fucking human. My sister has lost enough, do you hear me? Play time is over. You lost your little personal vision quest to find yourself or whatever the hell you told Tegan you needed to do before accepting the obvious and the inevitable. If you can't have the spine enough to admit you love her—all of her, not just the need to fuck her—you get the hell off this property and don't you look back. Don't so much as breathe in Tegan's direction ever again or I. Will. Kill. You. In time I'm told the pain of your mate's absence won't hurt as much. Certainly not as much as my killing you will. If it makes you feel better, I told her to get her shit together too."

Ben had always thought Lex was a badass but right then, he understood with utter clarity why Cade was Alpha and not Lex. A shiver of fear worked through him even as he was angry at the idea of being denied access to his woman.

Fuck. *His woman.*

"Tegan is my woman and I'm going to her. You can take your threats and shove them. You may be a werewolf but you can't outrun bullets."

Cade snorted. "I can." He shifted and moved so fast Ben didn't even see it until he stopped on the other side of the deck. "Accept that there are things in the world you can't explain but are true nonetheless. You didn't wish for the mate bond with Tegan but you have it. And you're a lucky man. She's the best and you've found something wolves, wolves like me, yearn for for decades. Go to her and grovel, dumbass."

Ben sighed. "Damn it. I hate when other people are right."

"Get used to it, Ben." Lex strolled onto the deck. "You think I get to be right with Nina? Now, the real question you need to ask yourself is whether you'd rather be with her or be *right* without her. Because being right and lonely sucks. Anyway, women aren't that hard to figure out. Listen to her, respect her. You'll fight a lot, she's been stubborn since birth. You'll make up, buy her pretty things, or in Tee's case, new weapons or somesuch and you'll go on. You can be *happy* and be *connected* and be right half the time. But don't you go over there if you can't commit. Because after Cade kills you, I'll kill you too."

Ben threw his hands in the air and stomped off, heading back to Seattle and toward Tegan's house.

Tegan felt Ben pull up outside and relief battled with fury. *The bastard runs off for five days and now he shows up?*

"Tee? Honey you okay?" Her sister Tracy touched her arm.

Josh, the Pacific Pack's Enforcer put his arm around her shoulder, concern on his face. "Tegan, did we do something wrong?"

"Get your damned hands off my mate!" Ben banged on the front door as he peered through the front windows.

"Oh, *now* I'm his mate?" Tegan ground her teeth.

"I can't believe that prick is here," Tracy growled and Nick looked up from his place on the couch.

"Let it be, sweetness. Tegan, darling, do you need Josh to kill him for you?" Even while threatening death, her sister's husband looked handsome and completely chill.

"He totally would," Tracy added hopefully.

Josh laughed. "Gladly. Or, shall I help make him realize what he's been blowing for the last five days?" He nuzzled her temple playfully and Ben's yelling got louder. "It's not like I'd have to fake finding you very attractive."

"As much as killing him would satisfy my initial feelings of rage at his behavior, I'd miss him in the end. He's actually a very good man. And thanks, a girl needs to feel attractive every once in a while." Blushing, she kissed Josh's cheek and moved to the door. Unlocking it, she stood to block Ben's entrance.

"What the hell is going on here?" he bellowed, trying to come into the house. She put a hand out to stop him and the shock of the contact made them both gasp. Her love for him, the way she'd missed him, ached for him, crashed through her.

With a cry of surprise, Ben moved her hand out of the way and pulled her to him, wrapping his arms around her tight.

She allowed herself to feel the warmth of his presence for long moments until she stomped hard on his instep and shoved him back.

"You don't get to ask questions, Ben."

"Ouch! What? Oh yes I do, Tegan Warden. Why was that asshole touching you?"

Josh laughed along with Nick but Tracy seethed at her back.

"There's only one *asshole* here and I'm looking at him. As for who was touching me when you decided to finally show up, you know Josh. He's a guest in my home. Unlike you. He's a friend. Why are *you* here?"

"Because I wanted to see you."

"You did? Well, thank goodness it's all about you then, isn't it? It's been all about you since day one. What *you* felt about the bond. What *you* felt about our connection. How *you* were going to deal with it. Lord, it must be nice in your world, all Ben Stoner-centric."

Ben's jaw shifted, clenched and unclenched and she felt his frustration, his anger and if she wasn't wrong, guilt too.

"I'm not sorry that I didn't let you beat a suspect in the street."

"We've established that. If that's all you've come to say, hit the road."

"I can feel what you're feeling, Tegan. I know you're happy to see me. You don't want me to leave." He had the audacity to smile at her and she growled, stomping her foot instead of slapping him silly.

"Do you now? Did you know what I felt every day this week every time the phone rang? How about when I answered it and it wasn't you?" She hated how her voice broke with emotion but she'd missed him, wanted him to miss her as much as she had him.

Nick whistled low in the background.

"I didn't know what to think after you sent me away!" Ben exhaled sharply.

"You might have if you'd called me back." Putting a hand at her waist, she cocked her hip and kicked the door closed in his face. She'd only made it a few steps when he stormed in moments later. He grabbed her arm, spinning her to face him, hauling her against his body.

Growls filled the room as the wolves all stood.

"You'd best let go of my sister right now." Tracy's eyes began to shine with that otherworldly light and the scent of wolf rose in the air.

"Your sister and I have a lot to talk about and we can't do it with an audience." Good Lord, Ben Stoner had a lot to learn about werewolves. Tegan sent calming energy through their link.

"You can't do it without a throat or a beating heart either. Now take your hands off Tegan. You're standing in a room with two pissed off females and two male wolves who feel the need to protect family. You've pushed as far as this can go without blood being shed." Nick slowed his breathing and Tegan saw the violence there in his and Josh's faces.

"Ben, let me go. This can't go anywhere positive. Not this way." Tegan traced the backs of her fingers down his jaw, leaned in to kiss him.

He let go and looked into her eyes, letting her see deep into his soul. "I'm not leaving until things are right. You're not afraid of me. You know I'd never hurt you."

"I'm not afraid you'd physically hurt me. But you ripped my heart from my chest. Where have you been?" Emotion filled her voice and she saw his response, knew he'd felt her pain.

"Please, won't you talk to me? Alone? Give me a chance, Tegan."

"Why?" she whispered and he dipped his head, brushing his lips over hers and her very DNA melted into a pool of need.

"Because I need you. I need us."

Tegan turned to the others. "I'll see you three later on back at Cade's."

Tracy approached, taking Tegan's hands in hers. "Tee, are you sure?"

Tegan nodded. "I am. One way or another we need to talk and all this testosterone in one room is distracting."

"Welcome to my world." Tracy winked and sobered again. "Listen, Tee, I've missed you so damned much. I looked up to you, came to you when, well *before*. I finally got you back and I can't lose that again. I need you to be my big sister. There's so much to share with you. Don't go. Don't *let* go. No matter what happens here tonight, you're still Tegan and you still deserve to live your life and be happy."

"I know. I remembered that and I'm not going to forget it again. Thank you, Tracy. I'll see you all in the morning when I come on shift." Tegan kissed her sister and hugged her mate and Josh, ignoring Ben's emotional bristle when she did.

Josh stopped at the door and turned back to look Ben up and down. "If you blow it, I'm going to make it my mission to help her forget you. You get me?"

Ben narrowed his gaze at Josh who laughed before closing the door behind him. Tegan locked up and set the security system before turning back to face Ben.

"I was just getting ready to make my dinner." She walked past him into the kitchen and began to pull things out of the fridge.

"Can I help?" He stood in the doorway and watched her greedily. "Talk to me, Tegan."

She pulled two steaks out of a plastic container and placed them on the grill of her stove which was nice and hot, and began to tear veggies for a salad. He moved into the room and cleaned and tossed potatoes into the microwave. Tegan liked their rhythm and gathered her thoughts as they worked side by side.

"Where have you been?"

He slathered butter with garlic and shredded parmesan

cheese on the bread and put it on a pan beneath the broiler before turning to her. "Trying to forget you. Licking my wounds. Not wanting to face how much I wanted you. Not wanting to face how much I needed you. I was pissed off and confused and hurt and guilty and I didn't know what to think about any of this shit and this woman I'd only just met was already making demands that affected my entire life! I was overwhelmed."

Stabbing the steak to turn it, she spun, furious. "Well, buster, how about me? Huh? What about what *I* felt about the bond? My life was turned upside down too you know. I've had a mate in the past, I know what it feels like when it's right. But I lost him. Lucas, a man who *celebrated* his bond with me. A man who cherished me and loved me and wanted to be with me. He died and I had *nothing* but emptiness. For four years. But you. You came inside me and it brought that back, that feeling of completeness and warmth that your mate, the partner of your soul can fill and it *hurt* as much as it felt good. Because I remembered what it was to be part of something so special it's like a fairy tale."

She took a deep breath and put plates and silverware on the table while he pulled the bread out of the oven and the potatoes finished up. "And you know what? The first day after the arrest I felt like I'd die. I felt empty and sad and so alone. By the third day I realized something important. I'd rather live with the emptiness of the last *five* days than feel second best or a burden or disrespected. I get that you and I will be at cross-purposes sometimes. I think I'm at the point where I can accept it. But I can't bear feeling off balance and not knowing what I mean to you."

"Talk to me then! You're the one who refused to see me."

"*Five* days ago. I needed some time to think. And I called you! But you clearly weren't as harmed by our time apart as I'd thought." And that hurt. She breezed past him and pulled the steaks off the grill, not caring if he liked his rare or not.

He was there then, his body pressed against hers, arms wrapped around her body, heart thundering in her ears. "I was scared, all right? Scared because it wasn't just my need to fuck you. It wasn't me just appreciative of having you around. I felt for you. I *feel* for you. Fuck, I love you. I do. I don't know how, it's too fast. But I do and I tried to fight it because it scares me. I've been with someone before, someone I thought I loved and what I felt for her, even when I'd asked her to marry me, was a shadow of what I feel for you. You're everything I think of and part of me is freaked out because a month ago I didn't even know you."

Relief poured through her as she turned into his embrace. "I know. It is fast and it is scary and I'm afraid you're going to think none of this is real because of the bond. I'm afraid you'll resent me. I'm sorry, no, I'm not sorry I found you because for me, it is real and I love you so much but I'm sorry you had no choice. If I could give that to you, even if it would kill me, I would."

He sighed, looking into her eyes, so pretty and green, a face he'd memorized every plane of and yet, each time he saw her, he noticed something new. He couldn't miss the emotion there even if it wasn't rushing through him. Cade had said it was a gift, so had Josh and for a time he'd thought it was a curse he'd been trapped by but with her in his arms, her scent, the sound of her voice in his ears, he realized they were right and he'd been wrong. No matter how he'd ended up there, he was there and he loved this woman. He knew for a certainty she loved him. The anxiety eased then as he realized he had no doubts of her love. In all the time with Sarah he'd had that worry and he'd been right to. With every woman since he'd held part of himself back. But with her there was no holding back. It was good even as it was terrifying.

"I don't resent you. I don't understand the bond but I accept it. Can that be a start?"

"Of what? Where do we stand, Ben?"

"You're my woman, Tegan. I'm your man, your mate. I want to be with you every day. I don't want to date you, I want to share my life with you."

"You should know female wolves are very territorial about mates. I'm very possessive."

He smiled, feeling positively feral. "Good. Because I've been entertaining thoughts of hunting Josh down and running him over with my car. Repeatedly. I don't share and from what I've heard about the tri-bond, I'm relieved to know you already have one from when you mated with Lucas."

Realizing the sound he kept hearing was her stomach growling, he pushed her in the direction of the table and she started eating. His appetite was back for the first time in five days and he joined her.

"We're going to have struggles over the cop in you and the wolf in me."

"Yeah. Tegan, I can't stop being who I am. I can't stand aside and let you beat a suspect."

She nodded. "I get that. And I can't not beat him if he aims to harm my family. Which means I may not tell you everything."

He froze. "That's not acceptable. I need to know you're safe, Tegan."

"How do you propose we do this then, Ben? Because I'm not going to let the next guy who stakes me out with a gun in his pocket just walk away."

"Things would be a lot easier if you were my submissive twenty-four/seven," he grumbled and she snorted.

"Well that's not going to happen. Ever." She took a drink of her water. "I'm not interested in making it easier for you to be a human cop. I respect what you do, which is why I'm going out of my way to keep wolf business in my territory, not yours. But I can't stop being who I am either. I'm a werewolf guard in the elite Enforcer corps of my Pack. *My* Pack run by *my* brother. People I love have been endangered and continue to be threatened by Warren Pellini. You know that. You know Sargasso sent an open threat against their neighboring Pack for protection money. Memphis called earlier today and told us Pellini is trafficking in drugs and prostitution in their territory. He's moving and getting more dangerous and that means I can't sit idly by and do nothing."

He did know. Lex had called him earlier to tell him about the rising threat of inter-clan war brewing with the stronger hold Pellini held on more and more Packs nationwide. He'd scoffed at the idea of a werewolf mafia a few years ago when he'd first met Lex and Nina, but he'd seen the damage firsthand. Knew something was brewing. But he knew that made things even more dangerous for Tegan.

"We're all having a meeting tomorrow. I imagine that's why Nick and Tracy are here. The FBI is involved as well with their paranormal liaison."

"I know. I'll be there. I've asked to be part of the team."

He sat forward. "Tegan, you don't have to. Lex has other people. Gabe has people in place in DC. You don't need to put yourself in danger."

"*You're* on the team."

Sighing, he tore into his bread. "Yes. But..."

"But what? You've got a penis and therefore you're rendered incapable of being injured? Or do your testicles confer super powers upon you?" Tegan's voice was sharp and he remembered what a formidable woman she was. Remembered how fast and quiet she'd been as she'd ripped that perp out of his car. Damn it.

"You've been around Nina too long. I don't want you harmed! Is it too much to ask to let me do my job?"

"Ben Stoner, I'm not the one asking you not to do your job. You're the one asking *me* not to do mine. I'm faster than you are, I heal quicker, I have a higher pain tolerance. In short, I'm a very high capacity girl."

He shivered at the double meaning of the phrase. An ache to dominate her rode him sharply.

"I've been on Lex's team for ten years now. I've trained even longer than that. I'm good at what I do, Ben. Most of Pellini's people can't do me any harm because I'm better than they are and because I'm more vicious. They're dull, blunt instruments. But he's not. And his inner circle isn't either. But we have to stop this now before it gets worse and I can't sit back and wait around because you're worried. Do you think I like it that you're out there every day as a cop? Soft, human flesh which is so much weaker than mine. Surrounded by people who want to harm you, Ben. That makes me crazy. But I understand it's what you do."

"I don't like it. I want you safe, damn it."

She laughed and tossed a piece of steak into her mouth. "Suck it up, human."

"Mouthy fucking wolf!"

The heat built between them as they argued back and forth. Tegan neatly maneuvered around him at every turn and despite his frustrations, he admired her intelligence and temerity. It was hot.

Standing, he knocked the chair to the ground and her eyes widened and then a corner of her mouth tipped up.

"Come here, Tegan."

And like a switch turned on, she stood, all liquid grace and his entire body tightened to watch her as she moved to him.

One hand centered itself at her back and the other gripped the back of her hair, holding her in place as he leaned in to plunder. To take what was his. What she surrendered to him.

Her hands gripped the front of his shirt as her head tipped back and gave him access to the line of her throat. Submitting in that way too. He groaned and ran the edge of his teeth over the sensitive skin there.

Picking her up, he walked back to her bedroom, kicking the door open and tossing her on the bed.

"Undress, I'll be back. My toy bag is in the car."

She sat up on her elbow. "Awfully sure of yourself."

"I..."

One of her eyebrows rose and he cursed the link at that moment. He'd had it in his car because he'd been headed to the Club De Sade. How the hell could he explain that?

"You what? You've been with someone else in the last five days?" Her voice rose and she scrambled off the bed and got in his face, magnificent in her fury.

"No! No, I haven't been with anyone else but you since the first moment I touched you. I...I went to the Club. But I didn't go in!" he added quickly. "I sat in the parking lot and knew there was no one but you and I headed straight to Cade's place to get you."

Hurt creased her forehead.

"Nothing happened, Tegan. Nothing would have. I don't want anyone but you. I got in my car thinking, *I'll find some sweet sub to push her from my mind* but that was just stupid. There is no one who could push you from my mind. You're everything inside me, Tegan. I'm sorry. I don't want to hurt you, I didn't mean to. I've been stupid but nothing happened, I swear it."

"You wanted it to."

"I didn't." He took her face between his hands. "I didn't. It was another way for me to pretend I didn't need you. But I do. I do, Tegan."

She sighed explosively and cocked her head. "Get on the bed."

He blinked and swallowed. "What?"

"You heard me. Get on the bed. You're not the top tonight." One corner of that luscious mouth rose and he fought the inevitable.

"I'm the top every night."

"Not if you want to fuck me and get back into my life after even considering shopping your wares to another female. I told you I was territorial, Ben Stoner. A bill has come due. Pay it or get out."

"Tegan."

"Clothes off. On your belly." She walked out of the room.

He'd never actually switched before. He had no desire to submit but the novelty of it, of having Tegan, a woman he'd so thoroughly dominated before top him—that intrigued him. And he knew she'd drawn her line and in truth, if she'd gone to the club intending to let another man top her he'd have been livid, even if nothing happened.

Peeling his clothes off, he moved to lay face down on her bed, the scent of her body there in her comforter.

Tegan paced her living room for a few minutes as she let the anger and hurt wash through her. She didn't want to go back in the bedroom until she'd processed more. She'd never touch him in anger, not ever. There were lines in her life, D/s wasn't ever about anger, only love and she couldn't go back to what they were until she'd exorcised her mad.

After she got over being pissed, she'd give him a taste of being topped and then the next time they were together, it would be on his terms again. But he had to give and give up his position as top to her willingly as penance. And anyway, it appealed to her.

She found his toy bag in his trunk and came back inside, feeling much calmer.

Leaving her clothes on, she went back into her bedroom and took in the sight of him, hard and all man on her bed. What an ass he had. Giving in to her desire, she stalked over, leaned down and bit one cheek and he groaned. Not in pain.

He smelled good, she'd missed his scent so much. Tracing fingertips down his spine she idly looked through the bag and lit upon a few things she'd be needing.

"Undress me, Ben."

Rolling to face her, he took her body in as he came up to his knees. Gently, he unbuttoned her blouse and pushed it from her arms. Leaning in, he closed teeth around her nipple and ripples of pleasure rolled outward through her.

"Mmm. Very nice, but I didn't say you could do that. You have a job to finish first."

"You're pretty good at this domme stuff." He stood and helped her out of her bra, jeans, panties and socks.

She didn't tell him she'd had two exemplary men in her life to learn from. It wasn't the time to tell him Lucas had had her undress him every night when he got home. That part of her life was over, a sweet memory.

Finding the chair in the corner of the room, she backed into it and sat.

"On the bed behind you. Bring me the cuffs and the blindfold."

She heard his breath catch and her own matched. Emotion swelled through the room between them as this powerful alpha male submitted to her. It was motherfucking hot is what it was. While she had no plans to repeat the experience, she liked bottoming too much, topping him did have its appeal and she wasn't the only one who thought so.

He brought them to her. "Kneel facing away from me. Hands at the small of your back."

His back was broad and muscular. She ran her palms, greedy for the sensation, over his skin there, taking his warmth into her own body before securing the blindfold. Then she slid the wrist cuffs on. She didn't use the leather ones with the hasp clasp, they felt a bit much for him even though she loved the way they felt on her.

"You've never been topped before have you?" she murmured in his ear after securing the Velcro straps at his wrists. It was more a mental binding than a physical one. He could easily break through the restraints if he chose.

"No." His voice held a slight tremor. She doubted he'd find subspace, he was too controlled for that. But he was turned on, if the state of his cock was any indicator.

Reaching around his body, she took it in her hand and slid her fist around him several times until a moan slipped from his lips. Nipping his earlobe, she whispered, "Turn around, Ben. Turn around and eat my pussy. Make it good and I'll hand you back the reins. If it's not to my liking, I'll paddle you and we'll do it again."

"I want to see you." He turned carefully. Her hand

remained on his shoulder to help his balance with the blindfold on. Perhaps he'd also realize what it was like for her.

"I know. But this isn't about what you want, Ben." She settled back, leaning into the chair and spreading her thighs. Holy shit it was hot, hot, hot to have this man between her thighs bound and blindfolded.

His lips found her knee and he kissed up her thigh, mouth skating over her pussy and kissed down her other thigh. He did that over and over until her scent was heavy in the room. The cool softness of his hair slid against the skin of her inner thighs was a direct counter to the heat of his mouth.

Finally, his tongue found her pussy and she sighed. Reaching down, she pulled herself open to him and he hummed his appreciation. He moved his mouth from side to side slowly, running lips and the flat of his tongue over her clit and labia, driving her up slowly.

Without the use of his hands, he had to fuck into her with his tongue, his mouth pressed against the flesh of her pussy hard and he used every bit of himself he could. No one could say he wasn't taking the job seriously. A whimper escaped her when he lapped up the honey from her inner thighs and down over her perineum and the star of her rear passage and back up to her clit.

Over and over until she panted with her need to come. Her nipples were hard as her fingers passed over them. "I'm touching my nipples, Ben. Imagining your mouth on me here as well as on my pussy."

He groaned and sagged against her for a moment and she smiled as she watched. Until he sucked her clit into his mouth, abrading it with his teeth very gently. It was the last bit of sensation she needed to push her into climax. Back bowing, a growl of pleasure rumbling from her, she came, pressing her

Lauren Dane

pussy into his face.

But he didn't stop until she reached down with an exhausted hand and caressed his shoulder and murmured for him to stop. He did, his head resting on her thigh until she managed to undo his blindfold.

He looked into her eyes and held her gaze. In that moment he gave himself to her more than when he'd let her bind his wrists. She understood. He accepted the bond between them and while she was sure there'd be more fights, many, many more fights between them, she also knew there'd be no moments of doubt about what they were to each other.

Leaning down, she reached around him and undid his wrists. But instead of surging to take back over, he waited until she smiled and said, "Go on then. Take over."

With a laugh, she found herself on his shoulder as he stood and then turned, tossing her to the mattress and diving after her.

His mouth met hers as his body covered her. Her taste slid from his mouth into her system, changed by adding his unique flavor to it.

"You're a wicked, wicked little domme. That was fucking amazing, Tegan." He spoke into her mouth before he kissed down her throat and to her nipples. "And now you don't have to imagine my mouth here," he murmured before biting down just this side of pain.

Tegan arched with a gasp.

"But I'm not a switch. *I'm* the wicked, wicked dom and there's only room for one of us in bed." He chuckled and moved to his knees, pulling her thighs up and plunging into her without preamble.

Stars lit behind her closed eyelids as her body convulsed around his invading cock. His hands slid down her torso over

114

and over like he had to feel every single inch of her skin.

"I've missed you, Tegan. Missed feeling like this with you. Missed your voice and the way you smell. Missed the feel of your skin beneath my hands."

Tears pricked her lashes as the depth of loneliness she'd felt since their fight five days before welled up. He gasped, caught in the pull of it, pressing deep into her body, his gaze locked with hers.

The hands sliding over her breasts and stomach found her hands and their fingers locked as he fucked into her body with ferocity and overwhelming tenderness all at once.

"Mine," he whispered and she nodded.

"Mine," she echoed.

He changed his angle, bringing his pubic bone over her clit, mashing against it with delicious friction as she spun out, letting the pleasure go and giving it to him through the link.

She heard him stutter a curse and thrust deeply as he came.

Chapter Nine

"We have to figure out the living situation, gorgeous." Ben watched her as she pulled on her boots, strapping a knife to her calf. "I'm going to pretend I don't see that."

"Good, don't look at this either." She pulled on an underarm holster and slid a sidearm into it.

"That cannot be legal." He stood and held out a hand.

"What's the hand for?"

"I want to see it."

She gave him one of those explosive sighs of hers and cocked her hip. "To try and do something stupid like take it from me or because it's a fabulously cool handgun?"

He laughed, unable to help himself. Funny that he'd ended up with a woman who was as rough and tumble as he was but who liked to be tied up and flogged too. Perfect. Well except for the whole werewolf thing.

"The latter."

Tegan handed it to him, butt first and he looked at it, trying not to oooh and aaaah. It was, exactly as she said, a fabulously cool handgun. And totally, absolutely illegal.

"Look, I know. I know, Ben and I'm sorry, I really am. There are going to be times when our worlds intersect. I'll try and keep it to a minimum but if we're going to live together and share our lives you're going to see more things that are illegal in your world."

He handed the gun back to her and she put it back in her under arm rig and pulled a zip-up sweatshirt on over it.

"I know. We'll work it out. As long as it's confined to wolf stuff, I can deal. We know, the human authorities do, that you've got your own system of laws and enforcement. I can accept the guns and knives and all the other stuff as long as it concerns your world. Humans on the street outside my house? Our worlds intersect and we'll have to work that out."

"You can't kill a fully changed werewolf with regular bullets unless you use a lot of them. The ammo for this weapon is special, made to take down werewolves. Now, if a human got in my way and tried to hurt me or those I protect, I will use this on them. I'm not switching out to a regular handgun because you'd feel more comfortable. My job involves hurting or possibly killing people who pose a threat. You know that. As for the other, the humans on the street outside your house? Okay, we can work it out."

He paused as he considered it. "All right. Agreed. Now, my house is bigger and closer to your job. I have a home office there where I do a lot of work so I don't have to be at the station all the time. Still, I'm willing to consider living here. I like the neighborhood and if it makes you happy, we can work things out."

As a cop, she knew his getting called into work all the time in the middle of the night was a possibility. She often had to go in at odd hours as well. In truth, while she loved the house and it was hers, it was inconvenient to have to commute and his house was nicer. Bigger. More convenient for both. But she had a few things to clear up.

"Did your ex-fiancée live there?"

"No. I bought that house after. But other women have been there. Spent the night. The weekend. But they aren't what you are. If you want though, we can buy a place together. I don't want you to feel uncomfortable."

"I don't know. I may have to spend the night a few times to see. My wolf doesn't like it."

He cocked his head, taking her measure. "Explain that. Your wolf?"

"I don't know if I can but I'll try. I'm one person. My wolf is a part of me like my skin, like my liver or my lungs. But she's primal. She's the least reasonable part of me. I'm not a different person when I shift into my wolf skin. I'm the same person just with four feet and fur. But my vision is different. My perception is different. I'm not out of control or in a killing rage like in the movies."

"I know that. I've seen Lex in wolf form when he tracked a suspect. He was..." Ben chewed his lip, "...still Lex. But different."

She nodded. "Yes. I'm still in there, and she's inside my human skin right now. And she does not like the idea that other women have been in a bed where I'll be. She doesn't like that at all."

He smiled. "She's got nothing to worry about. You have nothing to worry about. Tegan, I...I love you. There's no one else, there never has been anyone who meant to me what you mean to me. There never will be. I don't have a wolf inside me to know that. And yet, I'm utterly certain of it."

Tegan knew there'd have to be a lot of give and take if they meant to make a go of things.

"Okay, we can live at your place. For now. And I'm buying us a new bed. Today."

"Thank you, Tegan. I know this is difficult and I appreciate all you're doing to work with me. I've been meaning to get a new bed anyway. I don't suppose my luck has held out long enough for you to have reconsidered not being on this team?"

"I laugh at your feeble attempts."

Standing, he moved quickly to her, pulling her against him. "You need to be sure to get a four poster bed. Sturdy."

He loved the way her eyes blurred just a moment and a sexy smile curved her lips. "That so? You use those toys on any other women? Because the woman and the wolf won't be having *any* of that."

"No, ma'am. The toys I've used on you are all new, I bought them for you. I'll be sure to get rid of any old stuff. The rope is new but since that got shredded when, well when we bonded, I'll need more. We'll need more."

"Good. Now, I have to get to Cade's. I'll see you at two for the meeting." She rifled in a drawer in the kitchen and pulled out a ring with two keys on it. "Here. House and garage." She gave him the code to the security system but he walked out with her, leaving when she did. He didn't want her to be out there alone when he could be there too.

Tegan walked through Cade's garage and up into the house. Milton, Tracy's crazy three-legged dog, barked and bumped her with his head until she bent and scratched behind his ears and gave him a squeeze. Damned dog was nearly as irresistible as Ben was.

"So without further ado, are things okay?"

"Hi, Nina, good morning to you. No, traffic wasn't too bad today." Tegan poured herself a cup of coffee and rolled her shoulders. She hadn't gotten much sleep the night before.

"Har. Now that your attempt to be cutting has failed

miserably you were going to tell us about Ben."

Tracy, who'd wandered in and grabbed a bagel, sat at the table, laughing.

"Yes, things are fine. More than fine. I'm moving into his house this weekend."

Nina grinned. "I take it he finally admitted the truth of the bond? That he loved you and not just fucking you?"

"He did. We talked a long time in between other things. Anyway, we're good. There'll be trouble in the future, he's very much like a male wolf. He's as stubborn as Lex, if such a thing is possible. Not pleased at all I'm going to be on the Pellini team. I told him to get over it. Puhleeze, does the man not get that I'm a freaking werewolf? He's seen me change, it's not like he hasn't dealt with Lex in a full-on rage. Still, it's kind of nice in a stifling and yet sort of cute guy way."

Nina hugged her. "Yes. When they're not being annoyingly over-protective, they're good in bed, they carry groceries and are nice to look at. I'm glad he finally came to his senses. Tracy said he looked like he wanted to kill Josh last night."

Tegan told them about Ben's reaction and they were all still laughing as Megan came in and they traded notes between shifts.

Ben looked up as the wolves entered the conference room. He'd felt Tegan come into the building a minute or two before. Odd, like she came into his thoughts and he felt her as if she were in the same room. A whisper at first and then it grew stronger as she got closer.

He tried to keep in mind she was there in an official capacity but when she sat next to him, he reached out to squeeze her hand briefly under the table. The need to touch her rode him when they were together.

"Agent Harrison Benoit, you know everyone?" Ben motioned from the task force agent around the table.

Benoit nodded until he came to Tegan and sensual awareness seeped from him as he tipped his head in her direction. "Not everyone."

Ben wondered if he was feeling what Tegan picked up from Benoit or if it was just his guy sense picking up when another man scoped out his woman.

He neatly leaned over and touched Tegan in clear view as he looked Benoit in the eye. "This is my fiancée and one of Cascadia's Enforcer team, Tegan Warden."

Tegan's lips fought a smile as she nodded her head toward Benoit.

"Ah. Nice to meet you, Ms. Warden." Benoit looked back to Lex, who made no attempt to hide his gloating smile and Ben wanted to smack him.

"Getting down to it, shall we? We've received a coded message from Jack Meyers. Pellini has demanded the National Mediator position be filled by one of his own people."

Lex and Cade both looked shocked. That would make the Fourth, and the Third, the Mediator both positions held by Pellini loyalists. It was also commonly believed that Jack Meyers was on Pellini's side too even though he and Templeton Mancini, the National Pack Alpha, were working to stop Pellini. Essentially Pellini would have the entire top governance within the National Pack in his power. Or so he'd believe.

Gabe Murphy, Tracy's second mate and National's previous Mediator spoke over the phone line. "Well that's bad. What are they going to do?"

"Templeton has asked for an envoy from each Pack in the National Council to go to Boston to meet. Jack will supposedly try to corner you all to see where you stand but really, he'll be gathering strength against Pellini. The member Packs will have to rise up and demand the position not be filled by a Pellini loyalist." Benoit sat back in his chair and watched them.

"Explain to me please. National Council?" Ben had been working with the wolves for a few years but there were so many things he didn't know about their culture still.

"Well, you know the National Pack is essentially the one Pack that holds the most power. The other Packs nationwide are like satellites. Mainly they're left alone to do their own thing but National takes on issues like lobbying for laws to protect us, making sure each Pack behaves and doesn't prey on humans, that sort of thing. Within each Pack there's an Inner Circle—the Alpha and Enforcer are first and second and then a Third through Fifth are the next strongest wolves. They're the governance of each Pack." Cade took a sip of water before continuing.

"So there are forty-five Packs in the United States and of those Packs, the five strongest Packs have a seat on a National Council. A sort of Inner Circle of all the Packs. Cascadia holds Second. Calling for a meeting of the NC is a big deal. Templeton is exposing himself to challenge if wolves see him as weak."

Well yeah, Gabe was right, that wasn't good at all. "So each Pack in this council goes and you all tell Pellini to shove it and he's gone?"

"We don't know where two of the five Packs stand. Great Lakes, the largest and most powerful Pack is on our side. They're actually the most affected by Pellini as his *group* is a Pack that broke away from Great Lakes and they run a lot of their crap through Chicago, the seat of the GL Pack. We're pretty sure Yellowstone are in with Pellini. That leaves Granite and Siskiyou. Granite like to be left alone. They're going to be annoyed at Templeton's call to Council and they're very old school, fought coming out to the humans. Siskiyou are wild wolves, the Pack is large, the third largest in the country. I've never been able to get a very accurate bead on them." Cade looked to Lex, who sighed.

"We need to get a group together. Gabe, how many in an envoy?" Lex asked.

"I'd say you'd stay this side of not insulting if you took four."

"We'll have to call our own Pack Inner Circle together to discuss this. Lex will obviously decide who goes, this is a security issue."

"You won't be going? Ben asked Cade.

Tegan snorted. "No. Alphas don't go. You have no idea what it's like to deal with five Alphas in one room. Nothing would get done as they measured their dicks over and over."

Megan barked a laugh at Tegan's comments and Ben just shook his head.

"You know, I'm missing those days when you glowered quietly all the time." Lex sent Tegan a dark look but his lips twitched. "Most likely we'll send our Third and three from our Enforcer team. I'll stay back with Cade, as will all the other Enforcers."

"Jack also indicated he understood humans would also want to keep an eye on this. Ben, you'll go naturally as will I. Once we know where the meeting is to be held, we'll set up surveillance," Benoit explained, making notes on his PDA.

"Okay, I'm going to try to make contact with Jack, to let him know we're on it," Gabe said. "You know where I am if you need help or expertise. I can give you the specs on most of the Pack buildings they'd use for a Council meeting. Trace, babe, I miss you."

Ben looked up at Tracy Warden's face and she smiled. "I miss you too. We'll be home tonight."

"Good. I took my vitamins today."

Tracy laughed. "I love you."

Gabe returned the sentiment and hung up. The rest of the wolves got up and made for the door.

"It's near quitting time, Tee. Why don't you head home for the day? Inner Circle will want to meet tomorrow anyway. I'll double the shift." Lex touched his sister's shoulder and she leaned into him. Ben noticed they touched each other a lot but he was still glad the Pacific Pack Enforcer had kept his distance.

"You sure?"

"Yeah, you have some bed shopping to do, I hear. Nina would chew my ass if I made you come back to the house for twenty minutes. And anyway, you deserve a life."

Tegan hugged her brother, rubbing her face along his jaw. "Thanks, Lex. And thank Nina too." She turned to Tracy and hugged her baby sister and Nick as well. Josh laughed, winking at her and then Ben before nodding his head and leaving the room.

"I'm going back to my office. I'll talk to you tomorrow, Ben, about travel arrangements. Nice to meet you, Tegan." Benoit took Tegan's hand, shaking it. "Congratulations, by the way. When's the wedding?"

"We have to work out those details. You'll be invited." Ben put his body between them and Tegan laughed softly.

When the room emptied out, he pulled her against his body, breathing her in. His system calmed, nerves smoothed. "Hi there."

"Mmm. Hi to you too. Are you near quitting time? I

borrowed one of Cade's trucks to move the bed so you can come with me to shop for it."

"I have a few things to do. I did make you a set of keys though." He handed her a ring. "I'll try to hurry up or you can wait here. I have to meet with another officer on a case. I may be an hour or so."

"Nah." She kissed his jaw. "I'll go now. Am I sleeping at your place tonight?"

"Our place and I sure hope so. Don't even think about moving stuff without my help."

"Ben." She writhed against him, firing those quieted nerves and igniting his need for her. "I'm a werewolf. I can move a bed. Seriously."

"I'll call you when I'm done."

He walked her to her borrowed truck and kissed her again before she left.

Chapter Ten

But one hour had been six as something broke on a case Ben was on and he didn't get home until after she'd gone to sleep. She registered his body sliding against hers during the night and his murmured *I love you.*

She woke up the next morning and showered as silently as she could. Still getting used to being in his place. Her toiletries took up half the counter now and she liked the way it looked. Liked her stuff in his house.

Her wolf had been satisfied at the lack of any woman's scent but Tegan's as well.

She made herself breakfast and was sipping a cup of coffee when he stumbled into the kitchen.

"I'm so sorry," he said as she came into his arms.

"Ben, you're a cop. I get that your hours aren't going to be nine to five every day. It's okay. You called. I'm not mad. Shouldn't you be sleeping?"

"I have to go in this morning and interview some witnesses. The new bed is nice. Where's the old one?"

She poured him a cup of coffee and he helped himself to the eggs and bacon on the table, settling in next to her.

"In the garage. I covered it all but you'll want to get to it or it might get wet out there."

"I don't have any sentimental attachments to it. It's just a bed I picked up a few years back. There's a domestic violence shelter I work with from time to time, I'll give 'em a call today and see if they need one. You want to make a date for dinner tonight?"

"Lex called last night, the Inner Circle is meeting at eleven today. It should be over by the time my shift is up. I should be home by five thirty or so."

"Good. Because I have something I want to try on you." One of his eyebrows rose and she laughed, blushing.

"Well then, I'll rush home." She rose, rinsing off her plate and putting it in the dishwasher. "I've got to go. I'll see you tonight."

He walked her to the front door, kissing her soundly before she left, leaving her brain in a muddle the whole drive over to Cade's.

Ben was going to flip out. Tegan took a steadying breath before hefting the box of her stuff and moving to the front door.

"Hey, let me help you." He met her in the living room, taking the box and kissing her. The house smelled spicy and savory. "I just opened a bottle of wine. Where do you want this box? I'll put it there while you change into the clothes I left on the bed."

"It's a box of clothes so the bedroom I suppose. Hmm, you're going to dress me up?"

He laughed, following her into their room and putting the box off to the side. She saw the beautiful emerald green kimono style robe lying on their bed.

"I'd like to."

She turned to face him, saw the look in his eyes and a

shiver worked down her spine.

"Okay. It's lovely." She drew her fingertips over the cool, smooth silk.

"Like you. I saw it last week. Yes, while we were fighting. I had to have it because I knew you'd look beautiful in it."

"I suppose now would be a good time to establish whether or not we start this part of our lives and drop everything from the outside or whether we fight first and then fuck."

Sighing, he sat on the bed. "Well now, that doesn't bode well. I suppose I'd say we deal with the outside first and then move to the other. I prefer for the other stuff, our sexual life, to be totally separated from any strife. So go on, tell me."

It probably would have been easier if she'd been wearing some slinky robe. She began to move about the room, putting her weapon away, unpacking the box of clothes.

"I've been chosen to go to the National Council meeting."

"You have not!" He jumped up and moved to her. "You are not going to that meeting, Tegan. It's dangerous." He crossed his arms over his chest and gave her his bad cop face.

"At the risk of channeling Nina, duh. That's why I'm going. Recall our conversation yesterday and this morning about the whole danger thing being part of my job. I'm very good at what I do, it's why Lex is sending me. I know it upsets you and I'm sorry for that. But I'm not sorry I was chosen to go, it's an honor my Enforcer thinks so highly of me. Just like you being chosen to go means your boss thinks highly of you."

Thank goodness she'd spoken at length about this with Nina earlier. Nina had explained Ben would be mad and attempt to be bossy but cautioned Tegan not to lose her temper. Nina had been right that Tegan would keep the upper hand if she let Ben blow off steam but never let it be a question of her going.

Nina was positively, delightfully evil that way. No wonder Lex walked around confused but very happy most of the time. It was a matter of letting the dude be all bossy and pissy but never letting the argument be about something she'd never change her mind on.

"Why are you being so calm about this?" Ben thundered.

"I know you're upset. I know you're worried. But you'll be there too, we won't have to be separated, which is nice, don't you think?"

He snorted and began to pace. "You're avoiding the subject, Tegan. I won't have you putting yourself in harm's way like this."

She ignored that last statement. "No I'm not. The subject is not whether I'll go. I'm going. The subject is your feelings about it. I know you're pissed. I'm sorry for it. I don't want you to be upset."

"Then stay the hell here and be safe!"

She laughed. He was really quite adorable when he got this way. She moved to him, placing herself in his path to halt the pacing and slipped her arms around his shoulders.

"We've already gotten past that. It's going to happen, you know it. I've let you rail about it and it's over unless you want to have sex with your hand and talk to yourself because I'm done now. I promise I'll look way better in that green silk than your hand will."

"Tegan, please. This is insanity."

She kissed him softly. What was insane was the fact that she was a freaking werewolf and he was a human. He was the weaker one but he worried for her. So sweet, this gruff man.

"It is. But it's my job and you have your job and we already discussed that very salient point and agreed to work through it.

This falls into the category of my world. This is wolf business and this fucker has harmed my family and he threatens my people. He's got to be stopped."

His spine lost its stiffness and she knew she'd won.

"Fine. You're going to drive me to an early grave. Should of found myself a woman who listened. Who was all nice and took orders. Oh no, had to get a bossy one who shoots guns and likes hand to hand," he mumbled as he undid the button of her jeans.

"You love it and you know it."

He harrumphed and pulled her shirt up over her head.

"I do love that you wear sexy stuff under your work clothes." He kissed her pulse, his tongue filling the hollow of her throat just a phantom of a moment before moving away.

"Victoria's Secret but I know it's there. Makes me feel sexy."

"How could you feel anything but? You're the most beautiful thing I've ever seen. Stubborn woman. There's a card with instructions on it beneath the robe. I'll be in the dining room when you finish."

He spun after one last, hard kiss and left the room. Wicked man to leave her hanging and breathless.

The card bore the embossed stamp of a red wolf at the top. Made her slightly dizzy that he'd put so much energy into that small detail.

Going into the bathroom, she undressed and showered, using the gel soap he'd indicated, ginger and vanilla. She smelled like gingerbread but in a totally hot way. Who knew?

She brushed her hair out and left it down. It gleamed in the light. She applied red lipstick, the perfect red for a redhead so he'd looked in her makeup bag because it was her shade. A shade she'd bought on a whim just before she'd met him.

Always made her feel daring and wanton.

Thong panties the same green as the robe went on before she slid the silk against her skin and belted it at the waist. The color brought out the pale cream of her skin. He'd chosen well and, as she stood there looking at herself, she'd never felt more beautiful.

The shape caught her eye, black satin pumps that tied around the ankle with pretty ribbons.

Swaying out into the living room, the warm light of the candles he'd lit drew her eye to where he waited near the dining room table. He was shirtless and wore low slung jeans worn in all the right places, including a threadbare patch right at his cock.

Her mouth dried up at the sight of him even as her body tightened. So masculine, so beautiful and all hers.

"You look spectacular, Tegan. That color is just as gorgeous as I thought it would be on you."

He took her hand and kissed it, making her smile. "Thank you. It's lovely and the card—you remembered I was a red wolf. I'm very touched."

"Despite how angry I was at you, I'll never forget how magical you looked as a wolf. The way your fur felt when I touched you. Soft. I hadn't imagined you'd be soft like that. I shouldn't have been surprised you make as beautiful a wolf as you do a woman."

"You're making me blush. Can I say how sexy you look right now? May I touch you?"

"I love that you asked. You're ready then? We've cast aside all the outside stuff and you're submitting?"

She nodded.

"Yes, please touch me as much as you'd like." His voice

took on a subtle but obvious change. He was firmly in charge in that moment and the warmth of it brushed against her senses.

His chest called to her so she gave in and ran palms over it, reveling in the way he felt. So warm, hard and totally unique. No one else felt the way he did to her. Right. Like home.

She massaged his shoulders, brushing kisses across the width of his back as she moved behind him. The shoes brought her to his height so she licked and nibbled on his ears and neck as well. Unable to resist, her hands skimmed down and over the curve of the well-maintained, nicely muscled ass, squeezing through the denim.

"Tegan, beautiful, come around here," he murmured, voice thick with desire.

She obeyed and he indicated she kneel on the pillow he'd tossed at his feet.

Standing in front of her, he brushed his fingertips over her neck, moving her hair to the side. "I have something for you, will you wear it? Not a collar because it's not practical in public. I want you to always have this on, except when you're a wolf, of course."

She looked up and saw the necklace he held. Delicate and yet sturdy, it was a simple chain, the pendant was a Celtic knot.

"Forever. You and I."

Nodding, she tried to swallow past the lump of emotion in her throat. "It's beautiful."

"Platinum. I know you can't wear silver. I have a bracelet with the design, I thought, well I thought we could wear them in addition to our wedding rings. What do wolves do with their jewelry when they change anyway?"

Tegan laughed. People so rarely even thought about that

sort of thing. "When we go through the ceremony before the Pack, my grandmother does some funky mojo over our rings and whatever she does causes the rings to stay when we're wolves. I don't know how it works. They aren't on our paws or anything but when we take our human form again, they're there. Clothes will tear if you don't remove them but the rings she touches during the ceremony are always there. And thank you for thinking about the platinum. It's, well, you're very sweet and I love you."

He put the necklace on and she reminded herself to ask her grandmother about it, whether she'd have to take it off when she worked or not. Tegan would hate to lose something so special to her.

"While you're down there, suck my cock the way I like it, Tegan."

Anticipation shivered through her at the sound of his fly opening, even as his orders made her relax.

His cock, warm and heavy and ready for her, filled her hands as she leaned in to rub her cheek over it. He didn't know but more than her human needing to touch him intimately, the brush of a cheek against a loved one was something wolves did in submission and seeking comfort. It took on a whole new meaning when she did it right then.

His hands gently kneaded her shoulders, his fingers occasionally sifting through her hair as she gripped his cock at the root, angling him so she could take him slowly into her mouth.

He appeared to like it when she kept him wet and sucked hard and soon, she fell into a rhythm, moving forward and pulling back, slow and steady. When he gripped her hair, a shiver of delight broke over her skin and desire coursed through her, slow and thick.

Tegan loved the way his cock felt in her mouth, loved his taste, loved the way he grew harder as time passed. Loved making him feel good. Each time he groaned or whispered something to her, triumph flared through her system that she'd affected him.

"Mmm, that's it. God you're beautiful like this."

She took note of the strain in his voice, knew he was near climax. Dipping her mouth down, she licked across his balls, tight against his body. He jerked with a groan as her fingertips pressed just behind his sac, massaging that sensitive spot.

His thighs bulged from the strain of his muscles, the fingers in her hair tightened, urging her back to his cock. She licked up the length of him before taking him between her lips again.

Relaxing, she took him as deeply as she could, speeding up, swirling her tongue around the crown, over the slit over and over and over until he gasped and came.

She kissed him gently and he held still while she tucked him back in his jeans.

Ben had never seen a more beautiful sight as Tegan made walking toward him in that robe. Her breasts moved enticingly, her nipples pressed against the silk, daring his hands and mouth. As if he could ever get enough. Her legs were long and supple as she moved in those sexy heels.

And on her knees before him, her hair spread about her shoulders, her lips wrapped around his cock—amazing. The mere sight of his woman caught his breath, made his heart stutter in his chest. The way she set aside how dominant she was in the rest of her life and yet truly submitted to him was such a gift.

Breathing heavily after coming, he hauled her up to stand,

wrapping his arms around her and bringing her body close to his.

He kissed her slowly. Tasting himself layered over her sweetness. Loved that.

"Thank you, Tegan. Dinner is ready. Shall we eat? Afterward, I have some gelato, I thought I might eat it off your nipples while you used the vibrator on your pussy."

Smiling, he watched the way her pupils widened, her breath sped, knowing she liked the suggestion as much as he did.

He pulled out her chair and she sat, thanking him.

"I thought some salmon would be nice. A guy from work just got back from Alaska and this is fresh." He put some on her plate and the rest on his. "Nothing fancy on it, just some butter and garlic. Rice to go with and some spinach and cucumber and dill."

He realized, as he watched her eat, as they spoke and laughed, he'd finally found just exactly what he'd dreamed of. Tegan was his equal. She pushed back when he pushed too far. Sexy, intelligent, funny, tough and sweet, she was the woman he'd been afraid to hope existed and there she was, laughing at his jokes and stealing food off his plate.

He kissed her knuckles and she leaned in, resting her head on his shoulder just a moment.

"I love that soap. I feel like a gingerbread wolf." Her smile was shy. He brushed his thumb down her jaw.

"I like taking care of you. I have others for different days. You do smell good enough to eat. But you always do."

She blushed. "I...it feels good to be cherished like this."

"I love you, Tegan." He said it and meant it. No fear, no hesitation.

"I love you too. I'm sorry the bond was sprung on you, but I'm not sorry I found you. This feels meant to be."

"Well, after the initial shock, I agree with you. You were meant to be with me. I'm meant to be yours. You need me to keep you from getting yourself shot." He winked and she rolled her eyes.

They cleared up the dishes and he turned back to her. "I'll bring the gelato. Go and wait for me in the bedroom. Take the robe off and lay on the bed."

She swallowed hard and nodded. He watched her sway out of the room on those fuck-me-heels with a smile.

"Oh and leave the shoes on."

He heard her laugh as she walked down the hall.

She heard him coming, the clink of spoons on the glass of the bowl, the brush of denim from his jeans. Scented the pistachio gelato and his elemental being as he approached.

It was hard to lay still as he stood in the doorway and looked at her with a small smile. His eyes took in every detail from the pointed toe of the heels to the top of her head. She felt his gaze like a physical caress.

She waited while he put the bowls of gelato down and rustled around the room. She knew how he worked so she wasn't surprised when all the things he'd need where waiting in the drawer next to the bed.

Patience, hard won, settled in as she began to fall away from herself.

"Arms above your head. Let's see how sturdy this bed is. I'd planned on making you fuck yourself with the vibe but I've changed my mind. Good thing I'm the Dom and I get to make the decisions."

She couldn't help but laugh. "Good thing."

He cuffed her wrists to the bed, making sure the leather wasn't too tight but had a nice hold. Confining with wide straps that pressed into her skin but not in a painful way. As a reminder.

Each movement he made eased her deeper into subspace. She'd never gone into it as deeply and quickly as she had with him. He connected with everything she needed on a subconscious level as well as a physical one. Like a key in a lock.

Her breathing slowed and deepened as he put the blindfold on. Suddenly, with the loss of her vision, her skin surged to life, feeling everything tenfold.

"Open your mouth."

She did, trusting him totally.

Cold and sweet, the pistachio gelato played against her tongue as he gave her a small taste. She licked the spoon, loving the way he hummed appreciatively at the gesture.

He straddled her, his jeans still on, feeding her small bites of chocolate and pistachio. When he scooted down her body and closed his lips over one of her nipples she squealed at the cold touch of his tongue.

Not nearly as cold as the back of the spoon and then the drizzle of melting gelato. She writhed against the erotic delight of the sensation of his tongue contrasted by the liquid and the metal of the spoon.

Need built up in her muscles as they trembled. She arched into his mouth, against his teeth as she squeezed her thighs together to get some relief from that want but it wasn't enough.

Only he would be enough and she knew he'd give her what she needed when he decided she needed it.

A cold, wet trail dripped down her stomach and she only barely held back a sigh of relief. *Yes, down, keep going!*

He left her panties on, snapping the thong against her hip bone with his teeth. Warmth a brief moment as he breathed over her pussy through the material and then dribble and lick, dribble and lick as he moved down her leg and then back up the other one.

"What should I do next?" he murmured.

"Make me come?" she asked hopefully.

"Well that could be an idea, yes."

He pressed his tongue against her clit through her panties but she was so wet and so swollen it didn't matter. A deep moan broke from her lips as pleasure shot from her clit to her nipples, rippling outward to her fingertips and her toes.

The edge of cool metal slid between her hip and the panties and she felt the release of the thong on one side and then the other as he must have used scissors to cut them.

Who cared about ruined panties when her pussy was now bare and available to anything he'd like to use on it? Whee!

He leaned up over her body and put ear buds in. Her iPod. PJ Harvey began to murmur and growl in her ears as she felt him touch her labia with a vibe that burred and stopped. Before long she realized it was the vibrator hooked to the iPod, reacting to the music.

She waited to feel what he'd do next and she didn't stop the gasp when he shoved her thighs wide and then pushed her heels up against her ass. She was totally open to him and the cool air against the heated slick of her pussy.

He stretched her slow and easy with the vibrator, leaving it deep inside her, pulsing to the music when his mouth found her clit and she cried out.

Unable to process every bit of the sensory information bombarding her, she whipped her head from side to side, gasping and moaning as he concentrated on her clit with his tongue and lips and the vibrations inside her sounded through her flesh.

When she came, she bit her lip hard as the air and a hoarse cry rushed from her. Her body thrummed with energy as her orgasm went on and on.

After she'd calmed, he petted gently over her pussy and kissed her mound before removing the vibrator and the ear buds. Her blindfold was next and she blinked against the light in the room and the masculine handsomeness of his face as he smiled at her before kissing her lips.

Lastly, he undid her wrists, kissing where she'd been bound and snuggled into her side as she caught her breath.

"I love gelato. I think we should have it for dessert more often."

Chapter Eleven

"Please don't be nervous, they're going to love you."

Tegan had her doubts but she kept them to herself as they approached the front door of the rambler he'd grown up in and where his parents still lived.

He'd told his family they'd met a bit earlier than they had and they were engaged to be married. He danced around what they'd thought of that so Tegan was pretty sure they were dubious and hey, she'd have been dubious too in their shoes.

"I can't believe you haven't told them I'm a werewolf yet. I could kick your ass for that." She *wanted* to kick his ass for that. It wasn't something you sprung on people!

"I'll tell them today," he murmured as he brought the hand he'd been holding to his lips for a kiss.

"You will not! Is that why you haven't told them yet? You wanted to have me there when you did so they wouldn't flip out? That's not fair of you at all."

Before she could yell at him in a whisper any further, the front door opened and a sixty-five year old version of Ben stepped out and waved.

"Hey, Dad!" Ben hustled her to the porch where he introduced her to his father, William.

His father shook her hand as he took her measure. Tegan held his eyes as he nodded. She'd apparently passed some sort of test, goodness knew what, but she'd take what she could get at that point.

"Nice to meet you, Tegan. Please, come in. Bonita just took the eggplant parm out of the oven and Jillian is pouring the wine." He waved them through and Ben kept an iron grip on her hand as he propelled her to the kitchen.

She turned to him briefly and whispered, "You're going to break my hand if you hold it that tight. I'm not going to run off."

He laughed, kissing her again and when she turned again, a small, dark-haired woman stood in the doorway to the kitchen with narrowed eyes.

"I'm Bonita and you're obviously Tegan. Come on through and sit down while you tell us what the hell is going on. Wipe that frown off your face, Benjamin, you knew I would be curious about any woman you met and were engaged to in less than three months. Especially when we hadn't even heard you mention her until last week."

That might be true, but manners didn't cost a damned thing.

"Thank you for inviting me to your home. Ben says he grew up here. A sense of place is very nice to have." Tegan used *her* manners as she took her seat.

"I'm Jillian, Ben's sister. It's nice to meet you."

The younger woman who'd been pouring wine smiled and Tegan relaxed a bit as she shook her hand.

"Ben talks about you a lot. Says you're an amazing cook. It's nice to meet you too."

Jillian blushed. "That's quite the compliment." Leaning around Tegan, Jillian kissed her brother's cheek and hugged

141

him one armed. "He's one of the best cooks I know."

"Very true. He spoils me with all the great things he makes."

Bonita frowned. "You don't do any cooking?"

"When he lets me near the kitchen. Usually breakfast because I'm up before he is." Tegan knew Ben had told them they now lived together, she wanted the other woman to understand she wasn't going anywhere.

They all sat at the table and passed around platter after platter of food. The sheer variety and quantity was dizzying.

And delicious. Eggplant parmesan, marinated vegetables, fresh mozzarella in spiced olive oil, a salad of mixed peppers and onions, crusty bread that was chewy and delicious on the inside. Meatballs and pasta as well.

All was silent for several minutes as everyone chowed down.

"This is delicious. I can see where Ben gets his talent in the kitchen, Mrs. Stoner."

"You'll bring her to the restaurant soon, Ben," Jillian said. "Everyone is dying to get a look at the girl who finally caught you." She winked at them and Tegan laughed. At least one member of Ben's family liked her. The father seemed to be waiting for his wife to give the okay. And from the looks of it, Bonita Stoner wasn't an easy person to convert.

"Why so soon?" Bonita asked. "You just met the girl. Is she in a family way?"

Tegan choked on the bread she'd been chewing. Ben handed her a goblet of water before answering his mother.

"No, Tegan isn't pregnant. If she was, we'd tell you. It's not something we'd hide. I'm not trying to hide our relationship or how I feel about her."

"How do you know anything? You just met the girl. You're living together so obviously you're not marrying to get her to have sex with you."

Tegan continued to chew, trying to be understanding. After all, they didn't know her. She also thought it was important Ben handle it. Her family had threatened to kill him so she could take a bit of unpleasant on his behalf.

"I've known Tegan's family for some time now, nearly two years. I work with her brothers a lot. And I'm old enough to know the difference between wanting sex and being in love with a woman I want to be married to. I've been in enough relationships to know that."

"Oh? Are your brothers cops then?" Jillian interrupted, trying to change the tone of the conversation. Little did she know.

"No. My brother Lex is an architect, although he does security consulting for my oldest brother, Cade. Cade runs several businesses, including a chain of coffee shops in the Seattle area."

"Then how do you work with them, Ben? Are they snitches or criminals?" his mother demanded.

Tegan thought the woman was deliberately rude to see how much Tegan would take. Tegan wanted to pop Ben in the nose for leading up to what he was about to tell them with no prep at all.

"Oh, well." He looked to her and Tegan narrowed her eyes at him and gulped her wine down in two swallows. May as well get it all out in the open.

"Go on. You knew this would happen." She sat back, arms over her chest.

"I didn't, not like this. Cripes. I'm sorry. This is my fault. Let's change the subject." He rolled his eyes and drew his

143

thumb over her arm.

"Are you high? You can't change the subject now! Whatever they're imagining has to be worse than the truth. Ben, you're going to have to buy her something shiny after this. Just spill it already." Jillian threw up her hands

"Yes it's your fault. This was totally predictable. But your sister is right that you need to just spill it. Although I doubt they've imagined this."

"Don't talk to my son that way!" Bonita interrupted. "You come into my house and this is how you act?"

Tegan took calming breaths and told herself the woman was just a momma bear protecting her son.

"Mrs. Stoner, your son has a few things he needs to tell you. I've been urging him to do it for a bit now. He and I have had words about it because it's my concern this stuff he's held back will create unpleasantness."

"You were obviously raised by people who had no manners at all. How dare you speak to Ben in that tone, he's better than the likes of you."

The woman actually sniffed in Tegan's direction and with that, she was done being accommodating. Ben held her shoulder and she shook him off to turn to face the tiny little beast.

"With all due respect, ma'am, I'm acting with way more restraint than you'd be shown in my house with your atrocious manners." Whoops, well okay so her brothers wanted to pop Ben in the nose but they hadn't and they respected the bond, damn it. Her family accepted Nina, Gabe and Nick as well as Sid. All the people who mated with her siblings had been welcomed into the Pack. Clearly this woman hadn't the slightest idea of what that meant.

The beast's penciled-in eyebrows rose as she wrinkled her

nose and glared at Ben. "You're going to marry this? Benjamin, she's after your money. Her family is obviously part of the criminal element if you deal with them and won't tell us why."

She did *not* just say that. "I don't need his money. I've got a trust with three million dollars in it. I also earn a salary that's twice his. As for my family, why do you assume all this negative stuff about me? Yes, you don't know me and yes, I'm sure it's a shock to suddenly be told your son has a fiancée but what I don't get is why you're so all fired hostile from go when *most* families would be happy their son met someone he loved!" Tegan stood but pushed Ben to sit. "No. You sit and finish dinner. I've lost my appetite and I'm going to leave now."

"I'm not going to stay here without you, honey. How are you going to get home?"

"My sister Megan just lives about three blocks over, actually. I'll go to her place. Call me when you're done and you can pick me up."

He stood. "No. I said I'm not going to stay here without you. I won't let you be insulted by my family. I'm sorry, I didn't imagine this would happen."

"Ben, may I speak to you privately?" Tegan asked.

He nodded and she drew him out front. "Look, there's a whole lot of stuff not being said. I don't know what's going on in there but you need to hash it out without me. I don't want you to have bad feelings with your mother. Just talk it through. Is this about your ex?"

Shoving a hand through his hair he sighed. "I don't know. I've never seen her this way. Honestly, I don't quite know what to think. I'm sorry. I'm so sorry. It's unacceptable, I want you to know that. I'm going to make sure they know that too. You're my woman, my mate and you'll be my wife."

Tegan smiled and kissed him. "I love you. Now go in and

talk this out. You're going to have to tell them about me now, you know that."

He handed her the keys. "I know. That's going to be really fun." He laughed without mirth. "Take the car. I'll get a ride from Jillian when I'm done here. Go home and I'll be there in a bit."

After he'd watched her drive away and had cooled off some, Ben went back inside the house.

He held a hand up and sat at the table. "Don't. I'm serious about this. That woman means everything to me and I won't have her here if you all can't respect that. She's done nothing to you and I'm so angry right now, so ashamed I don't know how to put it other than that."

"Who is this girl, Benjamin? She's hiding something and you can't expect us to just accept that," his mother said.

"In the first place, what matters is that *I* know everything there is to know about Tegan. Your knowing and accepting whatever there is about her is not relevant, Mom. Now, I love you and she knows that. She came here tonight understanding you'd be wary because this is all sudden. But the way you acted means unless this gets resolved, I won't be spending much time around here. I'm marrying her in a week."

Chaos broke out as his mother shot up and began to pace, reeling off curses, half Spanish, half Italian. Wait until he told them the next part, she might even break out the Magyar.

"Wow." Jillian sat back in her chair. "Okay. What can I do? Do you need help planning? Do you have a caterer?"

He laughed. His sister always was fabulous. "Tegan's sisters are doing some of it. I'll have them get in contact with you. You'll like them. Especially Nina. Thank you, Jillian, it means a lot to me."

She blew him a kiss. "Congratulations, I mean that. I'm happy for you. You've been alone a long time. She's gorgeous and clearly she can handle herself which means she won't let you push her around. Now, you want to tell us the backstory? What does she do? How did you meet?"

"She's a bodyguard. I met her at a nightclub but when we were having coffee we realized we had people in common. Her brothers. Her family is very well connected in her world." He looked at his mother to drive that home. Tegan after his money indeed! Holy cow, she had millions?

"A bodyguard? She doesn't look like a bodyguard at all. For what? Why?" his father asked.

"For her brothers. And," he took a deep breath and plunged ahead, "she's a werewolf. Her family is the ruling family of the Cascadia Pack. That's how I know her brothers. I'm the liaison between the human authorities and the Packs you know. Anyway, the Wardens are very influential and trust me when I tell you Dad, she may not look it, but she's a tough cookie. She can handle herself very well."

Utter silence.

"Wow. Always tossing out the big ones, eh, Ben? Jeez, I guess I can do just about anything at this point. Join a biker gang, get a tat on my neck, get two boyfriends, can't hold a candle to a werewolf." Jillian laughed but his parents did not join her. His mother's lips moved in what he knew all too well was a prayer for his salvation and his father's mouth formed words but no sound came out.

"Ben, you...you can't mean to do this! You brought that thing into my home without asking? Without telling us what it was? An animal!" The light in his mother's eyes scared him nearly as much as hearing her say those things about Tegan hurt him.

147

"Let me make something very clear right now and please listen carefully because it's very important. Tegan Warden is my woman. She's the person I love and will spend my life with. She is not an animal or a thing. No one who wants me in their life will ever refer to her in such terms in my presence ever again. Moreover, she's not just someone I love but she's my mate. There exists between us, a metaphysical bond. Even if I could change that, I would not. She has made me a better person and filled my life with something I needed so badly I can't quite talk about it right now without wanting to cry. I was alone. For a very, very long time. My life was empty. I sought out meaningless encounters with women who meant nothing to me because I was afraid if they did mean something to me, they'd do me like Sarah did. Tegan Warden *knows* me in a way no one else does. I love her and, thank God above, she loves me." His hands shook with emotion and Jillian moved to sit next to him, putting her head on his shoulder.

"I'm glad for you, Ben. I support you. I promise. Are you going to convert?"

"He will do no such thing!" His father's fist hit the table, knocking over several glasses of wine. "If this woman loves you, she would not ask it."

"She hasn't and I have no plans to do it. Not because I loathe what she is, but because I'm fine with what I am."

His father nodded. "I'm glad to hear it. I don't know what to say, son. I've just never imagined this situation. I like it very much that this Tegan makes you happy but I've never met a werewolf before much less had one in my family. I'd be shocked if you married a Protestant girl, this is way out of my league."

"Did you drink after her? Eat after her? Oh my God, do we need to get treated?" His mother stopped her prayers and looked to him expectantly.

"You can't catch lycanthropy from drinking or eating after a werewolf. It's very difficult to catch actually. Tegan was born a werewolf although her sister-in-law Nina was a human who was changed."

"This is insanity! An abomination. They're not even human, Benjamin. She's done something to you to mess with your head."

"Bonita, this isn't helping," his father murmured. "Ben is in love with this woman. He's a strong man, it didn't look like she'd bewitched him to me."

"I know this is a surprise. She asked me to tell you first so don't be angry at her for that. She's not an abomination, Mom. She's a good woman, strong. She fights for her family just like we do. Why don't you just give her a chance? She's not human, no. She's something else, but no less good."

"You are not marrying this...this thing! I forbid it, Benjamin. God says to honor your parents and your parents are telling you humans are not meant to mix with animals. It's unholy."

"Mom, knock this off. You're out of control. Take a nap, take a pill, drink some wine or something. You're talking like a freaking Nazi. You didn't raise us to think this way." Jillian's voice was gentle but firm and Ben was so glad his sister was there to help. "You raised us to believe all people were equal until they proved themselves otherwise. This woman has made Ben happy. He loves her. What does that prove?"

"She's not people. She's—she's a mistake of nature."

The vileness of his mother's accusations made Ben sick to his stomach. He loved his parents, respected them. They'd been a foundation of his life and he'd never hesitated to turn to them. This woman pacing around the kitchen was a stranger to him.

"Mom, come on, this is crazy talk. I know you're upset and

I know it's scary because you don't know a lot about werewolf culture. I can teach you. I've been working with them for nearly two years. They have families, live in houses, run businesses, they barbecue on the Fourth of July and go to movies and eat pizza. Tegan's first husband was an army ranger, killed in action in Afghanistan four years ago. They serve their country and make your lattes too. Nina runs a big nursery, in fact a lot of the landscaping plants on my property came from her place. They're just normal people who, through a different DNA sequence, can shapeshift into a wolf.

"You can't catch it from being in the same room or even if her blood got on you or in you. Lycanthropy is transmitted through a bite when the werewolf is in wolf form. It's a mixture of the saliva and the blood in an attack. It's very rare. She doesn't deserve all this hate from you for what she is. You know better than this. You and Dad raised us better. Please, Mom, for me, give Tegan a chance."

"How can you expect me to do this? This is blasphemy."

Where the hell was this coming from? His mother went to church, yes, but she had never used her faith like this, not to be harmful or hateful.

"Bonita, don't. Please, don't do this. You're going to drive him away. Is that what you want? To be one of those parents who doesn't speak to one of their children? When they have kids, don't you want to be part of their lives?" He looked to Ben. "You can, right?"

"Yes. It's complicated and I don't know if they'd be like half wolf or not at all or what." Something he'd have to ask her about after they dealt with this whole Pellini mess. "Anyway, kids are a ways off. I want to be married a while before we have kids."

"Ben, she doesn't even have a soul. If you mix with her,

she'll take yours. You'll be damned!" His mother shook him by the shoulders and in his shock, Ben heard his father's chair scrape back as he stood.

"Bonita! Are you ill? You're not yourself right now. Calm down." His father pulled her into his embrace and tried to calm her but she broke away.

She rushed to the drawer next to the fridge and rustled around, pulling out several brightly colored sheets of paper and slammed them on the table in front of Ben.

"They came by two weeks ago and I talked to them. Nice boys. Benjamin, you don't know what these things get up to. They're creatures of the devil."

Ben looked at the papers and nausea boiled through his gut. Hate literature about werewolves. It couldn't have been a coincidence either.

"Mom, have these men been back here? Have you seen them before?"

"I see them around here and there. They probably live nearby. They said they knew Father Joe so they probably go to St. Michael's. Read it, Ben, it's all there. All that scientific stuff. They control the media. It's all lies. I can't believe it and you bringing her here. Lucky thing I had this stuff."

"Mom! I can't believe you. This is the same kind of crap they say about Jews and black people. This is...I guess human supremacy. I've seen this stuff around about the werewolves but you're the last person I'd have thought would buy into this. Mommy, this is crazy talk. Think about it." Jillian rubbed a hand up and down their mother's arm.

Ben scrubbed his hands over his face. "Did you let them in? Did they give you names? Do you have contact information?"

Bonita sat down. "Why?"

"Mom, a very bad man has been trying to harm Tegan's family. He tried to kill Tegan's brother Lex and his wife. He did kill Nina's younger brother Gabriel. I don't think this is a coincidence."

"Do you think they'll harm us? The werewolves?"

"Mom, knock it off. Not the werewolves, the Nazi bastards who came to the door with this stuff."

"No. I was in the yard when they came by. They chatted. I offered them some tea and coffeecake but they had to go. I saw them at the grocery store and one of them near the gas station on 175th. They haven't been back here though. What did she do to bring this on her head?"

He stood. "I can't deal with this any longer. The pod people have made my mom into a Nazi and I don't know what else to say. Wait, yes I do. Mom, you're out of line and ugly. This is not you and I want you to think on the stuff you've said tonight. Jillian, go and help Mom pack a bag. I want you two to go stay above the restaurant. It's a lot safer than here and it's just a few blocks from the police station and I'm going to have them just keep a close eye on you. Jillian, your building is very safe but Mom is going to give a description to the police sketch artist so we can get some flyers out to keep these idiots away from anywhere you are. I'll call now and have him meet you at the station tomorrow morning. These people are killers and they're using you to harm Tegan and me because she's mine."

"This can't be. They're such nice boys."

"They stole something that could kill millions of people. Humans and werewolves alike. They're the animals, Mom. Now go. I'll catch a ride with Jillian and escort everyone home and I need to call my people as well."

When Ben walked in the door, Tegan had mostly dealt with

her anger and sadness over the way she'd been treated by his mother. She'd listened to Layla be comforting and Nina threatening to kick ass. Megan brought over Dove bars and things had improved. It was just a bump in the road. To be expected.

Right.

But his face told her things had not improved. Instead he tossed down some of the vilest hate literature she'd ever seen and announced his mother had it in her kitchen.

"Wow. Um, so I'm guessing she's not keen to have me in the family and stuff, huh? Did she bleach out the glasses and flip that I'd shared spit with you?"

The look on his face made her sick.

"That was supposed to be a joke. Fer fuck's sake, why didn't you tell me your mother was like one of those white supremacist people? God, you set me up, Ben."

"She's not. Fuck, I don't know what to say. The woman in that kitchen tonight is like a total stranger to me. I was raised by people who took us to freaking protest marches the whole time I grew up. My mom read me books about Sojourner Truth and Mother Jones. If they'd been a bit older they would have been flower children. This is not her." He shook the papers. "And I wouldn't do that to you. How can you think that?"

"I'm sorry. Although why I'm apologizing when your mom is a brownshirt I don't know. But I don't think you'd deliberately sabotage me. Anyway, it's not like my family has been all welcoming until recently." She sighed and kissed his cheek.

"This stuff is sick. I want to kick the shit out of these assholes. It's got to be connected with Pellini."

"Ben, maybe. I assume you mean they know about me and you and tried to mess it up with your parents. But this isn't the first time I've seen this stuff. I've had my car egged, my tires slashed, I've had things thrown at me. Tracy was jumped when she was in third grade by junior high kids. We've lived with this stuff our whole lives. It could just be run of the mill racists."

"It's too much of a coincidence, gorgeous. And if I knew who those people were who hurt you, I'd kick their asses right now. It makes me so mad to think you've suffered because you were born different."

He was so passionate and scary in her defense, she had to smile. "Aww, you'd thump someone in my honor?"

"Don't try to make me laugh. This is serious stuff. I've had my parents move to a safer place and my mom is going to talk to the sketch artist tomorrow for a composite. My gut tells me this is about Pellini."

"Okay. I'm glad they're safe. I'm guessing they RSVP'd to the wedding as a no?"

"My sister wants to cater the reception. I told her one of your sisters would call her so she could help plan. My dad is on my side. He's wary, this is all totally new to him. My mom? I don't know. I considered grinding up some Xanax or something in her tea tonight. She's not right. I don't understand. But we are okay. Period. You and me, Tegan, we are just fine."

"Yeah. Drama though, huh? I bet you thought you'd end up with some quiet, sweet woman who had a normal family and didn't turn furry at will. I'm sorry this is so crazy. It's been hard for you, the suddenness of the bond and then all this. It doesn't seem like anyone I know can have an easy go of it right off."

He kissed her with a chuckle. "Tegan, I'm a kinky guy. I've never expected what anyone could call normal. I thought if I buried it, I could just live with it. But it came back and the first time I saw you at the club, I was hooked. You got under my skin because we were a match. Even before the Claiming or bond or whatever you want to call it. I never dreamed I'd be with a woman like you, no. But the truth of it is, you're better than anything I could have imagined. I'm going to keep at my mom because she deserves to know you, but I don't expect you to take any shit or to be around her until I've resolved things."

"Thank you. And now we deal with my family. You haven't met my grandmother yet." She laughed. "She's the one who presides over the ceremony that brings you into the Pack. Sort of the wise woman of Cascadia. Very woo-woo but she's the coolest."

"They're okay that I'm not going to convert?"

Tegan nodded. "Not everyone does you know. It'll be harder later, my lifespan is longer than yours but we'll deal with it when it happens. The ceremony will recognize you as Pack, give you the protection of the Pack but you don't have to be a wolf to get that. You're mated to me and that's good enough. You can assure your family that because you're not a wolf, the part where the couple shifts won't be included. Everyone will keep their human skins for the whole time. If you want to have a ceremony in a church later, when we return from the NC meeting, I'm fine with that. I want your family to be comfortable with our relationship. Or, as comfortable as they can be."

"I may feel differently in a few years, hell a few months. That's cool too, right? If I decide later I want to be converted?"

"I don't want to push you into anything, so of course you can change your mind later. Now, I think I need to call my brothers about this flyer thing. Is there some sort of way you can check to see if there've been any other situations like this? If flyers were dropped anywhere else?" She moved back into the living room and sat on the couch and he followed.

"We have a database, a hate crimes activity database. I'm one of the paranormal liaisons so I have access to it although it's not something I normally do upkeep on. I have a call in to the officer who works county-wide on this stuff, I'm hoping she'll call me back soon. I can log in to the database from here though. Let's look before you call Lex so we can give him a more complete picture."

They searched and soon enough, several hits popped up in southeast King County where the Stoners lived.

"I know this is your world and all, Ben, but it seems to me that this is the kind of thing you should be notified about. I mean, you're the liaison to the Packs, we need to know this."

He sighed. "Yeah, I'm a little agitated about that myself. I suppose I just assumed they'd tell me."

"Why don't you check this database like once or twice a month or so? Or have some sort of notifier set to ping you when this kind of activity arises? I know you're busy and you have other cases to work on that aren't paranormal community related and all, but I'm guessing we can't get access to the information ourselves so we rely on you all." Tegan found her phone and dialed Lex. It was late but he'd be up, he rarely slept anyway.

"I'll make it part of my schedule to check it regularly. No, you can't have official access but the computer here can look it up, I don't mind you checking it out while I'm around." He began to jot notes down as Lex answered.

"What's up?" Lex answered.

She explained the situation including the call in to the officer in charge and the plans for the sketch artist. Tegan heard the contained anger in her brother's voice as he questioned her about the whole thing.

"So, you're telling me his mother believes this shit? That we're tools of the devil and have no souls?"

"I don't want to talk about that right now. I just wanted to fill you in. I'll write up a report and send it along to National as
156

well when I get in tomorrow morning."

"Fine, you know I'll just make you tell me when you get here anyway. I'll set a meeting for the corps tomorrow morning around shift change time." Lex told her he loved her, urged her to be careful and hung up.

She and Ben stayed up a while longer, her appetite had returned so she made a late dinner while he checked in with his sister and his parents.

"Come to bed, red wolf. I get the feeling we're both going to have a very long day tomorrow."

When she looked up at him in the doorway after they'd cleaned the kitchen and he'd taken out the trash, she noted the light in his eyes, the way his gaze held only her. Everything else fell away as she nodded and moved toward him.

Chapter Twelve

Harried, Ben hustled through four witness interviews, wrote reports, took about two dozen phone calls, answered emails and did a scene investigation all before three that next afternoon. He'd also gone to the cop shop near the restaurant to be with his mom when she did the sketch. She'd seemed a bit calmer and more rational and he hoped that trend continued.

He hadn't even had the time to check in with Tegan although she'd been on his mind after the night before. Hell, she was always on his mind. Smiling as he finished a report, he remembered how she'd looked spread out beneath him, a sheen of sweat on her flanks, her back arched to meet his mouth on her sweet pussy.

Ooops, now he had a hard-on to deal with.

Still, that was easily dealt with when he paused to wonder how the meeting with her brothers had gone. He'd played phone tag with the county hate crimes liaison who finally just faxed him some information about anti-paranormal activity in the county, which appeared to be rising at a pretty steady rate since the same period the year prior.

He forwarded the info to Lex via email on his way out the door to yet another meeting and that had been several hours past.

The growling in his stomach and a sudden feeling of total calm alerted him. Looking up, he realized it had already gotten dark. He also caught a glimpse of his red wolf coming toward him, a bag of takeout in her hands and a smile on her face.

"Hi there. I figured you might be hungry. I hope subs from Sharky's are okay with you." She placed the bag on his desk and leaned down to kiss him. He had to grip the edge of his chair to keep from grabbing her and pulling her down onto his lap.

"You're very good to me. I didn't realize it'd gotten so late. I'm sorry I didn't check in with you today. Here, let's go eat this in the break room." He took her hand and the bag. He got a few looks from his co-workers and he wanted to laugh and tease them all about his good fortune.

"Sit, I'll get some plates and sodas," he told her as he moved about the room.

They settled in and he'd inhaled a foot long sub and a bag of chips before pausing to catch the amused look on her face.

"Hungry huh?"

He laughed. "Yeah, I skipped lunch. Thank you for this. I needed it."

"There's another one in the bag, I figured you might need two."

"If we weren't getting married already, I'd be proposing to you right now for that."

He polished off the second sandwich, this one with more manners than the first, and sat back with a satisfied sigh.

"That was marvelous. I feel way better."

"Good. Maybe I'll pack you a lunch or something every day. Why don't you have snacks in your desk? I have snacks at work. It's not good to go all day without eating, Ben. You need your reflexes sharp."

The concern on her face warmed him. Other than family, who'd ever worried about whether he ate regularly? His warrior-woman was going to make him lunch? Damn, the hard-on was back.

"...I have all kinds of stuff to tell you but I'll wait until you get home. You gonna be really late?" she'd just finished saying when he tuned back in.

"I have about another hour or two to deal with here. Then I'll be home. I'm sorry."

She packed up their trash and tossed it. "Don't be. It's your job. Mine is like that sometimes too. I'll be home when you get there. I have laundry to do anyway."

"I'll walk you out."

She paused and blushed, ducking her head quickly. "Oh. Thank you."

Ben liked being with her this way. Just normal couple stuff. Liked it that she seemed touched by the way he cared for her, God knew he was bowled over by what she did for him.

At her car, he kissed her slow and thorough, letting her taste slide through him, hoping it would hold him over until he could do a much better job in private.

"Be careful, red wolf. I'll see you in a bit."

Three hours later, he pulled into their driveway and realized how much better it was to come home when the lights inside were on. Knowing Tegan was in there, in their home, filling it with her presence made him pretty damned satisfied with his life. General insanity of his mother going nuts and the fucking werewolf mafia notwithstanding.

He found her drinking a mug of tea, tucked up on the couch and reading a book. Her hair was up in a messy ponytail and she looked like the best thing on Earth.

"Don't you dare apologize," she called out as he came toward her.

He laughed. "Okay, come to the bedroom with me and fill me in while I change my clothes."

She sat on their bed and told him about the meeting she'd had that morning. Lex wasn't convinced it was Pellini but they'd all agreed it would be something devious he'd get up to just to keep people focused on something other than his activities.

"I also spoke with Agent Benoit's assistant, who is a wolf. Did you know that?"

Ben nodded his head. "Never met him though."

"Nice enough, Midwestern wolf. Anyway, there's some supposition Pellini might try and stir some anti-wolf sentiment to keep the Packs fighting and worried about humans. Cade thinks Pellini would do it to make the Packs on the fence about him fall his way. All the Packs against him, the ones with the most power, are the ones who advocated coming out to humans to begin with. There's been a general rise since this time last year in this sort of thing. They're looking into it."

"Imagine all the good people like Pellini could do if they just applied their intelligence and energy toward something positive instead of this shit."

"No kidding. Man I love those boxer briefs. I'm buying you more, I love the way they hug your ass and thighs." She rolled on her back and waggled her brows. Her hair tumbled free from the ponytail and her beauty hurt him for a moment. She was so damned precious, essential to him.

"You're so beautiful."

"What brought that on?" She smiled, just a simple, pretty smile. From what he'd understood from Nina, she hadn't done

161

much smiling for many years after losing her first husband. He liked that she did with him.

"I just love looking at you. Love having you here."

"I love being here. I like the feel of this house a lot. Looks like my cousin Dave is interested in buying my house. Which is nice because it keeps it in the family. Oh and they've set a date for the National Council meeting. Three weeks from Saturday. The security plans will start arriving over the next few weeks so the groups going and know what's happening. Benoit's aide told me he'd be contacting you tomorrow about it."

Ice moved through him at the thought of how dangerous this would be for her but at least he'd be there too. He'd have climbed the fucking walls if she'd gone and he'd stayed back home.

"Okay. Oh and Jillian said she spoke to you and Layla on the phone today. Thanks for including her."

He flopped down beside her on the bed and she immediately laid her head on his chest.

"Jillian is a very cool person. She's going to fit into the mob just fine. That's what Cade calls my sisters and Nina. She invited us to the restaurant for dinner and drinks tomorrow night so we can talk about the wedding and also get to know each other. I wasn't sure it was such a good idea with your parents staying there but Jillian said it was okay. She told me she thought your mom might be having some sort of breakdown and your dad had made an appointment with her doctor tomorrow. Are you okay?"

"I think it's for the best actually and while I hate that he's sort of talking her around the real reason for the appointment, she's taking some medications Jillian looked up on the web and thinks might be causing some paranoia. Truthfully? I hope that's it because I just don't know what else to think."

Tegan kissed his chest and sat up. "On your stomach. Oh don't get that look, I'm not going to top you, I thought I'd give you a massage. Your muscles feel really tight."

She wanted to laugh at the look of relief on his face, the big baby.

He got settled and she moved to sit straddling his ass as she smoothed her hands over the hard planes of his back just to warm them both up.

She grabbed the bottle of almond oil and poured a small pool into her palm and rubbed her hands together to warm it before beginning to work it into the small of his back.

"Other than the stuff we've talked about, tell me what happened today. What was your day like?"

As he went over the details of his very busy day, her hands kneaded his muscles, fingertips pressing into the knots, the heels of her hands smoothing the tension away.

Ministering to him like that made her love him more. Touching him to care for him, to ease his stress, enthralled her. The heat of his skin, the scent of the oil mingling with his own unique smell, the way the muscles of his ass bunched against her pussy and inner thighs where she sat—all drew her in. The sheer normality of it, the way one lover took care of the other, was so sexy.

His voice rumbled through his sides. He laughed as he described his co-workers and the people he came across, got frustrated briefly when giving details of a case he'd been working on for the last six months and relaxed again as he spoke of his sister.

Ben Stoner was a damned good man. A keeper if there ever was one. Sexy. Smart. Big and strong. Hotter than the sun in bed. And all hers.

She leaned down and kissed the back of his neck, nuzzling the warmth there, her wolf breathing his scent in deeply, letting it mark her.

"Mmmm, you're good with your hands. That's very nice. I love you and I'm sorry about all this crazy. I just want you to be happy. You make me happy, Tegan. I've never felt so satisfied, so happy with my life. You do that for me."

He said the best things. Smiling she hummed her appreciation as she continued to work on his shoulders.

"Tell me about losing him. What was your life like with him and then after?"

She stilled a moment before moving again. "I love you. I'm very happy, I want you to know that. I knew him, grew up with him actually. But he was this totally hyper guy. Played baseball in high school, got scouted even. But he wanted to go into the army. That's how I had so much exposure to him, he idolized Lex.

"I never considered him more than a cute guy who had way more energy than I wanted to deal with. I went to college and decided to join the Enforcer corps so we got to know each other and we became close. An attraction started to bloom between us but I had a boyfriend at the time. Also, werewolves don't reach sexual maturation until they're eighteen, which is pretty darned handy so the mate attraction hadn't really shown itself that strongly. Anyway, I'd had this fight with my boyfriend. I came home and I was crying, it was my twentieth birthday."

Tegan laughed, remembering the sweetness of that night. "Lucas had joined the army and was home on leave. He saw me and hugged me and I got a load of his scent and it was all mixed with sex and well, we had this intense thing in Cade's garage. On his Mercedes. And well, you know what it feels like to bond. He was everything to me. We were young and in love.

We had a great time together. He wanted to be a ranger. I was freaked but he wanted it so I supported that. It was hell to be separated for so long. He finished ranger school and I bounced between here and Georgia. Then September Eleven happened. Everything changed. He went to Afghanistan and then came back. We toyed with the idea of kids and decided when he got back the next time, we'd try. He was KIA two weeks before he was due home."

Her voice caught and Ben rolled to the side, facing her as he pulled her to the bed with him. He brushed the hair from her face. "I'm sorry. I can't imagine. You don't have to say any more."

Tegan shook her head. She needed to say it all, to let it go. "The first year after Lucas died was awful. I don't remember all of it. I wouldn't have made it through the first two or three months if it hadn't been for Layla. I lived with them for a while. Every morning she brought me food, made me eat it. I sat in a daze and watched my niece and nephew playing and growing up. Knowing I'd never have that with Lucas. Abe, he's my anchor, he visited when he could. You'll need to meet him and Collette, his mate. But they had a baby during that first year and it just made things worse. The bond in place saved me from death but seeing him, knowing he wasn't mine, not the way he belonged to her, knowing I had no one who loved me like that, it just sort of made me numb. To cope, I suppose.

"And then I moved to Lex and Cade's and worked. For a long time, years, I lived in this middle place. Not really feeling anything because I was afraid to. I didn't date, didn't go out with friends, didn't laugh or let anyone hug me. I felt a few things from time to time—fear, loneliness and rage."

The unshed tears in his eyes made her swallow, hard.

"Oh, honey, I wish I could have been there for you sooner.

What made you turn it around?"

Tegan told him about the dreams, about how she felt Lucas himself told her to move on and start living again. And about his warning.

"Wow. Well, there are times when I feel threatened by his memory, you know? He's this perfect love for you. He was a wolf too. You had different bonds, older, purer. Sometimes when you talk about him your face gets dreamy. But I'm glad you had him. And I'm glad he found a way to get to you, to tell you to let go."

"He was very special. But so are you. He's this beautiful part of my past but you're my future, Ben. You're the reason I live every day. Will you tell me about her? The one who hurt you so much?"

He told her the story of the woman and how he'd caught her cheating. Of how he'd had dreams of forever and the way this Sarah bitch had dashed them and hurt him so deeply he'd never trusted again.

"She needs a smackdown. Does she still live around here?"

Ben laughed and kissed her quickly. "While the thought of you kicking her ass is enticing, she's not worth it. She married and lives in Olympia, or she did the last I heard six or so years ago."

"Well, the offer is open. That pisses me off. How could any woman have you and look for anything else?"

He sighed and pulled her close. "I was different then. I have more to give now. I realize what the cost is to not put all my energy into a relationship. We didn't start off very easily, Tegan but I'm committed to you and to us totally. I want you to know that."

"I *feel* that." She writhed against him as he swept her beneath his body. "Oh, I feel *that* too. Why don't you show me what you got, old guy."

Chapter Thirteen

Tegan returned from the firing range and then took a run to check the perimeter at the start of her shift. The air was crisp and clean as she trotted through the trees, her nose to the air every few feet when she wasn't sniffing the ground.

Something wasn't right. Outsiders had been there. Watching.

There wasn't anyone around then. The scent was cold. Whoever it was had been very good and it took her an hour of very intense investigation before she found the scent on a bent back fern frond. Not human, wolf and not Cascadia.

After she'd come back, Ben had arrived and was eating breakfast with her brothers. Dave followed Tegan in along with some of the other wolves from her shift. They'd noted her tension and knew something was up.

As did Lex and then Ben when they looked up to see her face.

"What?" Lex didn't say anything else. She loved that he trusted her so much he didn't need to, knew she'd tell him what he needed to know.

"Wolves were here. Probably after the last perimeter check." She looked to Megan who'd been drinking some juice before she went to sleep. She didn't want her sister to think she blamed her. "Two of them. Not Cascadia. I didn't recognize the scent at all. Which means it can't be any of the west coast Packs or National since I've scented members from those."

She explained the rest as she sat. Nina put a plate full of food before her and Tegan tucked in. The change took a lot of physical energy, she needed the fuel.

"We expected this. It was far enough from the house they couldn't have used a sniper rifle. But you know, anti-tank missiles are still a possibility."

Ben choked on his breakfast. "These fucks have anti-tank missiles? Jesus God, Tegan, I'm going to get an ulcer for sure."

Tegan held back a smile as she patted his back. "Honey, they're the mob. Do you think they have ethics? They've never used anything like an anti-tank missile but we did find RPGs at their headquarters back when we first busted Pellini. That's Lex being, well, Lex. He has to think of all the possibilities including dirty bombs and suitcase nukes. It's his special talent."

Nina snorted and Lex just shrugged and continued eating.

"I'd wager it's Pellini's people keeping an eye on us as the time for the NC approaches. He's not going to move here. He doesn't have to. He'll wait to see if he can get his person into the National Mediator position. He's a thug but he's not stupid. He'll try and do this with the veneer of following our laws. If that doesn't work, we'll all be on the alert because he'll be three times as dangerous as he was before. For now, I think we continue to stay watchful and I'll step up the patrols of the road. Nina just hooked us up with a really good camera system along the entrance feeder roads and paths to the house," Lex explained and winked at his wife.

"Small cameras hooked to a wireless system. It won't be ready to go online until later on today. I planned to run tests tonight to see how the infrared works. Guess I was a day late."

Cade patted Nina's arm. "You can't do everything, Nina. It's

169

fine. We'll get it up and running on schedule. We can't skimp here. Lex is right, I don't think we're in any danger just now."

"Well that's a good thing! We have a bonding ceremony to do and if anyone ruined that I'd be very unhappy."

Grinning, Tegan turned to her grandmother, reaching out to hug her. "Hey, Grandma. How are you today? Come and sit. Are you hungry?"

Megan pulled out a chair and everyone else moved to grab things and offer them to her grandmother who relished the attention with a serene smile.

She turned her gray eyes to Ben and raised a brow. "You're a fine looking specimen. You and Tegan will make very beautiful babies in a few years."

Ben actually blushed. Tegan put a hand on his shoulder. "Grandma, this is Ben Stoner. Ben, this is my grandmother, Lia Warden."

"It's an honor to finally meet you, Mrs. Warden. Tegan speaks of you quite warmly all the time. I can see where the Warden sisters get their looks now."

Now it was her grandmother who blushed and then giggled like a young girl. Tegan looked at Megan and Nina and they shrugged and watched, fascinated, as Ben charmed the hell out of their grandmother.

After about an hour of back and forth, her grandmother turned and nodded. "He's worthy. I'm going to pay a visit to your mother later this weekend, Ben."

Ben paled and Tegan grimaced. "Do you think that's such a good idea, Grandma? I mean, she's...well, not very happy I'm a werewolf."

"The ceremony is in less than a week. She avoided the lovely dinner at Jillian's restaurant the night before last. But from what I understand, she's been put on a new medication for her blood pressure because it might have interacted with her cholesterol pills and exacerbated her negative feelings about our race. And so there needs to be a set to. This cannot go on. This woman cannot be allowed to make what should be the happiest day of your lives one bit sad because she refuses to cooperate."

"Grandma, perhaps you should let Ben and Tegan work this out," Cade said gently but with the Alpha behind it.

She looked at him and rolled her eyes. "Cade, I changed your poopy diapers, boy, don't try that Alpha voice on me. Your grandfather was the Alpha of this Pack for longer than you've been alive and then your father, a man I raised. As far as I'm concerned, that makes *me* Alpha be default. So poo. It doesn't compel me to want to do anything but rap you upside your head for even trying to control me."

Nina snickered.

Tegan looked to Ben. "Are you okay with this?" She would defy her grandmother if Ben needed her to and she saw he understood that and relaxed.

"Like I said, I don't know what's going on with her. My dad says she's calmed down a lot yesterday. The doctor said it would be a bit before there'd be any difference if the pills were the issue. She and I talked for a while Friday night and she was still very opposed to the idea of me marrying you but she didn't seem so extreme about it. I hate this. I hate that she's hurting you and not welcoming you into the family. I hate that you can't meet my mother and have to deal with this stranger. If your grandmother can help, I'm all for it." He looked to her grandmother. "And I'm sure you'll be gentle with her."

Her grandmother waved that away and Tegan hid a grin. "In any case, I've spoken with Mrs. Stoner on the phone and she is meeting me for coffee at Jillian's restaurant in three hours. It's a public place and one she's familiar with so I'm hoping it being on her turf will help her. I won't have it. My girl has suffered too much and this day will be perfect. I will it and so it will be." That regal chin jutted high and Tegan got to her knees and put her head in her grandmother's lap. Like she had many times, her grandmother sifted her fingers through Tegan's hair soothingly.

"I love you, Grandma."

"I love you too, sweetheart. It's going to be fine, I promise."

"I hope so."

Ben went to work later on after spending a few hours first thing that morning having breakfast at Cade and Lex's place. He loved watching Tegan interact with her family. She was easier as the days went by, as she got used to her old self again and embraced her new life. He saw the change in her, it only made her more beautiful to him.

He went over some security stuff with them and Benoit via teleconference. Gabe had given the FBI some very detailed information about the building the NC would be held in. It was right in the heart of the city so on one hand, they felt it would be safe from too much overt violence from Pellini, on the other hand, Ben worried about how exposed the building was in general.

Benoit and Ben would go in a few days early to stake out the area and find some good places to dig in and observe. Gabe was also able to help with that. Jack had forwarded some information about a condo building across the street that faced where the meetings would be held and offered to plant some listening devices after the initial sweep the Packs would make upon arrival.

Now if only Tegan would stay home and far away from the

danger. Ben snorted as he walked down the hallway to another meeting, like that was gonna happen.

He tried not to think about the meeting that Lia Warden set up with his mother, only hoping it would go well and his mother would see some sense. If anyone could handle themselves it was the grand dame of the Pack.

Ben was sure he'd hear all about it one way or another when he got home from work that night.

Chapter Fourteen

The ceremony began at sundown on the third Saturday in April. It was brisk but not cold and Tegan's outfit had been top secret. Ben laughed with Lex and Cade as they all waited on the top of a hill looking over a meadow south of the house.

He looked back at the assembled crowd and smiled. His sister Jillian sat, flirting with her date. His father looked at ease as he sat with his arm around Ben's mother's shoulders. Ben didn't know what had transpired at the meeting but within the following forty eight hours, his mother showed up on his and Tegan's doorstep and they'd begun a tentative move toward acceptance. His mother wouldn't talk about the coffee date and Tegan's grandmother was equally tight lipped. He wondered if the old woman hadn't done some sort of witchy magic on his mother, but he supposed whatever worked was fine with him. His parents were there to share his happiness with him and it made Tegan happy to know that too.

He'd warned them, as well as Benoit, who also sat in the crowd, that there'd be some wolf type stuff going on. There'd be a ceremonial spilling of his blood on the ground along with Tegan's. Marking it with his scent so to speak and mixing his blood with the Pack's.

Two large wolves sat on the ridgeline high above the group, watching and guarding—Nick and Gabe, his soon-to-be brothers-in-law and Tegan's baby sister, Tracy's, husbands. Several Pacific Pack wolves, Tracy's Packmates, had taken over guard duty for the afternoon and had spread through the surrounding forest.

Every once in a while he heard a howl, answered by several more in order as they checked in. As Lex didn't look alarmed when that happened, Ben just assumed everything was status quo.

An arbor marked the space where they'd stand and the trees surrounding the area were strung with white lights that cast a soft glow on the spot. It felt magical.

The hair on the back of Ben's neck stood up and Lex tapped his arm. Ben turned to catch sight of his woman walking down the path toward them.

Her hair was loose, beautiful strands of red blowing in the soft breeze as the deepest blue of twilight settled in. The dress she wore was the same deep green as the robe she wore for him several nights a week. Only this dress moved about her feet like the ocean as she walked. The front dipped low, the necklace he'd given her resting between her breasts and the sleeves were tight, buttoned from her wrists to her elbow.

Once she'd gotten close enough, he saw her hair had green ribbons and shiny things woven through it. She looked like a faery queen or a goddess. His red wolf.

"Wow. You look amazing," he murmured before kissing her softly.

She smiled and be caught her blush. "Thank you. So do you. I like you in this gray color. I'm glad you went for a tux, very sexy."

Tegan didn't remember much of the ceremony once she'd rounded the corner and saw Ben standing there with her brothers. She'd done this once before with Lucas. They'd been young and of course both of them were wolves so the ceremony was different. But this time, it felt like she'd been away from home for a very long time and just seeing Ben there, his blue-black hair trimmed just for the ceremony, all buff and hard in that tux, a total sense of relief settled in. She was home, he brought her back from the edge.

As she'd been walking from the house, she caught sight of a gold wolf running across the path. Lucas had been a gold wolf. None of the Pacific wolves were gold like that. She'd stopped and her grandmother had hugged Tegan to her side a moment.

"You saw?"

Her grandmother nodded. "It's his way of saying goodbye. He's giving you his goodbye."

But she wasn't sad. It made her happy instead. She missed him, she always would, but he held only happiness for her now.

The night was clear and the stars winked overhead as her grandmother and their local pastor had said the ceremony and blessing. When Ben's blood met hers on the ground, she'd felt him weave his way through the Pack consciousness at the back of her mind. He was Cascadia now. It made her proud.

Her grandmother spoke words older than Latin over their hands where their rings touched. Tegan knew when she changed into her wolf skin, the ring would go somewhere else but be back on her finger when she let her human surface again. Her grandmother explained Ben would feel it when she changed and changed back through the ring on his finger and he'd loved that, knowing he'd have a way to feel her when they weren't together. She'd also done her thing on the necklace, which had eased Tegan's worry about losing it.

The pastor had them sign the paperwork after he'd

announced them husband and wife, and his grandmother had done her magical mojo and suddenly, they were married under human law and joined in the eyes of the Pack.

The party was lovely. Jillian had outdone herself with the gorgeous little appetizers. The cake was fantastic and plenty of wine and champagne flowed for the guests. They danced under the stars, laughed, kissed and loved.

Ben's mother even stayed until midnight, which surprised Tegan but made her very happy for Ben's sake. The woman had been trying in her own way and while Tegan was pretty sure they'd never be very close, she was relieved not to come between him and his family.

Layla pulled her aside later and hugged her tight. "I'm so happy for you. I wondered if I'd ever get you back, if I'd see that look on your face again. The Tegan who belonged to someone. You're just gorgeous tonight and Ben is spiffy and you both look so good together it makes me almost want to have another baby."

Sid had approached and put one arm around his wife and another around Tegan. "Ah, my womens. Did you let Ben know he had to share you with me?"

Tegan had to admit the men each one of her sisters had ended up with were pretty amazing and all totally different. Sid was a laid back rock and roll artist type but he adored Layla and had never blinked an eye when Tegan ended up in their guestroom for months after Lucas died.

"As long as it's in your living room and not your bed, I'm happy to share." Ben approached and kissed Tegan's lips quickly.

"If you say so, cop. You're the one with the gun." Sid laughed and Ben joined him. Tegan smiled at her sister. Back in those first days after they'd first bonded, Tegan wasn't sure moments like this were even possible for them. It made the reality all the more sweet.

"Did your parents get out of here okay?" Tegan turned to Ben and snuggled against him.

"Yeah. They were tired but my dad told me to tell you how much he enjoyed the ceremony and he meant that. Jillian of course had a blast and says she'll talk to you soon. I like that you're hanging out with my sister."

"She's fun and she's a really good cook. Those meatballs she made? I could have eaten about five hundred of them, like with a giant spoon in front of the television on a Friday night."

He chuckled. "Even you talking about pigging out is sexy. You're amazing and I love you so much."

"Oh you're so good with that mouth." She tiptoed up and kissed him. "We should go. Honeymoon suite with our name on it is waiting at the Salish Lodge."

They said their goodbyes and headed out.

Their room at the historic lodge was absolutely gorgeous. Rose petals on the bed, a fire in the fireplace, chilled champagne waiting and a lavender scented bath.

"Wow." Tegan walked through the room and took it all in. "Swanky. I'm guessing this was Nina's idea more than Lex's but it's a very nice wedding present I must say."

"Mmm."

She turned at the catch in his voice, the deepening of the timbre and the thick note of desire there. He leaned against the door, clicking the locks. His eyes never left her and she felt naked there as he devoured her with his gaze.

Her mouth dried up as he slid the tuxedo jacket from his body and casually tossed it on a nearby chair.

"Oh. Well then."

"Indeed. Come and help me out of these clothes. Then I'll get in the bath and watch you get out of yours. I'll tell you what's next after that."

A few steps and she met his body with her own, sliding her palms up the expanse of his chest. He was warm, vibrant, his sensuality echoed from him and into her.

She took his hand and undid his cuff, first one and then the other, moving away from him to put the links on the dresser. Moving back to him again, she slid off his cummerbund and tie, then unbuttoned his shirt slowly, kissing each new spot of bare skin as she went.

He relaxed as he stood here, his hands stroking up and down her arms.

When she took his shirt off, she moved to breathe him in, loving the scent of the night on his skin and the smell of Pack. "You smell like Pack now." She kissed her way across his shoulders as her hands caressed his back before moving around him and over his belly.

"I do?" His voice was lazy, sexy.

"You do. It's very nice. Sort of wild. It goes well with your natural scent."

She dropped to her knees in front of him as he stepped out of his shoes and then she took his pants off, followed with his socks and last of all his boxer-briefs.

"While I'm here, mind if I take a little tour?" She looked up at him and caught his smile.

"Who am I to refuse my bride anything she wishes?"

Tegan ran her hands up the muscles of his calves and thighs, loving the way they jumped as she touched him. The skin of his cock was salty as she licked around the crown. She took her time, leisurely kissing and sucking the head the way he liked it as she palmed his balls gently.

His knees locked and the muscles of his thighs bulged. Her body reached as she gasped softly. His desire for her roared into her system as intensely as if it were her own.

"Wow. Is it just me or is this very intense? More than our usual hotter-than-the-sun chemistry?" He drew her up his body as he held her upper arms.

His pupils nearly swallowed all color in his eyes, she tasted his heartbeat in her mouth. Her wolf pressed against her human skin, rolling against him through that metaphysical barrier.

"Holy shit," he gasped. "What was that?"

"I think the bonding ceremony made us as close as if you were a wolf too. We were already bound through the Claiming but whatever my grandmother did, your blood mixing with mine, the whatever she said over the rings, it's made us very linked." Tegan closed her eyes for a moment and her head lolled back as she rubbed against him. "My wolf likes it as much as my human does."

"Good God, I've got to have you now," he whispered, his voice taut.

He shoved the bodice of her dress to the side, freeing her barely held breasts, lowering his mouth to her nipples. Fire licked at her senses as he nibbled and sucked on them.

"Get the sleeves unbuttoned or I'm going to rip it."

She fumbled with the sleeves as he continued his plunder, finally getting loose.

"Zipper on the side. Hurry!"

He let her go long enough to get the zipper down so she could struggle out of the dress. He helped her pull it over her head and a flash of green as he tossed it with his jacket.

"Damn it, those shoes." He shook his head as he stalked to her. Her shoes were pretty mules with peek-a-boo toes in a green satin that matched the dress. She'd had a pedicure that morning so her toes were a bright, shiny red. "And Tegan, you naughty, naughty girl. No undies?"

"Well we don't do the garter thing so my skirt wouldn't be up in front of a room full of people. The only person who'd see my pussy would be you." She hadn't meant it to come out a squeak but it did as he grabbed her to him.

"If I'd known, I'd have shoved you behind a tree and tossed your dress up, fucked you senseless under the stars." He marched her backwards into the room until she felt the cool glass of the windows at her bare back. "Turn around."

She did and started to reach to close the curtains but he caught her arms, bringing them behind her back, holding her wrists in one hand. "Uh uh uh. I think we should leave them open, don't you? No one is out there, it's late. But what if there were? Hmm? They'd be standing in the dark at the edge of the forest watching as my hand cupped your beautiful breast."

He spoke softly in her ear as he circled his fingertip around one of her nipples.

Her head fell back against his shoulder and he moved his hand, pressing her breasts against the glass while he spread her legs, tested her readiness and guided himself inside.

She was caught between the cool of the window and the heat of his body at her back. He held her wrists tight as he fucked deeply into her body, the height of her heels making her fit with him perfectly.

Everywhere he touched her sang with their connection as their mutual pleasure ebbed and flowed back and forth between them. She'd never had such a powerful experience, not even with Lucas. It was as if everything the two of them had held back over the years welled up and up until it finally crashed over them when he barely brushed a fingertip over her clit. Her climax brought his as the reverberations of sensation fed back and forth until Tegan's teeth tingled from clenching them so tight.

"Holy shit," he gasped as they both folded to the ground, laughing.

They got around to the champagne but had to run the bathwater again to heat it up. Nice big tub, big enough for two. Tegan and Ben left two days later with plenty of memories to go with sore muscles and a permanent grin.

Chapter Fifteen

Ben staked out the building his wife would shortly arrive at with the rest of the team from Cascadia. His heart lodged in his throat as he watched the muscle from National move around the area. He hoped like hell they'd be all right.

Lex had promised him Tegan could handle herself and Gabe had assured him Jack had the situation under control on the inside. But Pellini was a freaking crazy man and who could trust that?

"She's going to be just fine, Ben." Benoit chuckled from his chair beside him. Benoit watched the video from the room feeding from the pinhole camera Jack had placed while Ben watched the comings and goings from the building.

"Easy for you to say."

"Sure it is. But I like Tegan a lot and I've been working with Cascadia for nearly as long as you have and I don't want anyone hurt either. She's a hard assed woman. Strong, smart. She's not going to go down without a fight. It's why she ranks where she does as a female. And she would be pissed off if she knew you didn't trust her to take care of herself."

"Shut up. Did I ask you to be all FBI rational guy over there? Just watch the monitor and let me worry about my wife."

Benoit laughed again as he continued to watch the screen.

"There she is. Damn that wolf in charge thing is hot," Ben murmured as he watched Tegan get out of the dark-windowed SUV. She was tall and lethal in black, her hair a fiery rope down her back. She even had the ear bud in.

Two beefy werewolves approached and Tegan handed them something, conversing with them as she did. He could feel her through the link that bound the two of them. She radiated calm assurance as she stood, feet apart, waiting to get clearance.

With a nod, one of the large National guards stood back and Tegan spoke into the mic near her mouth and she opened the door to the car. Melissa, Cascadia's Third and Eric, the Fourth stepped out along with Dave, another guard.

They hustled toward the side door and for a brief moment, Tegan turned and looked up, right at where they were. Just a fleeting glance as she continued to sweep the area before disappearing inside but Ben felt it to his toes, knew she knew he was there.

Tegan felt Ben's presence in the condo building across the street as she turned to scan the area. She took in everything, every window, whether it was open or closed, where the trees obscured doors or entries, points of ingress and egress.

Plenty of wolves in the area and when she walked inside, Melissa and Eric between her and Dave, the scent of Pack from all across the country slammed into her. It rankled her even as it comforted her. That was the nature of family she supposed.

Because this was a National Council, the First and Second of National were in attendance. Jack Meyers stood as they entered the large boardroom. Tegan inclined her head exactly as much as he deserved and not a millimeter more. She stepped to the side to allow Melissa to move forward.

"Melissa, National welcomes Cascadia. Please, come in and

sit down. We were all just having a drink. Can I get you something?"

Eric stood next to Melissa and a bunch of posturing took place. Tegan kept her eyes shifting around the room, taking in every possible threat, watching the way everyone stood or sat. Body language was a big tell with wolves. Some of them were definitely with Cascadia on repelling Pellini but others, not so much.

"Tegan, so good to see you. I hear congratulations are in order."

Tegan couldn't help but smile as Templeton Mancini strolled toward her, ignoring all protocol by addressing her first instead of the other higher-ranked wolves all around the room.

He chuckled and looked around at everyone. "What? You tell me what man can resist such a lovely woman? I have a thing for redheads, just ask Carla." Tegan shook her head, Carla Mancini was a lovely woman who'd rip the throat out of any female who had designs on her man. She'd also written one of the kindest condolence notes Tegan received after Lucas had died, she'd never forget that.

Tegan inclined her head and tilted it to the side, baring her neck to him. "Alpha, it's an honor."

He kissed her forehead. "So, come and talk with me. Jack will be networking and I'm totally bored. Everyone else here is so uptight they look like they have a stick up their ass, don't they?"

He held out his arm and she took it. It wouldn't do to seek permission from Melissa. This was the National Alpha and if she refused for safety reasons, she'd be insulting his promise of safe passage.

"You're a very naughty Alpha, Mr. Mancini," Tegan murmured as he led her away.

"Why, 'cause these wolves expect me to let them paw at me and slobber on my shoes?" He snorted. "Carla's down the hall, I promised her I'd bring you by," he said in an undertone.

He opened a door and Carla Mancini stood up with a big smile. "Come in here! Let me hear all about your new husband. I hear he's quite handsome."

Tegan let herself be enveloped into a hug and put on the couch next to the female Alpha.

"Carla, before you start in on the girl, let me say my bit and then you can natter on." Templeton patted his wife's hand and she waved him off with an annoyed look.

"Go on then."

"He's here and he's been seen last night with some of the Siskiyou wolves. Great Lakes is a no, Granite are with you as well. I need to get back out there. Carla, bring this fine young girl back when you're finished interrogating her about her mate. And Tegan, I sure am glad you got another chance. Does my heart good to see you happy. The last time I saw you, you had heartbreak written all over your face."

Choking back emotion, she nodded, trying not to blush. He actually came to the funeral at the military cemetery, bringing Jack with him. A great honor but he hadn't made a big deal of it at all. He just did what an Alpha did.

Carla saw and hugged her around her shoulders. "It's very cute isn't it? When they get all sweet? He's a great big teddy bear sometimes. Now, tell me all about Ben. I've seen his picture, I do like the salt and pepper thing at his temples. Is he as gruff as he looks?"

Tegan laughed and visited with Carla for several minutes more and then Carla took her back to the others with a kiss on the cheek. It made it look as if they had attempted to work Cascadia on behalf of Pellini so she expected they'd get some looks.

"Let's get this party started then, shall we?" Jack addressed the group. The guards moved back to flank the room while the various Inner Circle members sat.

"First I want to note Gina Sorrano's presence here. It is not normally our way to have Enforcers attend but Great Lakes' Third is just about ready to give birth so she received a special dispensation to attend in her place. For the purposes of this Council, Gina will have the rank of Third."

Tegan took note and mentally shrugged. Great Lakes had a lot of power, they got to bend the rules and that's how their world worked. Templeton wouldn't have chatted up just any wolf in that room either. But she was a Warden and a Cascadia wolf and she got to break the rules too.

"The Council was called to bring to the table, the manner of replacing the National Pack's Mediator. Gabe Murphy has recommended one of his staff, a very strong, very able wolf with great experience. Naturally, as Gabe held the position of Third in this Pack for so long and as he was the Mediator, his opinion holds high value with us."

Melissa shifted in her seat and the tension in the air began to build as the real issue surfaced.

"At the same time, we have another candidate, William Reed. He's not currently in the area but he's got strong backing. He's currently Sixth in Memphis and he's got a law degree. We're here to decide the issue between the two." Jack smiled benevolently at the group.

"Ah, here everyone is."

A cold finger drew down Tegan's spine as none other than Warren Pellini strolled into the room. She growled, as did many others. It was a violation of the rules of the National Council for any Alphas other than the National to attend. It was also only open to attendance from the top five Packs who made up the National Inner Circle.

"Now, now, it's not polite to growl at me, is it, Tegan Warden?" Pellini turned to her and she stood tall. He wasn't a power like Cade or any of the other Alphas who commanded the Packs in the room. She had no reason to act subservient to him. He wasn't even part of a recognized Pack.

She moved forward to Melissa's chair, standing with one hand on her shoulder. Dave followed with Eric. In fact nearly all the guards in the room had moved likewise.

"Stand down," Templeton ordered and reluctantly, Tegan moved back, but only two steps. She'd take a bullet for Melissa if she had to and she wouldn't give more than the steps she'd given. If Pellini could just walk into the meeting, things were spinning quickly out of control as it was.

"We are only here to speak in support of our friend, William Reed for the Mediator spot." The smile Pellini gave was oily.

"Let us be clear then," Gina interrupted. "Great Lakes is opposed to Warren Pellini and his band of thugs having any more power within the ranks of National."

"Cascadia agrees," Melissa added smoothly. In the years since Carter had been killed and Melissa filled his spot, she'd become a force to be reckoned with, a quiet power. Tegan liked her a lot.

"Well, that's unfortunate, isn't it?" Pellini's drawl was affected, annoyingly fake and Tegan didn't bother to hide a sneer.

"You've already violated the Palaver, Warren, that's what's unfortunate. Great Lakes moves the uninvited wolf in the room be asked to leave." Gina stood but Jack put a hand on her shoulder.

"This will end now, Gina. Yes, Warren has violated the rules of the NC and the infraction will be dealt with. But you will not stir trouble here or you're the one in violation. Now sit and be silent until we hear the votes of the other Packs."

With a heavy sigh, Gina sat.

Jack was playing this one close to the vest. Tegan understood it but it made her angry nonetheless.

"Moving along. Yellowstone supports the candidacy of William Reed," the Third of the Yellowstone Pack spoke, smiling at Pellini as he did.

Two more Packs to be heard from and both could go either way. Tegan breathed in deeply, centering herself and keeping alert. She'd made eye contact with the Great Lakes guards and knew they'd jump in if trouble started.

"Granite respectfully abstains. We feel it is not the place of the member Packs to decide the National Third position and we do not like being called down here to play power games."

Tegan heard Templeton's snort and tried not to smile. That's who they were and you had to admire a Pack of curmudgeons. Still, it could go either way. Knowing Siskiyou was out being wooed by Pellini worried Tegan. If Reed went into the Third position, it wouldn't be long before tensions rose to the point of inter-clan tensions and turf wars. Briefly, she wondered just what Ben was thinking as he and Benoit listened to all this insanity.

Ben spoke on the cell to Cade. Cade's furious bellow at Pellini's showing up and violating the rules of the Palaver, something their kind held sacrosanct, had Ben holding the phone away from his ear.

"I get you're angry, Cade. But what do you advise here? We're out of our depth. Is he going to attack or something if he loses?" God, would he have to run in there and save Tegan? Would that bastard hurt her?

"I don't know, Ben. I mean, it's bad enough he's there, but to cause violence would break so many of our laws, even Templeton would have to openly come out against him. The FBI investigation would go to hell because there'd be no more undercover anything. I have to think even Pellini isn't that stupid." Cade paused. "How's Tegan holding up?"

"She growled at that fucker when he walked in. Should have seen it. Pellini actually jerked back and she did that thing where she walked forward so fast you didn't even see it but there she was, right at Melissa's back. The other wolves followed suit. When Jack ordered them to stand down, she only took two steps back and didn't lower her eyes." Ben was damned proud of his woman.

"Shit, Granite abstained."

Ben relayed the info to Cade.

"We got company," Benoit said as he stood.

They saw fifty wolves approaching the building from two different directions. The National guards were nowhere to be found. The monitors inside showed no one else had entered yet.

"There are fifty fucking wolves here, Cade. Damn it. I have to go."

"You can't stand against that many wolves, Ben! Wait. I'll call and get backup. Gabe has people there, he can…"

Ben hung up as he saw the monitors. He and Benoit grabbed their vests and weapons as they ran out the doors.

"Siskiyou resents the power plays they've been involved in. We were already convinced Warren Pellini and his *group* were bad for our people but after the constant attempts at bribery we

190

side with Cascadia and Great Lakes. The last thing National needs is yet another Pellini lackey with power in the Inner Circle."

Tegan felt the ground under her feet vibrate. "Get them out of here!" she screamed to Dave.

Melissa stood and shoved a chair out of the way. "I stand with you."

Eric followed suit as the doors busted open and wolves poured into the room in a mass of fists and teeth.

"Stand down! Damn it, Pellini, call these dogs off!" Jack growled, half changed, toward Pellini.

"Fuck this. You can't handle these dissenting factions, I will. Kill everyone but National and Yellowstone wolves," he ordered in the direction of the wolves who'd been waiting behind him.

Tegan had trained all her life for this moment. She felt no real fear as she slid her guns from the thigh holsters, flipping the safeties off with her thumbs before aiming one hand and then the other.

Wolves fell and others waded in to hand-to-hand or teeth-to-claw combat.

In the background, Tegan heard Ben's yells and caught sight of two wolves knocking him back.

She waded through the melee to get to him, shooting, kicking and knocking the shit out of anyone in her way.

The wolves, thank God still in human form, who'd been beating Ben slid to the ground, lifeless but before Tegan could bend to grab Ben, her guns were knocked from her hands as she was sent wheeling back by a fist to her temple.

Two of Pellini's people attacked, one in human form, the other as a wolf. Out of the corner of her eye, she saw Ben struggle up, a smear of blood on the wall he leaned against.

"Get out of here!" she screamed around a mouthful of blood. Setting her balance, she delivered a roundhouse kick to the face of the wolf and sent him reeling.

"You get out of here. Fucking crazy woman. I'm not leaving without you."

"Isn't that touching?" Pellini said. "Grab her and Gina, take them out the back."

"Oh that's *so* not gonna happen!" Tegan fought back harder, watching Ben get the shit kicked out of him. He went down and she used the wolf in front of her as a launching point to try and leap to him. The transformation in mid-air took a lot of energy but she bounded toward him, ripping into his attackers. The blood and fear of those who tried to hurt her mate only fed her fury.

Ben's hand reached out, covered in blood, to caress her side, grab her fur. She whimpered and spun to snarl and protect his prone form. Melissa had turned but Dave had ushered her and Eric out. It was important to save them. Cascadia would live another day to declare vengeance on Pellini for this.

Other wolves rushed in, Tegan scented Pacific but before she could relax, she caught sight of Gina being hit over the head and taken, unconscious, out the side exit.

Two of Pacific's people bent down over Ben and she licked his hand. She heard him murmur, *no* but there was no other choice. She was a guard, it was her job. She roared into action, biting, clawing and snarling.

The last thing she remembered was a white hot pain in her side.

Chapter Sixteen

"I'm going to kill someone in two minutes if I'm not released," Ben slurred at the nurse. "My wife. Damn it, my wife is in danger."

She sighed and patted his hand. "They'll find her, Detective. You have to calm down. We need to prep you for surgery. I'll be right back. If you continue to get agitated and threaten people, I'll tranc you up so much you can't move."

"Ben? I'm Jack Meyers, we've talked on the phone. I'm so sorry."

Ben tried to focus on the man standing there, tried to commit his face to memory so he'd be able to track him down and shoot him full of silver bullets when he got out of the hospital.

"Fuck you. Your fault."

"You're right, I'm afraid. We had no idea." Jack shook his head. "Cade has already called first dibs on killing me but Lex is on his way out here so I don't think he'll get the chance."

"We're already looking for her, Ben. I swear to you, I won't stop until we find Tegan. But you're in a bad way. You have to let them operate." Tegan's cousin Dave came into the room. "If you die, Tegan will kill me and then Jack and probably everyone here in the hospital. So let's focus on what we need to do.

They're setting up the operating room now. The surgeons are on the way. We're assembling a team right now."

"I can't lay here while she's out there." Ben's head raced but his body wouldn't obey the orders to stand and go find his wife. He realized what he needed to do. "Change. So—someone bite me."

"Are you sure? God, Ben, Tegan won't like it if you do this and then regret it. You know how she is. And then Nina will be pissed." Dave shuddered in fear.

"To save her? I'm sure. Do it, damn it." He'd cut off a damned limb to save Tegan. Weeks of recovery versus a few days. He'd take being a werewolf to gain some time for his woman. It wasn't even a hard choice.

"My bite will be best. I'm older and stronger of us." Jack looked back at Dave. "You'll need to guard the door. It's good he's so weak already, the virus will react far more quickly this way. You have to protect me from Tegan though. She's going to be pissed when she hears."

"You have another choice, Ben Stoner." Another man walked into the room and Ben felt the power ride over his skin like a thousand bites of electricity.

"I am Templeton Mancini. Watch the door, Dave. Jack, hold him, get a gag in his mouth. If you're one hundred percent sure of this, Ben, I'll bite you right now. There's no time to waste."

Weakly, he nodded and let Jack put a wadded up washcloth between his teeth to keep him from crying out.

"This will hurt. I'm sorry. God, so sorry for all that's happened. Let this be a step in cleansing the way between us." Templeton spoke before transforming into a wolf so fast Ben's brain couldn't even register it.

He did register the feel of sharp teeth slicing through the damaged skin on his side. Things nearly destroyed were utterly

194

damaged as the last thing he heard was a gasp and a muffled growl.

Ben was eating a sandwich and sitting up when Lex pushed through the door and stopped, surprised. "Well now, I guess Templeton's blood supercharged the shit right into you then didn't it?"

"Let's go. I'm ready."

Ben shoved the rest of the sandwich in his mouth as he made to get up.

"Wait. Jesus, it's only been seven hours since the attack and what, six since you were bitten? My God, Ben, this is incredible. Nina was out two days when she was attacked by our Third. Hours is just unheard of."

"Whatever the case may be, I'm up and ready to go. My woman is out there and she's in danger and I'm here eating a fucking sandwich. This is ridiculous. I'm fine!" His voice shook as he yelled and Lex sighed.

"Just eat that second sandwich and rest for a few minutes, okay? I'm waiting for a call from Dave and we can sit tight here until it comes. I cannot imagine what it feels like. The mere thought of Nina being..." Lex shook his head sharply. "But Tegan is my sister, I love her and you love her and we are going to find her and bring her home. You don't get to feel guilty for eating just mere hours after nearly dying and then being transformed. Your body is going to need a lot of extra protein in the first month or so especially. If you don't take care of that need, you're not going to be strong enough to fight off any threat. Full moon is tonight. Man, it's going to be a wild one for you. I'm sorry this was all forced. Tegan is going to kill me. Nina is already all over my ass."

Ben shrugged. "I don't care about that. I don't know why

anyone would think I'd blow off the chance to gain more strength to save my wife. Where is Nina anyway? I can't imagine she'd stay at home. Didja lock her up in the bathroom and run for the door back home?"

Lex laughed for a moment. "Once you ran into the building, everything went crazy. I was out the door, running to the car when Nina jumped in the passenger side. She was already on the phone with our pilot and getting the plane ready. She stuck to me like a freaking barnacle until we got to Detroit. We had to refuel and since the plane took off so fast in Seattle, there wasn't much food. I told her to run into the airport and grab us something, shoved her bag and a wad of cash at her, sent Megan after her and we took off without them."

Ben stilled. "Whoa."

"Yeah, I'm gonna wear a cup. I have no doubt the two of them will get here soon but she won't be able to get a commercial flight right away. I hope. I just don't want her in the middle of this."

"I understand it. I truly do. I wish I'd thought of something like that with Tegan. Damned woman. She was safe with me but she saw Gina being attacked and once they started stanching the blood and giving me first aid, she jumped into the fray. Lex, I'm going to kill Warren Pellini for having his men shoot her the way they did."

"Was it silver? Do you think she's..."

"I don't. She kept moving, struggling as they hauled her up. It happened in slow motion. I tried to get up but I couldn't. Others rushed in to help but Pellini's people got out the door. You tell me what the hell Mancini and Meyers were thinking to let that bastard stay in the room that way?"

Templeton walked in at that moment with Jack. Jack who found himself with his back against the wall and Lex's forearm cutting off oxygen. "You fuck! I ought to rip your head off right now and toss it on the train tracks. My sister might be dead because of your gross incompetence. You have no right to hold this spot." Lex's voice was barely human.

Ben blinked at the fury rolling off his brother-in-law. He'd seen Lex kill men before but he'd never seen Lex this outraged and murderous.

Templeton hauled Lex back and stood between them. "Knock it off, Warden. You'll have me to contend with if you keep this up."

"That's all right with me. You're more at fault than he is. The minute Pellini walked into that Palaver and broke the rules he should have been removed. You let him stay. You violated your oath of safety to all those wolves in that room. Cascadia is not convinced of your ability to rule at this point, Alpha."

Ben moved to stand next to Lex. He felt odd; his insides churned and all his senses were turned up to twelve. Still, his wolf surfaced, pressing against his human skin and he understood exactly what Tegan had tried to explain before. He was no longer upset he'd been changed, he loved the way it felt, wanted to share it with his mate. And mate she was. He really felt their mate bond as a wolf. She ran through his veins like blood.

Templeton blew out a breath. "Look, I made a mistake. I thought he showed up to bluster but if he lost, we could handle it and keep him in the dark. I thought he'd blow off steam and storm out. I was sure his little show of self-importance would sway anyone who hadn't voted by then. He still thinks we're on his side, or in his pocket as it were. We can use this. I am Alpha here and I will find my wolves. I give you my word that I won't stop until we find Gina and Tegan. I'm just waiting for him to call."

"I'm sorry, Lex. You have every right to blood me for this. I would never want harm to come to any of our wolves, especially your sister." Jack got on his knees and exposed his neck to Lex.

The room got very still as everyone waited to see what Lex would do. He stepped back and sighed. "I will trust you. For now. And it's not me you need to beg forgiveness from. Ben may have lost his mate today. I swear to you if my sister ends up dead, you will pay. I will burn this city down."

"And I will help you." Ben stood tall. "You saved me and I owe you, Alpha. But my woman is out there because your people messed up. If I lose her, I'll have nothing left to hold me to any manners at all. Help us find these bastards who've stolen Tegan and let me have first crack at separating them from their lives."

"After I clean my teeth with their bones, you mean. Boy are you two nitwits." Nina strode into the room, looking Templeton and Jack up and down with disgust. Megan took a station near the door. Nina spun to face Lex, her hands on her hips, face a mask of fury. "And you! I can't believe you thought you could just ditch me when we had to refuel in Detroit. You left me there when I went to get some food. You will pay, buddy. By the way, I charged a private flight and drinks for everyone on the flight crew for getting me here so fast."

Lex closed his eyes for a moment and Ben felt Tegan's absence so sharply he wanted to howl in pain.

"We'll find her," Templeton said, seeing Ben's anguish.

"I knew it was too good to be true to hope you'd be safe just for once." Lex kissed Nina who pinched his arm until he winced.

"Wow, wolf looks good on you. Tee will be pleased." Nina winked before she hugged Ben. "I'm so glad you're all right."

"Come to the safehouse. It's not too far and Carla has a huge meal waiting. We can grab the call there as easily as here."

Templeton gave them directions and left with Jack. They'd follow separately so no one would know they were all together. Ben had no doubt Pellini would be watching.

Lex took a quick phone call while Ben settled up and checked on Benoit.

Minutes later, Lex returned. "Come on. We'll go to the hotel first. I need to check in with Cade and I don't want to do it with an audience. Dave is supposed to meet us there shortly. Your stuff has been moved there. Benoit okay?" Ben nodded as Lex hustled them out. The nurse was pretending she didn't see a darned thing and Ben waved and mouthed a thank you.

Once in the car, Ben leaned back and closed his eyes. "Do you think she's alive?"

"Can you feel her through the link?" Nina asked. "Open up, reach out. It may not work but I can feel Lex when he's out here and I'm in Seattle so distance won't stop it."

"I can do that? Why didn't anyone tell..." He shut up and instead focused on the thread that held him to his mate. And she was there, soft, muted, but alive.

"Yes. Thank God, she's...I can feel her presence. But it's weak. Soft. I don't feel pain. Do you think I could feel her pain if she was hurting?"

"I don't know," was all Lex said as he drove through the tangled Boston streets to their hotel.

"Hey there, red, how you feelin'?"

Tegan opened her eyes and stared up into the not-unfriendly face of one of Pellini's wolves. He put a hand on her arm and kept her in place.

"Look, you have to keep it together or you're dead. I'm doing everything I can but...you don't want to end up like Gina.

I'm begging you, I owe Lex my life so please keep your mouth shut. Don't push him." His voice was the barest of sound but she heard the urgency in it. The truth.

Swallowing, Tegan nodded slightly and he patted her arm before letting go.

Don't want to end up like Gina. God, what had happened? Was she alive? What had Pellini done to her? Every bone in Tegan's body ached and several of them were broken. Why hadn't they healed yet?

Tegan tried to reach out to Ben through their link. Was he dead too? Could she survive if she'd lost him? She never wanted to face that pit of loneliness again and the idea of not touching him again, of not hearing him call her red wolf or even of never seeing the way his forehead furrowed when he was pissed at her, filled her with despair for a moment.

But the flicker she felt, distant but there, alive and, she paused, *lupine.* If one of Pellini's freaks had bitten him and forced the change would he hate her forever because of it?

No, he wouldn't. He might resent it, but he wouldn't hate Tegan for it. She believed it for all she was worth. He would find her. She'd make it out of there alive, she just had to start figuring out a gameplan starting with being docile if she had to bite her tongue off.

"I'm putting you back under. Trust me, it's better this way. It's been a day since Boston. Chicago..." were the last words she heard as she felt the sting of whatever he'd pumped into her and she fell unconscious again.

Ben sat straight up as they'd been driving west along I-90. "Shit. She's, I think she's awake or something."

Jack was driving so Lex sat in the passenger seat with Nina next to Ben in the back. Megan and Dave took the very rear.

Lex turned to look over the seat. "What do you mean?"

"I've been reaching through the link as often as I can. It's been sort of, I don't know, muted, muzzy. It's sharper now. I felt her energy touch mine." Ben kept his eyes closed as he concentrated on her. "She's worried but planning. I can feel her resolve. Hurting. Fuck. My bones hurt. She's...shouldn't she be healed by now? How can they let her hurt?" He slammed his fist into the seat and felt the leather and stuffing give under the force. Nina's hand went to his neck and he felt calmer. Megan's hand grabbed his shoulder and Dave took the other shoulder.

"Calm down, Ben," Nina ordered softly. "You can't help her like this."

"She's slipping away. It's all soft again. Damn it."

"We'll be in Chicago in just a few more hours. We're going to get to her in time. Know that, Ben. She's strong. Really strong. They're probably keeping her drugged," Lex said, pain clear on his face.

"Why is she hurting?"

"Do you really want to think about that?" Jack asked softly.

"YES! Would it be easier if I didn't? Sure. But she's my woman, I love her, I hate not knowing. I have to think about it so I can prepare myself and do the best I can for her. This isn't the time to hide my head under the sand." Anger cleared Ben's mind.

"All right. There are a few reasons. First, they could be beating her repeatedly every time she heals. Each successive time it will take her longer to heal because she'll be weaker than the last. Or, and this is a favorite of Pellini's, he's using silver on her. Not enough to kill her, most likely a hugely diluted injection right into the break. It won't heal that way. It'll keep her hobbled though." Jack's delivery was flat but Ben noted the man's knuckles were white from how tight he held onto the steering wheel.

"Will she heal ever?"

"She'll need to change but she'll be very weakened. Weakened enough to need her wolf lured up by someone else."

"What does that mean?" Nina asked.

"I'll have to force the change on her. It won't be pretty and it will hurt her. A lot. But it takes a wolf near the top or at the top of Pack hierarchy to do it. I'm hoping I'll be enough as Second at National. If not, we'll have to get Maxwell to do it. He's the Alpha of Great Lakes." Jack kept his eyes on the road and Ben wanted to do something to get there faster.

"I'll call him, Ben. We'll have him meet us when we start tracking. I think Jack will actually have a stronger wolf, but Maxwell is very powerful too. He'd do anything he could to help and his Second is missing too." Lex grabbed his phone and began dialing.

They'd gotten a call sometime after midnight, right after they'd returned from a wooded area outside the city where Ben had made his first transformation. He'd then wept for the first time in years as he lay in bed, alone, knowing Tegan was out there, scared and hurt and he'd changed for the first time without her.

The caller had been very brief, stated a zip code and hung up. They'd waited in the hotel room until Templeton called them about two hours later and told them Jack was on his way. Pellini had checked in, told Templeton he'd gone to Chicago to hole up. So it was to Chicago they'd head.

The zip code encompassed a large area of Chicago but as Nina began researching, they saw a lot of that part of the city had no buildings or houses. They'd have to track once they arrived but it was closer than they'd been just a few precious minutes prior.

Jack arrived, they'd stopped at a drive through on the way out of town, and drove west. They would have flown but Lex's plane had some mechanical problems and Templeton's was in use and by the time it reached them, they'd be nearly to Chicago anyway.

Ben tried to sleep on and off, they stopped to get gas while someone ran in, stocked up on food and they hit the road again. A normally fifteen hour drive would take them just around ten with the way Jack had pushed the SUV the whole time.

"Wake her up."

Tegan heard the order, knew the wolf who'd been helping her would have to obey. She steeled herself, knowing once she fully surfaced to consciousness, the pain of her broken bones would slam back into her.

At the same time, she felt Ben. His consciousness brushed against hers and she reached out with all the energy she had. He was nearer than the last time, some hours ago, when she'd become conscious last. He was coming to her. She had to hold on. She *would*.

The hands on her were gentle enough but it still hurt when whatever he'd injected her with pulled her from that quiet place she'd been resting in. Her wolf was far, far down in her consciousness, so far down Tegan knew she wouldn't come even though Tegan had been calling her. She needed to change to heal.

Facing the music, she opened her eyes and stared into Warren Pellini's face.

"Look who we have. Not so tough now, are you, Warden bitch?" He jammed a knuckle into her femur where it had been broken and she barely bit back a whimper of pain.

Nervous laughter erupted from the wolves behind him.

Lauren Dane

Wolves whose hearts she'd eat when she got hold of their worthless carcasses. They were werewolves, noble, strong creatures but she scented their addictions even in her own addled state. Junkie werewolves. She shuddered.

"Got anything to say?"

She held her tongue. Ben would come for her. She had to be alive and right then, she was in no condition to fight with anything more than her wits.

"Well, wouldn't you like to know where your friend is?" Pellini pulled a chair near and sat. She knew from the look on his face and the way the other wolf's fingers tightened just momentarily on her ankle she had to play and she hated it.

"Is she all right?" Tegan's voice was like sandpaper. At least her throat had begun to heal from where Pellini had nearly torn it out.

"She was quite feisty, that one. Gave my boys a good time."

Revulsion settled in Tegan's gut, even as guilt kept it company. She was glad if she couldn't have helped, she didn't hear it. It might have made her a coward but it was there nonetheless.

"Will you grieve for her? A female you barely knew? You gave your life, or you would have given your life for her. Why?" Pellini had no idea but he expected to be answered. He was not an Alpha though, she had no compulsion, other than wanting to survive long enough to kill him, to obey him.

"I will grieve, yes. She died with honor like a wolf of her station should." *Like he wouldn't* but she didn't add that.

"Why give your life for her? Your mate was there in the room. You abandoned him."

She hadn't! He was safe, she'd made sure of it. "He was safe and it's my job. My position. To not have tried to help would have shamed me and my Pack." Tegan burned with the effort to keep her voice as emotionless as she could. She knew she had to answer his questions to a certain extent, and keeping him talking meant they weren't doing to her what they did to Gina, and also gave Ben time to find her. She had nothing to send him but her presence. She hadn't been conscious when they'd arrived so she knew nothing more than Chicago and it wasn't like she could send an address through their link. All Tegan could hope was he'd feel her, know he was moving in the right direction.

"Position, shame, bah! It's this attitude that keeps us where we've been for way too long. Do you think I care about any of that shit? I care about me and mine. The new way of the wolf is coming, Tegan Warden. Profit, muscle, dominance and our rightful place which is not alongside humans like your mate, but over them. I heard he wouldn't change." He snorted derisively. "Why did you ask him? Who does he think he is to turn down such a gift?" We're better than they are. They should beg us to gift them with a wolf."

He stood abruptly, beginning to pace. "I told Maxwell but did he listen? No. Him and his precious honor and position. Of course he didn't. He didn't have to. He got the lake house. He got the Pack. When I threatened to leave, he waved at me and laughed. Bastard shunned me and my entire family! Well he's not laughing now that I hold part of his city. And he's not laughing when the cops are suddenly all over homeless people showing up having died from the change."

"What?" Tegan hadn't meant to ask but shock brought the hoarse question from her despite herself. Stupid.

He smirked. "Oh I see he hasn't told Cascadia, or even National I'd wager. Not that Templeton would do anything about it, he's in my pocket you know. Let me stroll right in and take over that meeting. Bet Siskiyou is sorry they sided with you now

205

that their Third is meat. But I've been trying out our little renewed cocktail on the downtrodden. We're working on refining it. Naturally until we hit right on the formula there'll be mistakes. Humans who pretend to be so noble don't seem to get too upset when their street people go missing."

Her leg throbbed and her two broken ribs made it hard to breathe, she tried to shift to be more comfortable when he zeroed in on her.

"Another lovely little thing we cooked up. Just the smallest amount of silver and purified water. Injected into a wound, especially a broken bone, it impedes healing indefinitely. Hurts I bet. I love this lab. It makes me so happy to be here."

The dude was batshit crazy. Tegan's head swam but the connection to Ben grew stronger. He *was* on his way to find her.

"I've been wondering what it would do if we injected it into the brain. So we shot Gina in the chest and then injected the serum into her brain to see if she'd heal when her brain couldn't react." He laughed, a near giggle, filled with glee. "We've tried it on other wolves of course but it's not every day we get a Second who's willing to be experimented on. Well, I suppose willing is an overstatement. My boys did get mad because they had to play with damaged goods but they like blood."

Tegan couldn't hold back the retching. Nausea roiled through her but she'd eaten nothing so it only hurt her body even more. She tried to shut down, didn't want to hear any more of it. Would they do that to her? She could live if she had trouble walking for the rest of her life, but her brain?

As they edged up to the building Ben doubled over and began to shake.

"What? Ben, is Tegan...tell me!" Lex ordered urgently, his

own hands trembling as he whispered.

"She's so fucking scared. God, let's go. She's so afraid now. They're going to do something to her."

Maxwell Williams, the Alpha of Great Lakes shook his head. "We move now." He gave a hand sign to his wolves and looked to Jack and Lex, who nodded. As a group, they moved into position, took out the guards and with one as a hostage, got into the building.

Megan and Dave destroyed the surveillance cameras as they continued down a long hallway.

Ben scented her, scented Tegan, sickness and blood, smelled her fear and her anguish.

"Don't rush in there, Ben. Be patient," Lex warned him. Ben knew that, he'd been on enough of these raids as a cop to know the score but his wolf itched to go and grab his mate.

Suddenly, he heard a shout and they all began to run. Jack kicked open the door and Ben tore his way through three wolves as he rushed straight to a table where Tegan lay, pale and barely conscious.

"Wait, don't, not that one," she mumbled as Ben started to snap the neck of the wolf nearest her bed. "He's been helping."

"I have. Pellini left using the back door. Be careful, that hall has booby traps!" he called out to Maxwell's people as they ran to follow Pellini's retreat.

"I knew you'd come." She began to cry and Ben didn't know what to do. His strong warrior woman, his red wolf crying in fear? He locked his knees and leaned over her body.

"You will fix her now or I will kill you," he growled to the other man.

"I can't. She's got silver in her. Pellini used it before he left. It's killing her. She has to change. I can't make her wolf answer."

Nina heard and with a gasp, she ran, shouting Jack's name. Megan went to her sister's side as Ben kissed Tegan's face over and over, murmuring to her.

"Come on, red wolf, come out. I need you to change. I'm a wolf now too. It's so beautiful and I want to share it with you. Please, don't you leave me. You can't. I demand you change right this instant!"

Jack came rushing back and Megan moved so he could get to Tegan on the other side.

"Tegan, I'm going to make your wolf rise. You have to help me. I know it's painful out here but you'll be better once you change." He put his palm on her heart and the other on her forehead.

She was so pale, sweat poured off her as she began to tremble.

"Silver seizures. She only has a few minutes now. You have to get her to change or she will die."

"If she dies, you do," Ben growled, never taking his eyes from her face.

He felt her wolf stir and his pushed at him. He opened himself up to it, if his wolf felt he could help, Ben would let him through. His wolf burst up through his consciousness and stood, looking at her.

Barking over and over, he grabbed her wrist with his teeth and bit, not too hard but to make her notice.

Jack mumbled and Maxwell ran into the room. He moved next to Jack and placed his hands on Tegan as well. Her wolf jerked closer to the surface.

Ben turned and barked at Lex. Lex had to help too. He rushed in with Nina, saw them all and with an anguished cry, he joined them, Nina following suit.

Her life grew dimmer and dimmer until Ben barely felt their connection. He howled then, loud and clear, howled his pain, his anguish, his fury and his passion. He felt it all leave him and fill the air.

The air around her shimmered for a moment and suddenly, a red wolf lay on the table where Tegan's human form had been. Lex and Jack picked her up and put her next to Ben, who curled around her body protectively, placing his muzzle against her chest, feeling the rise and fall.

After a few minutes, Ben changed back and got dressed in borrowed clothing. They left Tegan in wolf form and went to the Great Lakes compound. A series of buildings on the lake surrounded by woods.

Chapter Seventeen

Tegan slowly recovered in the hours after they'd brought her back to the Great Lakes compound. She'd only changed back to human form a few minutes before and still slept comfortably in the guest suite Maxwell had given them.

Ben hadn't left her side for hours, first when she was a wolf, her breathing shallow but gradually deeper and more relaxed, and then when she'd changed back to human form. He couldn't believe she was there and really all right. The fear still coated his mouth, stung his senses.

He couldn't let go of the memory of her on that table, nearly dead. Couldn't let go of her fear, her pain, that she'd been so devastated and he hadn't helped her. Would she hate him for it? Resent him?

"They want you down the hall, Ben. Nick, Gabe, Cade and Templeton are calling in in just a few minutes and you need to eat something. Nina and I will be here with her. I promise if anything changes we'll come get you. It's just two doors down. She's going to be okay." Megan hugged him. "You saved her. You got to her in time. She knew you wouldn't give up until you found her."

"But not before they hurt her." His voice was a whisper.

"You can't think that way. Ben, she's a guard, it's what she does. You're a cop, it's what you do. You both have dangerous jobs. She worries for you too. But you can't not let her do what she was born to do. She'd be very unhappy if you did," Nina soothed. "I know where you are right now. Every time Lex walks out the door I know something could happen to him. It tears me up sometimes. But we work it through. You two will as well. She loves you, you love her. You accept each other and that's what counts. She can count on you. She'll need that when she wakes up. Just keep being there for her."

"I wish I could have..."

Nina interrupted him, "But you can't. You can't change the past so stop it. Don't do this to yourself. She doesn't want you to. Nobody blames you. You're Pack, you protected Pack. You're *family* and you protected your wife. Forgive yourself, Ben Stoner because no one else blames you."

He nodded. Bending down, he gently tucked Tegan's hair back and kissed her cheek. She still smelled of blood, pain and fear. When she woke up he'd personally take her into the bath and clean her up.

"Any change at all you come get me." He moved to the door and looked back to see Megan carefully get into the bed with her sister, curling against her back and Nina settled in on the other side. They both nodded to him and he quickly moved down the hall.

"Come in, Ben. Please, you need to eat. Help yourself, my staff has brought some dinner in. We're getting everyone connected now." Maxwell indicated a side table where sandwiches, salads and protein drinks sat.

His stomach growled as he hustled to eat. He hadn't realized how hungry he'd been and still wasn't used to his new metabolism.

"I just looked in on Tegan. Tracy is on her way. Maxwell has sent people to the airport to get her. Tegan will be happy when she wakes up. Layla arrives shortly after that so they'll ride in together." Lex grabbed a sandwich and ate as he sat next to Ben.

Cade and Templeton finally got connected on the line along with Gabe and Nick.

"Everyone on?"

After the assenting answers, Jack got started. "Pellini is gone. He rushed out a back door as we stormed the front. Unfortunately he's taken Gina's body with him but the Pellini Group wolf who'd helped Tegan and gave us the tip on her location told us Gina had been experimented on and then murdered. It wasn't a pretty story. It looks like he was in too big a hurry to get much else though. One laptop near the door had been taken apparently but the other computers in the lab remain and have been shut down. Nina will look them over when we get them back here."

"My people are still combing over the lab buildings, gathering evidence. We'll work with Ben while we have him. I'm sure he'll be a great resource." Maxwell nodded at Ben. He was eager to help so that was fine and dandy with him.

Maxwell paused a moment and then cleared his throat. "I have to tell you all we've got a problem here. Besides, well, because of Pellini. I was trying to handle it myself but I only realized today just exactly what has been going on. Pellini has been grabbing street people and experimenting on them. The police came to me twice in the last two weeks about finding dead bodies of partially changed humans. No bites. They don't know what was going on and I'd thought they were wolves who'd changed but it never took hold or died in mid change. Something like that. Pellini has been so busy with drugs and money laundering, I just didn't think. I...it's stupid and I suppose I just didn't want to face it. No one thought to tell us, the biggest Pack in the US, that Templeton wasn't really in the pocket of the mob so I hesitated. It cost lives. I'm sorry." Maxwell scrubbed hands over his face and Ben wanted to punch him.

"I told you people to share it with Great Lakes months ago," Lex said angrily.

"I know. We made mistakes and that led to a very high cost. We wanted to keep it as quiet as we could. We know Great Lakes has spies and Templeton didn't want to risk it." The exhaustion in Jack's voice showed on his face as well. "This is a clusterfuck of epic proportions."

"No shit. But my sister was taken at a Palaver. One of my wolves, Ben Stoner, was nearly killed. Another man under my protection, Agent Benoit had to undergo two different surgeries and nearly died. This cannot stand. Cascadia cannot be silent any longer," Cade's voice rang clear over the line.

"Great Lakes aligns with Cascadia," Maxwell said and Ben looked around the room, not knowing what was going on.

"Pacific aligns with Cascadia," Nick and Gabe said as one from their end.

"National will lead. War is declared. Warren Pellini and any wolves aligned with him will be eradicated. They will be bones and dust," Templeton said over the phone line.

"War? I'm sorry, I've been a wolf for a little over twenty-four hours now. Not enough time to know much. What the hell is going on?" Ben asked.

"We've just declared inter-clan war for the first time in a hundred and ten years. Pellini has broken many laws, his behavior cannot be tolerated. I was willing to cooperate with this undercover thing to try and bring an end to the threat without this drastic step but it ends now. We must take a public stand and the other Packs will align with our side,

Pellini's side or they'll attempt to abstain," Lex explained.

"Abstainers will be considered the enemy in this case," Cade said and Ben, again, heard the Alpha in Cade's voice. Took a lot of restraint to only wield that kind of power when absolutely necessary. Ben understood Cade and Lex a lot more now that he'd seen them under pressure. He admired them both a lot more too.

"We agree. To stand aside when a law breaker of this magnitude runs free is to be as negligent as Pellini is guilty." Maxwell poured them all some whiskey. Ben drank his quickly and was grateful for the warmth spreading through him. He'd come very close to losing it several times over the last day, he was barely holding on by that point.

"A council will be called, factions declared. Jack, I need you back here," Templeton said quietly.

"On it. My plane leaves in about forty-five minutes." Jack stood. "It will be an honor to stand beside you in the coming days." He held his hand out to Ben, who shook it. The man had helped save Tegan's life, they were even.

"I have no idea what will be happening but if it's about taking out Pellini, I'm in."

"We'll get the Call made today. Gabe's choice for Third has been appointed and Tina has been taken into Pack custody for Jack to question. Our Fifth has stepped into Tina's spot in the interim. As we're entering dangerous times, I expect votes to be tallied by phone and mail. Once factions are drawn, we will appoint a Council of War. I'll be in touch. Please keep us apprised of Tegan's health and when the funeral will be for Gina." Templeton hung up and the room was still for long moments.

Jack said his goodbyes and left.

"I'm going back in to Tegan. The doctor said she should be

waking up soon and she should eat."

"Ben, I wanted to invite you and Tegan to stay here as long as you wish. You're welcome in Great Lakes territory. Today, I was incredibly impressed with your skills leading up to the assault on the lab and once in the room where Tegan was." Maxwell clasped his forearm.

"Trying to steal him?" Lex sounded less than amused and Ben realized there was more going on than he'd been picking up.

"Tracy and Layla are here," Megan came in to announce and Ben reluctantly disengaged himself after thanking Maxwell for his offer.

Ben saw his other sisters-in-law as he entered the room. Relief hit him as he saw no blame on their faces, only relief and happiness to see him.

"Ben, hi honey. How are you feeling? I can't believe you're up and around so quickly." Layla pressed a hand to his forehead and frowned. She turned to Nina. "He needs to eat more. Can we get him some food up here? A steak and some greens, a milkshake too. Don't argue with me, Ben, or I'll tell Tegan on you. Sit down now." She turned back to him once Nina had gone with a chuckle.

"Bossy. All you Warden women are bossy," Ben muttered but his smile belied his cranky words. He liked that they'd taken him into the family. Liked that they'd rushed to be there for Tegan.

"You've met my grandmother. Why don't you sit in bed next to Tee? I can see you're itching to touch her and she'll need the attention too. Her color has improved a lot in just the last few minutes." Megan moved so he could take her place. "You look a bit tired too."

"I changed three times in the last twenty-four hours, I

215

suppose that makes a guy tired." He casually sifted Tegan's hair through his fingertips as he spoke.

"They'll bring up some dinner for all of us in just a few. The cook here appears to have a crush on Ben. She said it was *dreamy* how devoted he was to Tegan." Nina snickered. "Lex is going to join us after he's done with his phone call to Cade."

"You changed three times? You mean from human to wolf to human?" Layla asked, her eyebrow raised.

"No. Lay, from human to wolf for the first time last night. And then today, twice more. He helped Jack and Lex track and then at the lab, he helped call Tee's wolf to the surface with the others. He changed back just a few minutes later."

Ben shrugged as he listened to Megan explain it to Layla. "Not a big deal. She needed me and it's a snap to change. Feels good even."

"Your first time it felt good?"

He winked at Layla. "Well sure. Didn't know what the hell I was doing at this either though." He took in their surprise. "What? Why are you all looking at me like that?"

"Because, Ben, it's unheard of for a newly changed wolf to make that many transformations in one day. Not for the first six months or so. Some wolves can never do that many a day. Who changed you?"

Startled, Ben looked down into the big green eyes of the other half of his heart as she stared at him. Her voice was low and rough, scratchy even.

He leaned down and kissed her face over and over. "Red wolf, you're awake. No, don't sit yet! You sound like you smoke a pack a day and you're trying to get up? My God, woman, lay down."

"She should sit up and eat. Really, it's all right." The Pack doctor came into the room with Lex and Maxwell right behind.

"The hell you say. She nearly died!"

"She's a werewolf, a prime werewolf from a powerful line. She has spent hours as a wolf and then back as a human, her body has healed itself and now she needs to refuel." The doctor checked Tegan over after helping to sit. "Your vitals are fabulous. How do you feel?"

"Good. Much better. Starving. And do you think my voice will change soon?" Tegan scrambled into Ben's lap, needing all the contact she could get. His arms encircled her immediately and his scent calmed her. But her wolf scented his and she felt that metaphysical roll against her human skin and then his wolf responded. Gooseflesh rippled over her body and everyone else in the room shifted uncomfortably.

"Okay, stop it. I don't want to know this," Lex said as he looked everywhere but at them.

When Tegan turned to see Ben, his eyes had glazed over a bit. "Ben, control it a bit better. Just sort of put a lid on it," she said softly.

His eyes cleared after a moment and he nodded. "Sorry. I don't know what happened."

"Don't be sorry. It's beautiful. We'll talk more later, okay?"

He licked his lips and her body tightened. Jeez, even after she'd nearly died he did this to her. What a man.

"Why don't you get cleaned up. Nina said dinner is on the way. We'll all eat with you if that's all right?" Lex looked so worried and so sweet Tegan wanted to cry.

"That sounds good. I need a shower."

"I'll help you, red wolf." Ben stood and picked her up easily, carrying her into the attached bathroom and slamming the door

217

closed with a foot.

He fiddled with the water a moment and, after making sure she hadn't moved from where he'd placed her on the counter, he peeled his clothes off and she sighed.

His Adam's apple slid up and down as he turned to face her. With gentle hands, he pulled the hospital style gown off her body and helped her down and into the shower stall.

"Sit on that bench there and I'll do the work."

He moved around her body as he slowly and carefully cleaned her up.

"I knew you'd come for me. When things got bad, very bad, I felt you inside me and it helped." She didn't bother to hide the tears in her voice. "I just kept thinking to myself, Ben's going to find me. And you did. Thank you."

He knelt and looked at her. His eyes held so much emotion. "I would crawl on my knees to the ends of the Earth to get to you. I'm sorry. So sorry."

"Sorry? For what? Are you upset about the change?"

"The change? You mean into a wolf? No. God, no. It was a way to get out of the hospital faster to find you. It's made me faster and stronger and my bond to you, I can't believe how intense it is now. It's not that I love you more, but I *feel* you more. I'm sorry I failed you."

She jerked back in surprise. "Failed me? Ben, I'm sitting here, alive because of you. How is that failing me? You saved me. Honey, didn't you hear me? I knew you were coming for me. I never doubted it for a single moment."

"In that room when you jumped toward where they were attacking Gina. Pellini took you right in front of me and I did nothing." His voice broke and tore her apart.

"Oh Ben, honey, part of your intestine was hanging out.

You'd apparently been changed by one of your attackers. I made sure you were taken care of and then I did my job. My job, Ben. You ran in to the room and did yours as a cop and my mate and I did mine. You did *not* fail me. Stop that right now."

"I love you so much. But I wasn't changed by my attacker. Templeton changed me at the hospital. I thought you knew but I guess you haven't been conscious very long." He stood and finished up.

As he dried her off, she pushed him against the wall. Her wolf pressed against his, wanton and hot.

"I need you, Ben. Right this second. If you don't fuck me I'm going to scream." Reaching down she grabbed his cock, pumping her fist over it a few times as she dragged her nipples over his chest.

He panted as he sought control. "Wait. Fuck, don't do that! Tegan, you nearly died. Stop it."

She climbed up his body and when he caught her to keep her from falling, she reached around and angled him, pressing down on him.

"Christ! Tegan, fuck, fuck, fuck."

"Yes, that's what I'm trying to do." Her voice, still whiskey rough, was low and the magic of her wolf tinged it. His wolf was close as well, she felt him, saw the flicker in his eyes. "I can't wait to change with you. I'm so sorry you had to be without me when you took form the first time. God you feel good. So damned good. I'd scream but I'm hoarse and I can see you're embarrassed. They all know what we're doing so let's get to it. I don't want foreplay, I don't want finesse. I want you to fuck me hard. Top me, please, Ben. I need it."

An anguished sound broke from him as he spun and pressed her back against the wall. Thrusting hard and fast into her body, he dropped kisses, hot and wet, open-mouthed, across her collarbone. Every few kisses he nipped just the right side of painful. One hand fisted in her hair, the other arm banded around her waist to hold her up.

"You're so beautiful I could die from it. Looking at you makes me ache. Feeling the way your pussy holds me, welcomes me, you're more than I ever imagined wanting, more than I ever imagined having. You're alive and you're mine," he murmured, voice thick with emotion.

"Always. I'm yours. And you're mine." And he was. Unbelievably, wonderfully, he was. She tipped her head to the side and he moved quicker than she'd ever seen him move and bit down where neck met shoulder.

Orgasm rocked her foundations as she clamped her lips together to keep from crying out. He muffled a deep groan, his teeth still holding her still as he came.

After they'd gotten their breath back and kissed, long and slow for several more minutes, he helped her into pajamas Layla had brought and she put her hair back.

"You're not going out there without a shirt, Ben." Tegan grabbed him before he moved to the door. He looked hard and hot, his hair tousled and wet from the shower, skin tawny and stretched tight over muscle. The change had made him even sexier. She was going to have to beat the females off with a stick even harder now.

"The shirt I brought in is tight. I wanted to get a new one." He winked, knowing just why she'd stopped him.

She handed him the shirt and he put it on. "Guh. Just guh. You look so sexy right now I want to take a bite. Or five." Reaching up, she touched the mark on her neck and shivered.

"Sorry about that." He winced.

"It's so not anything to be sorry about. It's considered very special when a mate marks the other like this. A badge of adoration. Thank you."

"Oh. What about other marks?" His voice dropped an octave and her thighs tingled with the sense memory of the last time he'd flogged her—right before he'd left for Boston.

"Mmm, well those will be just between us. Come on. I smell food and I'm starving."

"Oh shit. Come on." He picked her up and took her into the next room where the food had just been delivered. Ben tucked her into bed and put a lap table on for her before giving her a plate. He brought his own and snuggled in beside her.

"Nice love bite." Nina snickered.

"I thought so. So Maxwell has told you about the homeless victims of Pellini's experiments, right? I will be very cross with you if you haven't," Tegan said around her first mouthful of steak.

"Yes. I told everyone."

"I'm sorry about Gina. She fought hard, and with honor."

Ben squeezed her hand briefly and she told them what Pellini had said, every horrible detail about how they'd used the silver in her brain.

The room got very still. Her breathing was uneven as she tried to hold her emotions back. Ben folded her to him and rocked her for a while, whispering into her hair until the horror passed enough to go on. The others let her work through it, quietly speaking amongst themselves for some minutes.

When Tegan sat back up again and took a sip of her milk, Maxwell heaved a pained sigh. "I'm sorry, so sorry you had to bear the telling of that tale. Thank you for doing it. It just means Pellini has another strike against him. He dies either way. You did us a great honor by stepping in to aid her in Boston. And your man did the same today when we hunted for you both. I've offered him our compound and the safety of the Pack for as long as the two of you desire."

Lex growled but kept his mouth shut and Tegan realized that now that Ben was a wolf, he'd be a much lower position in Cascadia than his strength and power would warrant. He was a cop, he'd hate the diplomacy of Third, even if he wanted to challenge Melissa. Eric was strong but if Ben could change three times in his first day as a wolf, he was no match for Ben at all.

"Would someone like to tell me why the hell every time Maxwell offers us a place to stay while Tegan gets better Lex growls and his hackles rise?" Ben demanded, not missing a beat with the steak he demolished.

"He's offering you a place in his Pack, Ben. Us a place in his Pack." Tegan looked at his face to see his reaction. Surprise and a rejection of the idea. He hadn't begun to think about his place in Cascadia, she'd wager. It wouldn't be anything he'd contemplate. How would he even have that frame of reference?

"Honey, you're an incredibly powerful man. You were before you changed. But now that *the* Alpha of National was the one who changed you, you get aspects of your sire so to speak. With Cascadia, with you as a human, it wasn't an issue. But everyone in the Inner Circle will be threatened by you and your power and you're far too strong to be happy at my rank for long. There's no place for you at Cascadia."

"Bullshit. I don't care about this ranking stuff. I have a job already. I don't want to take anyone's rank in the Pack." Ben shoved the last bite of steak in his mouth and began to attack the greens.

"How many detectives are werewolves in Seattle, Ben? Here in Chicago it's zero. Many police departments say they don't discriminate but you and I both know people still have a lot of prejudices about werewolves," Maxwell said. "And how long will you have your job once people find out?"

Tegan closed her eyes. Maxwell had no way of knowing about Ben's mother but the point hit the bullseye as Ben's shoulders slumped a bit.

"And when war begins in earnest, there will be a Council of War appointed. Everyone of power will be needed in the best place he or she can be," Maxwell added.

"War? What the fuck?" Layla exploded.

"I'm sorry. I expected you'd know by now but I didn't think to tell you." Lex pushed a hand through his hair. "Tonight war was declared. National will lead. Cascadia, Pacific and Great Lakes are all aligned. Templeton will call a vote to see where the other Packs fall."

"What does this mean? Will there be a draft? Will there be battles? How the hell does war work between werewolves?" Ben shifted uneasily. "Humans are not going to be pleased and I can't see something like werewolves savaging each other in the middle of the street being kept secret."

"We haven't had inter-clan war in a hundred and fifty years so it's not like we've got modern experience with it. But at first there'll be posturing. A show of strength. I imagine most Packs will align with National. The two biggest Packs are aligned together as it is with National. The Packs are already freaking out over what happened at the Palaver. Siskiyou lost members and they'd already voted against Pellini, my guess is they're with us." Maxwell paused.

"Yellowstone helped Pellini. Their guards helped the attack." Tegan remembered seeing it happen and the helpless rage that burned through her.

"There'll be an accounting. Anyway, Ben, first comes the posturing. Politics. The bigger faction will offer to let the smaller surrender. This goes on a while. Growling, snarling, small fights will break out especially in areas where two opposing Packs have territory in contact. Most of the time, after some skirmishes, the smaller faction will surrender without full fledged war breaking out."

Tegan watched Ben take it all in before he asked Lex to follow up.

"Two things—what happens if they surrender and what's full-fledged war?"

"If they surrender, their territory will be taken from them and re-distributed. Spoils of war. Full fledged war means lots of dead wolves on all sides. In Europe, thirty years ago, there was war between Packs in Spain. They lost half the werewolves in the country in pitch battles and surprise attacks. Here, we'd have to deal with drive by shootings and car bombs from the likes of Pellini. Assassinations. That kind of thing." Lex sighed heavily. "It won't be pretty."   •

"If they surrender and territory is redistributed, what happens to the wolves from the losing Packs?" Ben asked.

"They're given amnesty." Lex's voice was flat.

"Most of them," Maxwell interrupted. "There will be trials in this case if there's a surrender. I won't allow anything else. Warren Pellini will stand trial or be killed in war. He cannot be allowed to live and get away with what he's done."

"I hear that. Okay, I'm in one way or another. That bastard can't be allowed to be free after this." Ben moved closer to Tegan. His energy vibrated from his skin. She brushed her lips over his shoulder, snuggling into his body. She needed him as much as he needed her.

"Does that mean you'll consider joining Great Lakes? We need an Enforcer and I think you'd fit the bill. Our Third doesn't want the job and none of the guards are capable of holding the spot I don't think." Maxwell avoided looking at Lex and Tegan was torn between a host of competing concerns.

"I need to think about everything you've all said. Tegan and I need to talk and weigh a lot of stuff. I can't answer you now." Ben looked to Tegan. "We can't answer you now."

After the discussion, everyone left to rest or clean up. Tegan turned to Ben and hugged him.

"Want to go for a run?"

"Jogging? Now? It's three in the morning."

She laughed. "No, not jogging! As wolves. I need the change to help chase the last bit of stiffness from my body. You'll feel better after a run too and it's selfish of me but I want to see you, want to be at your side as a wolf. I didn't see you the first time and I don't remember when you changed at the lab."

He smiled. "That's not selfish. After we got back from changing I lay there alone, so fucking alone, wanting you there with me, wanting to share it with you. If you're sure it won't tire you, I'd love to. And honey? I like your voice that way. I know you're upset the doctor said it may never go back to the way it was before but it's very, very sexy."

She led him out the back doors to the trees where Maxwell said they'd be welcome to run.

"That's so sweet." And it was. He was such a bundle of contradictions. So tough and hard but loving and gentle too.

"Will that mark go away when you change?" His voice dipped low when he shed his clothes.

Her breath caught when she took him in, always affected by him. "Yes, most likely." Her fingers sought the spot, touching it, sending tingles through her body.

He undressed her, kissing her softly as he did. "Well, I'll have to do it again then."

"Mmm, if you say so. I'm all yours. Change first please so I can see you in color."

She stood and watched as he fell to his knees. The air shimmered for moments and then a big black wolf stood before her, gray hair at the ears.

Running her hands through his fur, she bent to kiss the top of his head. Her wolf practically burst through her human skin, wanting to be in charge so she let go and gave her the reins.

The ran for miles and Tegan remembered the joy of what it meant to run with your mate at your side. She remembered what it was like to hear Lucas run with her. Allowed herself some celebration and a last bit of mourning too. She would love him until she died. But she had a second chance and it was all the more special because Lucas had been a part of that too.

Chapter Eighteen

Two weeks later

Ben paced through the small house they'd been given in the weeks after Tegan's attack. Just a mile from the main house but still on the grounds of the Great Lakes compound, he'd admittedly begun to feel at home.

"How many?" he asked into the receiver as he spoke to Benoit. Bodies had been found in New Orleans. Transients, same thing as in Chicago. Partially changed. Only these had been burned.

"Six. You can't keep putting the FBI off with Pack business as an excuse, Ben. I know you're all dealing with some crazy shit but the Nashville office has a report of a possible serial killer of transients there and it looks like that's werewolf shit too."

"Okay. You're right. I'll talk with Lex and we'll get back to you."

"You goin' back to Seattle or what, man? Your leave of absence is up in a week isn't it?"

"I don't know. I really don't. My family is there. Tee's family is there. But my life has changed drastically. Hers too. I don't want her to feel pressured but...I don't know." And he didn't. They'd avoided the topic but it had to be dealt with soon. They'd returned to Seattle briefly to pick up some of their belongings but it had felt foreign and he definitely felt weird about how the other wolves he'd run into had reacted. For the most part, Cade had asked him to stay away from the Pack house in town and to not interact with wolves beside their immediate family.

"Okay, Ben, I feel you. It's got to be tough. I can't imagine what it's like to be a werewolf." Benoit snorted. "The talk on the street says you're all supercharged too. Wolves in Seattle are uneasy with you coming back."

"So I hear. I can't explain what it's like other than to say it's sort of like that moment right before you go on a raid. Right before you take that first step and your body is amped and your brain is screaming and yet all quiet and focused. So fast, you can move, even as a human, so fast and you're strong. It's pretty damned amazing. But you know I'd never do anything to cause trouble in Cascadia. They're Tegan's family, *my* family. I want to protect them, not hurt them. It's why I'm still here. Cade wanted us to sit it out for a while so he could lay the groundwork for me to come back. But I've made some good friends here. Human cops as well as in the Pack. Tegan has too." He sighed again.

"All right. I'll try and hold my superiors off for a few more days. Let me know and I'll keep you updated on Nashville and New Orleans." Benoit hung up.

"Hey."

Ben turned to see Tegan standing in the open French doors. The patio led to a fabulous view of the water. He heard the birds singing and the scent of the trees and the earth hung in the air. But she edged it all out until all there was, was Tegan.

The light on her hair made it appear she had a fiery halo. Her skin had returned to that pearly glow. She wore a pretty, filmy pale blue dress and her feet were bare.

"You look like a fairy. A beautiful fairy come to steal my heart."

"You're good. Although I'll keep that secret or your Dom privileges might be revoked." She walked into the room and clambered into his lap when he sat. "I heard the call with Benoit."

"I expect that's why you look the way you do."

"You're the one who's avoided any conversation about staying or going back." She kissed him quickly.

"I don't want to pressure you. Your family is there. My family is there for God's sake. I grew up there, you did too. I can't ask you to leave that behind for me."

She growled at him and he raised a single eyebrow.

"Yeah, yeah, you've been giving me the *punishment is coming* face for two weeks, and yet, not a single bit of ass smacking or shackling or anything remotely punishment, well fun punishment, related has been delivered."

"You nearly died!"

"But I didn't and I'm alive and I need you to be yourself. All of you. I need you to talk to me about this situation and I need you to own me, to top me. I..." she shook her head, "...I feel so safe when you're totally yourself with me."

He nuzzled her neck. "I've held your wrists and bitten your neck." His cock came to life, pressing against his zipper.

"Mmm, God that's good." She undulated, grinding her pussy against his cock. Her heat found him through her dress and his jeans. "Not enough. Not for you either. You're holding back. Don't."

"I wasn't a werewolf before. What if I hurt you?"

The rich scent of her pussy tickled his senses as she stroked him through his jeans. "You won't. You didn't before.

And you won't hurt me by telling me you want to be here either."

"Tegan, my gorgeous red wolf, war is here and I can't expect you to be away from your family." He bit down on her nipple, her stuttered breath skittered through his senses.

"Shit. Oh, more. Ben, that's so good. Take me like you want to. No more training wheels. I'm a big girl, I can say, *whoa boy too hard* if that's the case."

Fisting the front of her dress, he yanked, pulling it apart and baring her breasts to his mouth. Her heartbeat sped, he tasted it on his tongue along with her desire, her need and his own, mixed.

"You're my family. You can't be what you need to be within Cascadia. You know that." Her head dropped back and she moaned deep in her throat as he sucked hard on one nipple and then the other. "And, well, Cade is going to have enough to deal with without having to constantly deal with how the other wolves will react to you. We're predators...yes, oh yes, that..." Her sentence trailed off into an inarticulate squeal and then a sigh.

He'd sort of gotten that feeling from Cade when they'd spoken. Cade clearly felt conflicted. He loved his sister and liked Ben but there would be problems with Ben remaining a lower ranked wolf.

"There will be infighting. You're too strong to be outside the Inner Circle and yet unfit for any role but Enforcer." She managed to breathe this last bit out as she held on to his shoulders, back arched to press into his mouth.

And there was the unspoken. His mother had refused to speak to any of them once they'd given her the news about his change. She'd gone crazy, accusing Cascadia of kidnapping Ben and changing him against his will. Going so far as to make a police report. He'd had to admit to being a wolf, which technically shouldn't put his job in jeopardy but his boss didn't hesitate when Ben asked for leave time.

His father had been in regular contact as had Jillian but his mother wouldn't take his calls at all. It hurt deeply but he had the best thing in the universe right there on his lap and truth be told, he knew he'd be an excellent Enforcer for Great Lakes. The rest of the Pack had already accepted his dominance and he worked great with Maxwell. Chicago would be a good city to live in, to raise a family in. They could be happy but he didn't want Tegan to have regrets. She'd lost so much, he couldn't bear to take anything else from her.

He stood, keeping her wrapped around him as he headed into their bedroom.

"Go get the toy bag. It's in the closet."

When he put her down, she moved quickly to the closet, her dress falling away from her body as she stepped over it, leaving a pale blue puddle of fabric in her wake. He knew she'd let it fall that way to entice him. Loved that she seduced him even as he seduced her right back.

"Pretty panties," he said as she returned, dropping the bag at his feet. He drew a fingertip over the front of the silky material, her wetness scorching him. Flicking idly over her swollen clit he smiled when her hips jerked forward.

He pulled the panties off her body and breathed her in, watching her pupils widen, hearing her intake of breath, knowing it turned her on to see him that way. The panties were cool against his lips for a moment before he tossed them to the head of their bed.

"I didn't bring everything of course. But let's see what we've got in there." Kneeling in front of her body, he admired the long, pretty line of her, her strong legs, the naked pussy, the slight flare of her belly and hips, coral colored nipples, hard just for him. Her eyes were glassy, her face calm. She'd already begun to slip into subspace and he'd barely touched her.

So responsive, so beautiful and strong. And all his. That she gave herself to him so completely went through him. He knew she was a gift, every moment he was with her, he knew that. Resisting truly topping her had been so difficult and as he knelt there, looking in the bag, he wondered what had taken him so long. Perhaps a fear she'd react to him differently since she'd been so harmed, or maybe a fear he'd harm her himself. But he wouldn't and she knew it. Suddenly everything was all right again.

"Spread your pussy open for me," he ordered, leaning in to lick her clit fast and hard, stealing her breath as he filled himself with her taste. She made a sound, low, needy, deep in her throat.

He'd start her off with orgasm and then give her a few more because he loved to make her come, loved the sounds she made, loved the way she writhed, loved the way she became languid and sensual as endorphins flooded her body. He made her that way. No one but him would ever bring her that kind of pleasure.

Her clit bloomed under his tongue as he teased it, tasted it, tickled it. Their link, made all the stronger since he'd been made into a wolf, flowed to bursting with her pleasure

She trembled as he pushed her straight into climax. He put an arm around her ass to hold her up as her knees buckled and her breath came in short, hard, jagged pants.

Giving her one last lick, he stood and met her gaze. "Christ you're beautiful," he mumbled before he captured her mouth. She opened to him immediately as her arms circled his neck. Her tongue danced lazily along his, letting him lead and take from her. She gave herself completely and he took, plundered, even as he gave back. He sank into her warmth, into the way she gave him safe harbor, into her trust and the gift of her submission.

With one last nip of her bottom lip, he moved away as he caught his breath. And then he watched her eyes clear up when he held up the nipple clamps. Her breath puffed out softly as she made a small *ooooh* sound.

"Mmm. Your nipples just got even harder." He thumbed them and she moaned. "Hold them for me so I can put the clamps on."

She cupped her breasts and the way her breathing quickened, once he touched the rubber-covered metal to her nipple, shot straight to his already ridiculously hard cock.

Carefully, he set the tension with the small screw. Just tight enough the weighted ornament on the chain that hung between her breasts would tug but not hurt.

Tegan looked down and watched, mesmerized as he attached the clamps. The sight of his large, olive-toned hands against her pale skin as she held her breasts out to him deeply moved her. Something about the juxtaposition of all those things—his work hard hands, her smooth, pale skin, the delicate color of her nipples and the shiny steel and black rubber of the clamps—rolled what they were to each other into that one brief moment.

Hard and soft, tough and vulnerable. Both of them were a lot of things at different times but she realized she could trust him to be what she needed, when she needed it. That sort of surety was breathtaking.

The tension on the clamp was just barely shy of painful as a dull throb settled in. She adjusted her breathing, knowing when he took them off, usually right as she came, sensation would burst through her body. The way he knew her, manipulated her senses to bring her more pleasure was so sexy. He never took too much, always pushed just far enough.

He looked at her closely, making sure she was okay before moving on. The half-lidded eyes and the small, wicked smile let her know he had plans. Anticipation slid through her, and relief, she'd missed this with him.

A few steps back and he backed up to a chair in the corner. "Knees."

She swallowed hard and moved to him eagerly. He put a pillow down for her to kneel on and the case was cool against her skin.

"Undress me."

He'd been shirtless and barefoot, looking totally rakish and devastatingly corrupted. She shivered as she looked up at him and leaned in to rub her cheek against his cock through his jeans before running her hands up the muscled calves, the hard thighs and cupping his ass a moment. Her fingertips dipped below his waistband, between the scratchy denim and the smooth, hard, warm skin of his abdomen.

Inhaling deep at his belly button, she slowly unbuttoned and unzipped his jeans and slid them down his legs, along with his boxers. His cock, gloriously hard, slick at the head, tapped his belly. The scent of his maleness wrapped around her and squeezed until she thought she'd explode with it.

He fell into the chair, widening his knees for her to move closer to him. "Beautiful woman, all mine." He ran a gentle hand through her hair before drawing a thumb down the line of her jaw. "Suck my cock. Don't make me come just yet though. I'm going to be fucking the hell out of you when I come."

Holy shit the man knew what he was about.

She let his scent, the timbre of his voice, the way he stroked a hand over her hair, draw her in and let the pace. She leaned in and palmed his sac, drawing her thumbs over it as his balls began to tighten against his body.

Long, slow licks with the flat of her tongue over his balls and up the line of his cock followed. She loved every inch of his cock, making sure to pay extra attention to the places she knew he liked best. A dig of the tip of her tongue just beneath the crown. A she sucked hard on the head, she slid her thumbs but the stalk of him from root to her lips, using the slickness she'd created with her mouth to ease the way.

"That's so good, Tegan. Beautiful. I could sit here like this forever. Looking at you, your mouth wrapped around me, your hair sliding against my thighs. You're so sexy."

His nails scored her back, making her gasp with delight and arch to get more. She loved it when he did that, the burst of sensation that rode the line between pleasure and pain with such a sweet edge. She also loved the way there'd be faint marks some hours afterward. Because he was a wolf now, they'd stay longer. The thought brought a warm flood to her gut, her pussy heated as she groaned.

"Mmm, I love when you make that sound. Dreamy, needy. I love making you react like that."

His nails gently raked over her scalp, massaging it as she sucked his cock. The throb in her nipples returned as she rocked back and forth to take him in her mouth again and again, sending the little weight swinging. Her clit began to throb in time and she writhed a bit to ease the building ache.

"Do you need to come, Tegan?" Grabbing her hair, wrapping it about his fist he pulled her away from his cock. His eyes glittered and she knew he was as turned on as she was.

She nodded.

Lauren Dane

"On my lap. Face away from me."

She obeyed, he helped her to stand from kneeling so she wouldn't lose her balance.

"Legs outside mine, I want your cunt spread wide open for me."

Her heart pounded as she adjusted how she sat. He moved so his cock rested between her legs, up against the folds of her pussy.

"Hot. Scorching hot and creamy wet. My favorite," he said in her ear before biting down on the lobe. "Use my cock to make yourself come."

Desire for him ran through her like honey. Sticky-sweet and warm. Languid, she moved, undulating while she held his cock against her on the opposite side as the full length of him stroked against her.

"Tell me how it feels," he gasped.

"Good. Oh Ben, so good. Your cock is rubbing over all of my pussy. I'm so slick and my clit is so hard."

"Mmm, I can't wait to angle you just right and slide into your cunt. After two orgasms you'll be nice and ready. Swollen and juicy. I'm going to pound and watch that weight swing back and forth, knowing it's tugging on your nipples. You know I'll make you finger your pussy, I love the way you feel when you come around me. At some point, I'll pull the clamps free and you know what you'll feel then. You do remember, you just spilled honey all over me. Close now, hmm?"

She swallowed back something utterly incoherent as the ridge of his cock stroked back and forth over her clit again, sending spirals of pleasure through her, blinding her.

It was then he bit her on her shoulder, prolonging the orgasm as her wolf stirred, loving that bit of dominance she could understand as well.

He helped her to stand and did as well. While she watched, he stroked himself, still bathed in her honey while his eyes never left her face. She whimpered and he stopped.

"What is it?"

"I want it to be me doing that."

He chuckled darkly and then licked his fingers, nearly sending her to her knees. "Go stand next to the bed. Palms flat against the mattress."

She moved, knowing what was next. Her body trembled in anticipation. He hadn't flogged her in weeks. She felt as if she'd drown in the intensity of his need for her. But his very being anchored her, kept her from slipping away completely.

Anxiously, her body attuned to the sounds she knew would come. First the creak of the handle as he gripped it. Then the slither of the tails as they slid against each other when he weighted it properly in his grasp. She scented the leather, the oil from his hand on the handle. The combination of the sounds and scent of the flogger in this man's hand devastated her in a way little else did.

And then the first, cool, feather-light touch of the tails as he lightly drew them over her shoulders, down the line of her back, across her ass and up her thighs.

By the time he shifted subtly behind her, moving back to get full extension of his forearm and wrist, she'd slid deep into the narcotic bliss of subspace. Limbs heavy with pleasure, she registered the first sting on her left thigh. And then her right. Over and over again, in multiple places from the tips of her shoulders to the backs of her thighs. He'd spread her stance wide enough that he tickled her pussy, swollen and sensitized with just the barest tip of the tails.

Heat built over her skin as the percussion sent blood to the surface layers, making it more sensitive to every touch.

Dimly, she heard the thud as he tossed the flogger to the side, felt the wetness of a tongue sliding down the line of her spine, down the seam of her ass and straight to her pussy.

She cried out, beginning to rise from the heady languor she'd been in, arching toward him. "Please, your cock, please," she begged, her voice a slight slur.

The blunt head of his cock was pressing into her gate before she'd even realized he'd stood. He'd truly become fast since his conversion.

"Cripes, you feel good." He adjusted her, one hand at her hip as the other grabbed her hair the way he knew drove her insane as he made good on his promise to fuck her so hard the weight between her breasts would swing.

His cock slid in deep, retreating with a wet, slow sound. She didn't want him to leave, moved her body with his with a sound of entreaty and he leaned down, careful not to put pressure on her back and with the hand that'd been in her hair, pulled the nipple clamps off.

She gasped at the wave of sensation, first pain and then the warmth of pleasure flooded through her. Her nipples throbbed with sensation, driving her close to coming right at that very moment.

"No, no. Not yet, red wolf. I want to feel the way the muscles on your forearm cord as you make yourself come."

His voice was everything. Dark and velvet, filled with longing, with adoration and love, with arrogance and self assuredness that absolutely marked him as an alpha man and a very Alpha wolf.

She gave herself to him as she did every time he asked because she loved him. Because he took her love and the gift of herself and he made her feel as if she were the most special, beautiful creature alive. Even with Lucas it had never felt so intimate, so intense and loving even as it felt deliciously wicked and taboo at the same time.

As her fingers danced around her clit, he spoke to her low and intense. Told her he loved her. Told her how beautiful she was, told her he lived to wake up to her face each day and she knew he meant every word. Those words, the reverent way he spoke to her, treated her, sounded in her ears as the mammoth climax hit, sucking her under with an anguished cry as she shoved back to meet him, to take him in as deeply as she could while her body clutched his.

Three more hard thrusts into her and he stilled, the fingers at her hip digging deep. Leaning down, he took the back of her neck between his teeth, the warmth of his breath against the cool sheen of sweat on her skin when he came.

He put aloe on her back, soothing the heat before they took a shower together. Before capturing her lips he looked at her for long, silent moments. "Am I what you want?" His words were soft, gentle.

Her heart swelled as she nodded, emotion making words hard to come by. "Yes. From the first moment you touched me at the club, before I'd even seen your face, you were what I wanted. You're what I need too. You didn't hurt me tonight. It was," she paused trying to think of the right thing to say. "It was amazing. Raw. I feel like tonight was the first time you totally opened up and didn't hold back."

"That's probably true. When I thought you were human, I held back because what I felt for you was so intense and because I didn't want to harm you. And then after the Claiming I was afraid to confront the intensity of my feelings. After that, it was intense and hot, sexy and wonderful but when I changed, I feel like our bond has become deeper, more, I don't know, integral perhaps. But then you'd had this terrible experience. I realized tonight you knew I wouldn't hurt you. You trusted me and if you can trust me, I can trust me too."

"You're what I need, Ben. What I crave. You fill me up in every way. You accept all of me and make me whole."

They had a meal. Took a run and came back home. As she stood on the deck, overlooking the water, scenting other Pack wolves as they ran on the compound property, she knew this was home now. Knew this place was theirs and from then on, Seattle would be a place they visited.

The rightness of it settled into her as she leaned into his side.

"We need to be here. I feel it. This is where we're meant to be. I'll be on your Enforcer team."

"We're going to have to talk to Cade and to Maxwell. You need to talk to your parents and your sisters too. I hate you having to lose anything else."

She turned to him, cupping his cheeks in her hands. "You're everything. You're my family and this is the way it has to be. There are airplanes. War is here, there's no more time for indecision."

Ben watched the stars and listened to the steady breathing of his wife as she lay sleeping in his arms. Out the window, the world was changing. He had no control over the war brewing, no control over the very real possibility he'd never be able to be a cop again. But he had Tegan. He had the ability to be a cop for the Pack and that could be good. If they could survive the coming storm.

Ben vowed he'd protect the woman in his arms with his dying breath. Yes, she'd be on his Enforcer team, she'd be his right hand man. They'd be together so he could keep her safe and that was all there was to it. Pellini would be dead, one way or another, for what he put Tegan through.

The rest they'd have to take one step at a time.

About the Author

To learn more about Lauren Dane, please visit www.laurendane.com. Send an email to Lauren at laurendane@laurendane.com or stop by her messageboard to join in the fun with other readers as well. www.laurendane.com/messageboard

The end of a curse is the beginning of a magical love.

Reading Between the Lines
© *2007 Lauren Dane*

Celtic language expert Haley O'Brian is thrilled when she gets the chance to translate a scroll written in Ogham, an ancient Celtic text used in magic and divination. While translating the text, she unwittingly frees Conall macCormac's Fae soul from a millennia-old curse that kept him imprisoned in a human body, lifetime after lifetime.

The end of the curse is just the beginning of the magic for Haley and the ridiculously sexy Conall. He takes her into the world of his people, the Daoine Sidhe, where she begins to learn of her own Fae heritage, carve out a new path for herself, and embrace her new-found power.

But their happiness is marred by Ninane, the jealous Fae who cursed Conall a thousand years ago. She will stop at nothing to have him for her own, including the murder of Haley's family.

Determined to bring Ninane to justice, Haley must ask Conall to undergo the ultimate test of love—to stand aside and let her fight her own battles.

Available now in ebook and print from Samhain Publishing.

Enjoy the following excerpt from Reading Between the Lines...

The look in Conall's eyes seared her deep. Such love there. Adoration. Trust. Admiration. Joy. Fear too.

She felt it as well. How fortunate she was to have this. However it came about, whatever brought it to her she couldn't feel resentful or distrustful of it. It simply was and she wasn't going to question it.

She shared his love, his adoration, trust and admiration. And his fear. Fear that this bitch who harmed him would come back to hurt him again. Fear she'd lose the best thing she'd ever tasted. And what would her world be like without Conall now that his life had touched hers? Bleak.

"Haley? Are you all right?"

She focused on his face, saw his concern. Unable to speak she nodded but a tear fell anyway and he sat up and scooted back to lean against the headboard, staying seated within her.

"What is it? Am I hurting you?"

"No," she managed to whisper. "I don't want to lose you. She won't come back will she? Teach me how to fight her, Conall." She could bear a lot, but losing him seemed totally unimaginable and yet, the anticipation she'd felt in the glade where the ring stood just a few days before remained and she had a strong suspicion it had everything to do with Ninane.

He smiled and kissed her tears away. "Lady, you slay me. So precious to me, sweet, sweet Irish witch. Ninane may try to come back. I won't lie. But she doesn't have the element of surprise she had before. She won't succeed if she tries to harm me. And I'll kill her before I'd let her harm you."

She nodded. "Okay. I love you, Conall. I know it seems

soon. Hell, it *is* soon, but I do."

He kissed her lips softly. "Me too. I love you too. Now, if you're not going to do your job, you can't be on top."

Haley undulated on him, rolling her hips as she raised one eyebrow in his direction.

His breath stuttered. "Where'd you learn that, Irish witch?"

She continued with the movement, slow and sure. "I took a belly dancing class. I've never tried it this way. Pity."

Leaning in, he nipped her bottom lip, making her yelp as she laughed. "You'd better not have!"

"Conall," she continued, breathless from laughing, "you may have been forcibly chaste for a thousand years but I'm not so stupid I don't know you got it on with loads of chicks before that."

Putting a hand to his chest he gasped theatrically. "Got it on? You wound me! Are you suggesting I was loose?"

"A man whore? A floozy, or is that moozy if it's a guy? Oh get that look off your face! I'm guessing you were a connoisseur of women rather than a moozy."

"If you didn't have such talented hips I'd be vexed." He totally blew it when he started to laugh, rolling over and landing on top of her body, continuing to stroke into her.

He felt so damned good Haley thought she might die from it. The heightened sensation her magic gave her now that she was Fae was incredible. Like having her skin turned on to ten on the dial. Everywhere they touched was like a brush of her clit. Every inch of his cock sent ripples of pleasure through her pussy. Stretching her even as he caressed her internally. He existed within her, not just with his cock, but with their connection to one another. He was all around her and inside her. She was awash with him, with desire. Love filled her to overflowing. To say sex with Conall was mind-blowing would be an understatement. In truth she wasn't sure there were words adequate to describe the feeling of his cock as it pressed in and then retreated.

Haley arched her back, needing more of him. She raised her knees, wrapped her calves around his waist and dug her fingers into his shoulders. His hair caressed her bare chest and neck, his scent settled things within her even as it excited her.

Her orgasm began to build again and she let go of one shoulder to slide a hand between them. He groaned in her ear. "Goddess it's sexy when you do that. Soon, Irish witch, soon I'm going to put you on the table and sit back and watch your fingers coated in your honey, playing over your clit."

Her breath caught in her throat when her middle finger reached her clit and pressed gently. She didn't need to move, he provided the friction as he fucked into her body.

"Your pretty pale skin will glow with pleasure and I'll take my cock out. Lightly stroke it because I'll want to concentrate on you, with those fingers sliding into your pussy. Your head will fall back, you'll catch your bottom lip between your teeth the way you do and you'll make soft, needy sounds." With each word, his voice became deeper and more strained. She knew he was close and she was too.

"Oh, yes!" she gasped as orgasm rushed through her, sucking her under as her body gave over to endorphins designed to make her feel as if she floated in desire. His body on top of hers anchored her, kept her from drifting away as he arched back, thrusting into her hard and deep, and came as well.

Long moments later, he let out a satisfied sigh and rolled to the side, holding her against him as they caught their breath.

"Now, my family will be here in about half an hour. There's

to be a large meal and everyone will ooh and aaah over you."

Haley sat up with a gasp. "Why didn't you tell me? Conall, I have to get ready. Shower. I don't have any clothes here. Oh man."

He grabbed her and pulled her back to him, kissing the top of her head. "I tried but you jumped me. Minx. And I saved you from a trip to my parents'. You should be grateful. They'll all come over here because my mother won't hear of you going anywhere for a day or so. Now, we will shower together. No, don't get that look, you're still weak and I shouldn't have had sex with you just now but I don't want you to fall. I can wait a few hours to have you again." He winked and tumbled out of bed, helping her to stand.

GREAT
CheAp
FUN

Discover eBooks!

THE FASTEST WAY TO GET THE HOTTEST NAMES

Get your favorite authors on your favorite reader, long before they're
out in print! Ebooks from Samhain go wherever you go, and work with
whatever you carry—Palm, PDF, Mobi, and more.

Printed in the United States
150839LV00004B/7/P